About the Author

Neil Coley resides in the Staffordshire City of Lichfield with his wife. He has written several books about its rich history. They are:

NON-FICTION
The Lichfield Book of Days
The Beauty and the Spy
Lichfield Pubs
Lichfield People
Secret Lichfield

FICTION
Lichfield Stories
An Alien Autumn
The Cold Distance

A Blood Winter

The Ashto and Atia Chronicles: Book Two

Neil Coley

Copyright © 2024 Neil Coley

The moral right of the author has been asserted.

Apart from any fair dealing for the purposes of research or private study, or criticism or review, as permitted under the Copyright, Designs and Patents Act 1988, this publication may only be reproduced, stored or transmitted, in any form or by any means, with the prior permission in writing of the publishers, or in the case of reprographic reproduction in accordance with the terms of licences issued by the Copyright Licensing Agency. Enquiries concerning reproduction outside those terms should be sent to the publishers.

This is a work of fiction. Names, characters, businesses, places, events and incidents are either the products of the author's imagination or used in a fictitious manner. Any resemblance to actual persons, living or dead, or actual events is purely coincidental.

Troubador Publishing Ltd
Unit E2 Airfield Business Park,
Harrison Road, Market Harborough,
Leicestershire LE16 7UL
Tel: 0116 279 2299
Email: books@troubador.co.uk
Web: www.troubador.co.uk

ISBN 978-1-83628-037-8

British Library Cataloguing in Publication Data.
A catalogue record for this book is available from the British Library.

Printed and bound in Great Britain by 4edge Limited
Typeset in 11pt Adobe Garamond Pro by Troubador Publishing Ltd, Leicester, UK

To Thomas and Anna

1

Renewed Acquaintances

'Margot, do you really think that it's a wise course of action for us to pay a visit to the local policing authorities again?' First Commander Ashto had a worried look on his face as he walked along the crowded Whitechapel High Street arm-in-arm with Apprentice Commander Atia. Both of the undercover explorers from the planet Jara were well wrapped up against the chill of an early morning in January. To anyone observing them as they strolled along they appeared to be a normal, well-to-do, handsome looking, married couple from the West End of London taking a walk in the streets of the busy, working-class area of one of the less salubrious parts of the capital in this year of 1889. No one at all was aware that the two alien visitors had been living alongside Earth people for the last six months gathering information on all aspects of life in this region of the planet. One day their superiors back home on Jara would use their findings to assess the viability for the Earth's possible induction into the organisation known as the Galactic Federation of Planets.

'Well, Trevor, we have discussed this issue at some length over a fairly long period of time. I thought we had both agreed that the best thing to do was to visit the Inspector and simply ask him to return the computer terminal he took from you when you were arrested last November.'

'Yes, Margot, that is true but we know, do we not, that Inspector Reid is a most perspicacious individual who is bound to question us about what the computer terminal actually is and the functions it performs.'

'Trevor, I think we simply have to keep to the explanation I put forward when he asked me on the occasion he briefly kept you as a prisoner in one of his police cells. At that time I told him the computer is in fact a new type of timepiece, which has recently been invented by the notable American scientist, Thomas Edison. My explanation seemed to satisfy him at that particular time. My only concern is that he, or someone else, has decided to investigate the computer's function or has taken it apart to discover technology that does not yet exist on this planet and we know what the attitude of the Explorer Executive is towards lost or misplaced pieces of equipment.'

First Commander Treve Pacton Ashto, known as Trevor Ashton while stationed on the Earth, nodded but still looked a little concerned as he climbed the four steps that led up to the main entrance of the Leman Street police station.

Inside they introduced themselves to the heavily bewhiskered desk sergeant who told them they would have to remain in the waiting room until Detective Inspector Reid could find time to see them.

As it turned out the Jaran pair didn't have to wait very long before Reid joined them in the austere room with its row of rickety wooden chairs and whitewashed walls on one of which hung a large photograph of a regal but rather dour looking Queen Victoria. Greeting the couple a smiling Inspector Reid directed them to his office. The Inspector, short in stature, especially compared to the two tall Jarans, was nevertheless an imposing figure in his own right: burly, mustachioed, with highly intelligent eyes and an incisive, determined manner. He invited Ashto and Atia to sit down while he seated himself behind his desk, leaned forward and proceeded to stare inquiringly at them.

'So, Mr and Mrs Ashton, what is it that I can do for you?'

'Well, Inspector,' said Ashto, aware that the eyes of the senior police officer were fixed on him, no doubt analyzing every nuance of his current behaviour, 'last November, when I was briefly your guest in this building and before I was taken to one of your cells, you took from me an item that I would very much like you to return, if it would be convenient for you to do so.'

'Do you mean this object?' Inspector Reid took the small, silver coloured computer terminal that was about the size and shape of a cigarette case from his desk drawer and held it up for the Jaran pair to see.

'Yes, that is it Inspector Reid, may I have it back please?'

'In just a moment, Mr Ashton, but first can I ask you to

inform me what this… this thing… actually is? According to your wife it is a new sort of clock developed by an inventor in the United States.'

'That is correct, Inspector,' said Ashto.

'It's just that I and one or two of my fellow officers have looked at it on a number of occasions and discovered that when some of the raised areas on the object are pressed part of it emits a strange glowing light on which various unusual markings can be seen. Also every so often the object makes a strange sound, almost like the squeaking of a mouse. I have to say we are baffled by it and wonder why any inventor worth his salt would bother to spend his time constructing such a device.'

Ashto held out his hand and was relieved when Inspector Reid placed the computer in his palm.

'Thank you, Inspector; actually I believe that the said inventor, Mr Edison, employs something of a scattergun approach to the process of invention and that this timepiece was one of his least successful undertakings.'

'I understand, Mr Ashton, although that does beg the question as to why, if the object in question is not particularly useful, you were carrying it on your person when we arrested you in the Britannia public house last year?'

'Er, only for purely sentimental reasons I can assure you, Inspector,' replied Ashto, 'it simply reminds me of my home in the United States, a place I will be not be returning to for the best part of the next five years.'

The police inspector smiled and shrugged his shoulders, seemingly in resignation. 'Well, that seems to solve that particular mystery. Is there anything else I can do for you, Mr and Mrs Ashton?'

'No, Inspector, there is nothing else… just this,' said Ashto holding up the computer before slipping it into his coat pocket. 'Thank you for your time, Inspector, we will take our leave as I am sure that you having many other pressing tasks to perform. Thank you for seeing us so promptly,' said Ashto.

'Think nothing of it, Mr Ashton; it has been a pleasure to meet you and Mrs Ashton again. I do hope that your researches for your book continue to bear fruit,' said Inspector Reid walking over to his office door and holding it open for Ashto and Atia.

After exchanging several more polite goodbyes with the Jaran pair Reid stood in the doorway of his office watching with interest as they left the building.

'Bill!' Inspector Reid shouted, 'come here please.'

Sergeant William Thick, a man Edmund Reid trusted implicitly and someone who in Leman Street police station and throughout the East End had gained the universal nickname of "Upright Johnny" joined the Inspector, a quizzical look on his face.

'What is it Sir?' Thick said.

'I've just had the Ashtons in my office.'

'Yes, I noticed. What did they want?'

'They had come to pick up that so-called clock or whatever the hell the thing was we took off him back in November.' Reid looked thoughtful. 'I still don't trust that pair – particularly him. There's something not absolutely kosher about them, something not quite right. I feel it in my bones, Bill. Have you still got that list of passengers who arrived on ships from America that docked in Southampton in August of last year? I'd like to take another look at it.'

'Yes, Sir, I'll go and get the file from my desk. Oh, by the way, some more of those counterfeit sovereigns have turned up in the district.'

Reid frowned. 'Righto Sergeant, let me have that report as well.'

Inspector Reid went back to his desk and sat down. Things had become very much quieter in Whitechapel since the latest Ripper murder two months ago, but everyday he expected someone to charge into his office to tell him there had been another hideous murder at the hands of the killer. So far, however, there had been no further atrocities committed. Was the Ripper just biding his time? Was the last gruesome murder, where parts of the unfortunate woman Mary Jane Kelly had been placed around her room, some sort of grand finale that meant the murders had finished and, for whatever reason, Jack the Ripper had ceased his bloody activities? Reid winced as he remembered entering that room in Miller's Court. What he saw then would be imprinted on his mind's eye forever: the blood, the piles of flesh on the bed and table, the hideously mutilated body of a poor young woman lying on the blood-soaked mattress, her face totally destroyed by the Ripper. He shivered. Bill Thick appeared in the room with the files he had requested and Edmund Reid was pleased that he would have something else to think about other than the horror of that room of death in Miller's Court.

Inspector Reid quickly flipped through the papers contained in one of the brown cardboard files.

'Are you sure that there's no record of a Mr and Mrs Ashton on any of these passenger lists, Bill?'

'Quite sure, Sir, I've been through them with a fine-tooth comb and there is no one of that name on any of the lists throughout the whole of August arriving at Southampton.'

'And Mrs Ashton has told us that they had docked at Southampton arriving on a ship called the SS Elbe, a steamer belonging to the North German Lloyd shipping line.'

'That particular ship did arrive at Southampton from New York on Wednesday the 15th August last year but there is no mention of a Mr and Mrs Ashton on its list of passengers.'

'That is very interesting, Bill. Have we still got someone following the Ashtons?'

'We have, Sir. I put Perkins on it. He's one of our best; young but very sneaky and skillful.'

'Good. Have him report to you and then let me know of anything that pair get up to that is in the slightest bit out of the ordinary.'

'Certainly, Inspector. Anything else?

'No that'll be all for now, Sergeant, thank you.'

Inspector Reid sat back in his chair as he watched Sergeant Thick close the door to his office. He looked at his pocket watch and sighed deeply at the pile of reports in front of him. If only there were a few more hours in the day he told himself and sighed again.

The Jaran visitors to Earth: First Commander Treve Pacton Ashto and Apprentice Commander Atia Mo Margo felt relieved as they left Leman Street police station.

'Well, Margot, hopefully we will never have to visit the inside of that building again,' said Ashto.

'Agreed, Trevor. I think it most unlikely that our

activities over the next few years will cause us to have to talk to Inspector Reid again in the future.'

'Let us hope you are correct in that assumption, Margot.'

The Jaran explorers walked the short distance to Whitechapel High Street where they hired a hansom cab. Their continuing gathering of data on behalf of the Jaran Federation had now taken them out of the Whitechapel area and into other districts of London. Today they had decided to journey to the West End of the city. It was an area they had come to know reasonably well during the previous few months but where they were yet to do an in-depth trawl for information that was going to be useful to them during their five-year stay on the planet Earth. During that time they would be busily compiling their report to send back to their superiors on Jara.

The hansom cab's horse clip-clopped its way through the city streets, past the landmark structures of the Tower of London and St Paul's Cathedral and into the busy West End. At Covent Garden the cab stopped as directed and Ashto, now fully conversant with the monetary system employed in this the most important city in the foremost nation state on the planet Earth, paid the driver giving him, as he usually did, a large tip. The cab driver smiled and touched his bowler hat with his whip by way of gratitude and drove on leaving Ashto and Atia in the already crowded market area.

The Jaran pair liked London's markets. They particularly enjoyed the sights and sounds they came across in such places. The unfamiliar fruit, vegetables and blooms on display; the mixture of the different languages, accents and dialects that existed side-by-side in London all gathered together in this place of business and retail commerce.

There was English of course, often spoken in the confusing cockney vernacular, but there was also Yiddish, Romany and various East European tongues mixing with a smattering of Italian, French, Spanish and German, a truly polyglot meeting of people from various places on the planet Earth. As a Jaran, Ashto was supposed to look forward to the day in the future when the people of the Earth, as members of the Jaran Galactic Federation, would be united and fully embrace the highly logical Jaran language along with the many other benefits that membership of the Federation would undoubtedly bring. However, having spent the last few months getting to know the Earth and its people, at least those in London, he had started to believe that it would be something of a shame if or when the languages here on Earth were consigned to the dustbin of history. He knew that life on Earth, after the involvement of the Federation into the everyday lives of its people, would fundamentally change the planet and be an improvement on the current generally confused situation but secretly he rather hoped that some provision could be made to preserve at least some of the languages he could hear all around him today.

The Jarans walked through the crowded market place looking with interest at the many trestle tables, barrows and baskets full of oysters, nuts, cheeses and cakes as well as various ironmongery and knick-knacks the purpose of which was a complete mystery to Ashto and Atia. In the flower, fruit and vegetable market inside the colonnaded building with its great glass roof Ashto bought two apples, which he and Atia preceded to munch on as they continued their progress through the market. As they did so they smiled at each other both remembering their arrival in London, the previous summer, when the first food they ate on this new planet were apples bought from an elderly female street vendor.

As the First Commander and his Apprentice Commander walked through the market, Ashto dressed in his favourite tweed suit, Inverness cape and deerstalker hat, Atia in a black, stylish feathered hat and a long purple coat with fur collar and cuffs, they became aware that someone was following them. Stopping by a vegetable stall Atia whispered in her First Commander's ear, 'Trevor, I do believe we are again being followed by an old acquaintance.'

'I thought so, Margot. I first saw him as we entered this building. Shall we make it known that we've spotted him?'

'I think we will, Trevor,' said Atia smiling widely.

Quickly turning around so that they faced the way they had come they both waved at the man who was half concealed behind a stall piled high with apples and oranges.

Rather sheepishly the man emerged; it was the second time this individual had been caught following the Jaran pair in a market place.

'Good morning, Mr Rogers, how very nice to meet you again,' said Atia holding out her hand and walking purposefully towards the man.

'We meet again, Mrs Ashton. Good morning to you and of course your husband Mr Ashton.' William Rogers, a reporter for the London Evening Standard newspaper, shook the hands of the Jaran explorers in turn. It was the first time they had seen the young journalist in this brand new year of 1889. In the previous November Rogers had been important in helping to obtain First Commander Ashto's release from Leman Street police station where he was being held on suspicion of being Jack the Ripper. Not until after the Ripper's final murder had taken place did the police agree to Mr Rogers' request that Mr Ashton should be allowed to leave police custody.

'Well, Mr Rogers, you seem to be following us yet again,' said Ashto smiling. He had never really taken to the reporter mainly because the newspaperman had shown an undue amount of interest in Atia even to the extent of taking her out to dinner one evening. However Rogers' willingness to help out at Leman Street while Atia was secretly dealing with the Ripper at 13, Miller's Court had caused him to modify his feelings towards the young reporter just a little.

'Ah, this time I have to admit that I *was* actually following you both. I saw you emerge from Leman Street police station and was wondering what you were doing there.'

'That is a little on the presumptuous side, Mr Rogers,' said Atia, 'considering our dealings with the police are a private matter.'

'That is completely true, Mrs Ashton, but I was in Leman Street heading towards the police station on newspaper business when I noticed the two of you emerge and as I consider myself to be a rather good reporter who is always on the lookout for interesting stories to write I decided to follow you to see if I could pick up any details regarding the reason for your visit to that particular building.'

'Well, I doubt very much if you would gain any intelligence regarding our visit to the police by following us all the way to Covent Garden market,' said Atia.

'Again that is so true, Mrs Ashton, but I was rather intrigued by the fact that as soon as the both of you exited the police station you were followed by an extremely expert individual who I know is a police officer, despite his rather impressive down-at-heel disguise. He tracked you all the way here and at present, as we speak, is lurking behind us at a market stall examining in detail a long string of onions.'

Ashto and Atia could not resist glancing over to where the man stood seemingly fascinated by the vegetables.

'Are you sure he is an undercover police officer?' said Ashto.

'Oh, most definitely, Mr Ashton, and if I'm not mistaken he is one of the Leman Street detective constables, a young chap by the name of Philip Perkins I believe. I have seen him in the building many times in the course of my search for stories to put in the Standard.'

A look of concern passed over First Commander Ashto's face as he wondered why Inspector Reid would still be sending one of his officers to follow Atia and himself. Atia must have read the expression on his face as she quickly suggested that she and Ashto ought to leave the market.

'Well goodbye then, Mr Rogers, we must get on with our researches,' said Atia shaking the newspaperman's hand. 'Until we meet again; which I'm sure on past evidence will be sooner rather than later.'

Rogers smiled. 'Goodbye Mrs Ashton and Mr Ashton, I do hope that you are not too bothered by being followed by one of Leman Street's finest.'

Ashto nodded at the young reporter and shook his hand before walking out of the market arm-in-arm with Atia. Rogers watched them leave and then walked in the opposite direction quickly turning back to watch the undercover police officer follow the Jaran pair. A thin smile played across the lips of the Evening Standard journalist.

Report Number 0012 to the Glorious and Munificent Jaran Galactic Federation High Council (Planetary Exploration and Viable Exo-Planet Evaluation Committee – Sector 2007 Sub-Committee) by First Commander Treve Pacton Ashto.

My greetings and utmost felicitations to the esteemed members of the sub-committee.

Several days ago a new calendar year began on this planet and here, as is also customary on Jara, there was a certain amount of celebration connected with the turn of the year and the beginning of a new seasonal cycle. London is now in the depths of the winter season although to be honest there doesn't seem to be a great deal of difference between the winter weather and that of the autumn that preceded it. The temperature is several degrees lower certainly but the instances of precipitation and thick fogs seem to occur at much the same regular rate as before.

After the turmoil that was caused last year by the series of brutal murders that took place in our adopted home region of Whitechapel things seem to have returned to some sort of normality although it is fair to say that the area will probably never get over the hideous nature of those terrible killings.

Apprentice Commander Atia, although physically recovered from the wound she suffered when she confronted the male who had become known as Jack the Ripper, has found it difficult to shake off the feeling of horror and dread she felt on the night she dealt with the killer by reducing him to his component atoms with the disrupter weapon she had carried on her person. At the scene of the final murder she was forced to witness the hideous mutilations that had been inflicted by the killer on a young Earth woman Atia had got to know well. The Apprentice Commander now often wakes up distressed in the middle of the night, assailed by vivid and unbidden dreams that cause her to relive that traumatic experience. I have to comfort her and provide her with emotional support so that she can drift off again into a hopefully untroubled and dreamless period of rest.

Meanwhile we have, of course, been continuing with our mission to collect data and assess how the people of the planet Earth would generally react to a visit by the representatives of the glorious Galactic Federation. Having been here for about half an Earth year we still have four and a half years in which to continue our investigations at the end of which we will of course supply the sub-committee with our substantive findings and recommendations for future contact, or not, with the people and authorities of Earth.

To follow the above course of action Apprentice Commander Atia and I have decided to stay on in the Whitechapel area of the city called London at least for the time being. The location at which we have been staying, called Mrs Smith's Select Guesthouse, leaves much to be desired in terms of its facilities and comfort it offers, but it has suited us well so far due to its location and general anonymity. If we moved to a more salubrious area of London we would probably find that local residents would be far more inquisitive about our origins and antecedents. In Whitechapel, as a rule, few people are interested in us. Local individuals go about their own everyday business and we can carry on unchallenged in our assumed guises of married couple Mr and Mrs Ashton, a writer and his assistant from the relatively faraway country of the United States of America, here in London to write a book that would act as a travel guide for other Americans visiting Britain and its capital city.

Our mastery of the local language called English has continued apace and we are certain that we appear to others as ordinary members of British society, albeit ones who are relatively wealthy. Any slight mistakes we have made in our understanding and communication of the English language can be put down to our cover story that we come from another country called the United States of America where, by all accounts, a slightly different type of English is spoken.

I am pleased to say that we have had no contact with the police so far this year. The members of the sub-committee will no doubt remember that I had dealings with a police inspector by the name of Edmund Reid during the time when the police were hunting Jack the Ripper. A most formidable human, Inspector Reid is the type of individual that any future Jaran diplomatic or trade delegation would be well advised to win over in any attempt to persuade Earth humans to agree with the concept of becoming willing members of the Galactic Federation.

So now Apprentice Commander Atia and I continue to gather data and intelligence about the people of London and the society in which they live and work. Having got to know the Whitechapel area very well we have begun to discover more about the other regions of London and the humans residing there. The Apprentice Commander and I will continue to send data about the Earth and its people directly to the sub-committee as well as these regular reports. I will submit my next report soon, of course.

With my utmost loyalty to the glorious Jaran Galactic Federation,

First Commander Treve Pacton Ashto.

2

A Horrible Discovery

Metropolitan Police Constable 282H Joseph Dragge looked at his police issue pocket watch. There was still another hour remaining of the first half of his nighttime shift before he would be able to return to the warmth of Leman Street police station, have a cup of tea and put his feet up for a while. He pulled his cape around his neck in the hope of shutting out some of the biting cold that surrounded him on this freezing January night. His nose, reddened already from the head cold he had developed earlier in the day, felt raw and frozen. He wrapped his gloved right hand around it in a vain attempt to warm it up. One more hour before he could have his break, drink a nice hot cup of tea and endeavour to get warm again, he told himself. His ice cold feet would certainly appreciate the warming effect a roaring coal fire back at the station would have on them.

He was still daydreaming about the welcoming atmosphere of the staff room at Leman Street nick when he heard footsteps behind him and a plaintive, urgent voice calling to him.

'Officer, officer, this way, come quick, the Ripper's bin at it again!'

PC Dragge's spirits fell. He had been dreading this moment ever since November when the most recent of the Ripper murders had taken place. Throughout the month of December most of the East End had been on tenterhooks waiting for Jack the Ripper to strike again. Older coppers had told him to be on the lookout. They had said that once a killer starts they'd only stop when they're caught and so far no one had been arrested and charged with the five or maybe six killings that had been attributed to the Whitechapel murderer.

PC Dragge, with a certain amount of difficulty, got his frozen feet to break into a run and pursued the man who was frantically gesturing for the constable to follow him. The man stopped with his arm outstretched pointing at some wooden fencing that cordoned off a section of Whitechapel Road near to the Whitechapel and Mile End underground railway station. Constable Dragge had passed by the fence earlier in the evening and hadn't paid much attention to it plastered as it was with old posters and handbills advertising cheap eating and drinking establishments as well as the attractions that could be enjoyed at the local music halls. The man was pointing at a large hole in the fence that someone had obviously created so they could get a look at the building site beyond, no doubt in order to assess the thieving opportunities therein. Police Constable Dragge shone his bull's-eye lamp through the gap in the fence and peering through saw the hideous sight that had so alarmed the man who stood beside him and who was shaking and still pointing at the hole, a look of horror on his face, noticeably pale even in this darkest of nights. Dragge took out his whistle and blew three loud blasts on it. This was something with which he would need some help.

Detective Sergeant William Thick stroked his impressive bushy mustache as he looked down at the headless and naked corpse. 'It don't look like the work of the Ripper an' that's for certain.'

'Not unless he's changed his approach,' said Inspector Reid as he knelt down to get a closer look. It was undoubtedly the naked body of a man minus his head.

'It's a young man's body. Good muscle development, sparse chest hair, no saggy bits, apart from the obvious items that is. He would probably have been about 5 foot 8 inches tall if he could stand and if he had his head in place,' said Reid.

'An' no mutilations except for the missing noggin,' replied his sergeant.

'Let's turn him over and see if there's any marks on his back.'

Reid and Thick turned the pale body on to its front.

'A small tattoo on the right shoulder,' said Reid wiping some mud away, 'looks like a butterfly or a moth. Fairly unusual wouldn't you say so, Bill? As you say there's no sign of any mutilation though. Let's turn him back again.'

'Clean cut through the neck – no hacking away at it – must've used a pretty good sharp saw to take the head off – perhaps a surgical instrument?' speculated the sergeant.

'Yes, you're right, Bill apart from this mark on the side of the neck. What do you make of it?' Bill Thick peered closely at a small but deep v-shaped indentation on the neck just below where a saw must have been used to remove the person's head.

'Hmm, it could be where the teeth of the saw caught the skin just before whoever it was began to cut the head off.'

'Yes possibly, a bit too large for that though. Could be part of a bite? Look, it's almost tooth shaped.'

Sergeant Thick looked closer at the mark: 'It could be I suppose, it seems unlikely though.'

'Well, one thing is certain with no blood about, it would seem that the murder was committed somewhere else where the head was taken off and the rest of the body brought here and hidden behind this fence.'

'Not very well hidden though, Inspector. There'd be plenty of workmen here on the building site on Monday morning when the body would have been quickly discovered by them.'

'Yes, so the body was meant to be found. What's also interesting is this.' Reid had lifted the corpse's right arm and was looking carefully at the hand. 'See here Bill, small writing callous on the top of the middle finger as well as some ink stains on the thumb and under the nails. I believe what we have here is a young office clerk who spent much of his time sitting at a desk writing letters or adding up figures in a ledger.'

'Plenty of them about, Sir.'

'That's right, Bill. We need to find out if any such person has been reported missing recently. Then we can start to work out why someone killed him and decided to keep his head. We'll know a bit more after the coroner has done his work. Make sure you get his report to me as soon as possible.'

Inspector Reid stood up, groaning slightly as he did so and dusted off his hands. After instructing two waiting constables to fetch a handcart and wheel the body to the nearby Whitechapel morgue, he and Sergeant Thick began to head back to Leman Street. They were stopped by a gaggle of newspapermen who stood outside the fence, prevented from entering the scene of the crime by a burly uniformed policeman.

'Is this the work of the Ripper, Inspector Reid?' said one of the reporters.

'We'll let you gents know once we've got the report from the coroner,' answered Reid, who then realised that such uncertainty could lead to members of the public in the area panicking, stopped and addressed the group of journalists as a whole. 'The unmutilated torso is that of a man and there is absolutely nothing to associate this death with the Whitechapel murderer. Killers do not usually change their pattern or method of operation and so I can categorically state that this murder has nothing to do with Jack the Ripper.'

'Why has the body got no head on it?' asked another of the reporters.

Inspector Reid looked at his Sergeant and shook his head in mock disbelief. 'Because whoever killed this young man removed his head before dumping the body on this building site; *why* he did that is something we'll have to find out. Good day gentlemen.'

And with that Inspector Reid and Sergeant Thick walked

off towards Leman Street leaving the gathered reporters jotting down notes in their notebooks and chatting excitedly among themselves.

The Scottish Play

'Shall we go to another theatrical presentation this evening, Trevor?'

Apprentice Commander Atia was sitting at the battered writing desk in the Jaran pair's very basic room in Mrs Smith's Select Guesthouse in Bell Lane, in the heart of Whitechapel. She was reading the day's edition of the London Daily News.

'That's a marvelous idea, Margot. I very much enjoyed our recent visit to the theatre to see the play entitled Dr Jekyll and Mr Hyde. What production do you propose we should view this time?'

'Well, Trevor, two of London's leading actors are currently performing at the Lyceum theatre in a play called Macbeth. It is the work of a very famous British writer, a male called William Shakespeare.'

'I have heard of that individual, Margot, I believe he is very well regarded. What is the play about?

'Well, from what I can gather from our ship's data bank the play is set in the Earth's distant past in the area known as Scotland and tells the story of a military commander whose blind ambition causes him to kill the reigning monarch in order to take his place. His equally ambitious wife spurs him on in this regicidal endeavour.'

'Well, we were able to glean some interesting insights into the psychological make-up of Earth humans in our last theatre visit. Hopefully this production will allow us to do likewise, Margot.'

'Yes, Trevor, hopefully it will. It begins at 7.45 this evening with the preparatory overture starting 5 minutes earlier.'

'In that case Margot, I would suggest that we spend the afternoon making observations in the West End after endeavouring to obtain tickets at the box office of the theatre. We could perhaps go to Fortescues' restaurant before going on to the Lyceum.'

'A wonderful idea, Trevor, I shall very much look forward to it.'

Fortescues' was the rather expensive restaurant in the Strand to which Mr Rogers had once taken Atia, much to the chagrin of First Commander Ashto who had experienced a certain degree of jealousy at the time. Since then he and Atia had visited Fortescues' together and enjoyed the roast meats and vegetables followed by a selection of delicious cheeses that were served in the restaurant's extremely ornate surroundings.

'Before we go out, Margot, I must use the replicator to produce some more gold sovereigns; we seem to be running short of them.'

'Well remembered, Trevor. It would be quite embarrassing to eat at Fortescues' and then not be able to pay the bill.'

Both Jarans chuckled at the thought. The last thing they ever wanted to do was to draw unwanted attention to themselves. Their mission required them to keep as low a profile as possible whilst they went about their business collecting data and intelligence about the inhabitants of the Earth. The fact that their replicator, a portable model they had brought with them on their shuttle craft that had now safely returned to their spaceship currently in orbit around the Earth, could produce facsimile gold coins had enabled the Jaran explorers a good degree of purchasing power while they went about their Earth-bound tasks.

Atia turned the page of the newspaper and immediately her eye was caught by a disturbing news report. 'Trevor, there has been another murder; a body has been found on a building site on Whitechapel Road.'

'Oh no not again, Margot. Why is it these Earth humans cannot stop themselves from slaughtering each other?'

'I do not know, Trevor. This latest body had its head missing.'

'That is horrible, Margot. Do the police know anything about the person who has committed this heinous act?'

'Apparently not, Trevor, either that or they are not disclosing all the information at this stage.'

'Well, Margot hopefully this terrible killing will be a one-off occurrence that the police will get to the bottom of fairly swiftly.'

'Yes I do hope so, Trevor. Let us further hope that we are not seeing the beginning of another series of murders in the local area.'

Ashto and Atia looked at each other, their expressions full of concern at the very possibility that such a thing could happen again so soon after Jack the Ripper had caused such murder and mayhem in the East End of London.

Later that day, the First Commander and the Apprentice Commander, having obtained their tickets for the evening presentation of Macbeth, were strolling down Regent Street making a visual record of the shops and shoppers by using the micro cameras they had attached to their clothes. In Ashto's case his camera was located in one of the buttons of the tweed cape he wore while Atia's was fixed to her fashionable brimmed and feathered hat. The Jaran pair would upload the information stored in these cameras to their ship's computer when they returned to their guesthouse room later that evening. Both Jarans also kept notebooks to hand in which they occasionally made notes that were somewhat superfluous. These were felt by Ashto and Atia to be necessary just in case they were again being followed by one of Inspector Reid's officers, which if the evidence of previous days was anything to go on, was highly likely.

Outside the Liberty and Co. store in Regent Street they stopped and looked in the window at some of the latest fashionable clothes on display. 'Trevor, do you think it would be a good idea to go into this particular retail emporium? Just to analyse Earth human's reactions to the goods on sale?' said Atia, hopefully.

'If you would like to enter this store, Margot, then of course we must if you believe it will furnish us with some useful data.' First Commander Ashto smiled broadly.

'Thank you, Trevor, I also believe it would also be an

interesting diversion for the undercover police officer called Perkins who I have just noticed is following us again today.'

'I understand, Margot. Perhaps we could endeavour to rid ourselves of Reid's man once we're in the store by some sort of subterfuge?'

'Perhaps, Trevor, but it might be a wiser course of action to go about in the store making copious entries in our notebooks. That way when the undercover officer reports back to Inspector Reid he will have nothing of substance to tell him apart from our normal activities.'

'A splendid idea, Margot,' said Ashto taking a pencil from his coat pocket and checking to see if it was still sharp.

Once inside the large department store the Jaran pair stood for a while looking at the collection of objects d'art on the ground floor of Liberty's. As they made notes they were also able to identify the young undercover policeman as he too examined the artistic and pricey items for sale in the exclusive store pretending to show an interest in them.

Ashto and Atia then headed for the stairs and the female clothing area of the store. Atia spent some time looking at dresses and ball gowns, many of which were made from expensive silk imported from India. Ashto still found it quite incredible how complicated, uncomfortable looking and how immensely fussy the clothes of Earth females were. He remembered to make notes in his notebook as well as record a visual record of the garments. He smiled at the reaction those in the sub-committee on back on Jara would have when they viewed the elaborate and intricate style of clothes worn by the inhabitants of this planet, at least those wealthy enough to afford them. Jaran clothes were always simple and comfortable, the exact opposite to those worn by the people of Earth. Ashto smiled again when, out of the corner of his eye, he saw Reid's man lurking in a doorway looking rather embarrassed and out of place among the displays of women's dresses and under-garments. He almost felt sorry for the undercover police officer now looking bemusedly at a display advertising "The Victoria corset" that was, according to the nearby description, known for its "Perfect Shape, Elegance and Durability."

That evening Ashto and Atia made their way to the Lyceum theatre in Wellington Street in the West End of London. They had thoroughly enjoyed their meal at Fortescues' restaurant and both felt well fed and satisfied as they walked through the impressive colonnaded frontage of the theatre and entered the crowded lobby of the theatre. After depositing their outerwear with the theatre's cloakroom attendant they headed towards the narrow, plushly carpeted corridor that led to their seats in the stalls. Atia was dressed in her long, dark blue gown with a short jacket of the same colour and as usual gained many admiring looks from the men present, some of whom were reprimanded by their accompanying females for staring too long at the tall and striking looking Jaran woman. Ashto wore his black evening suit and top hat, a particular fashion item he still found absolutely ludicrous, although with his height and dark good looks he too was the recipient of a number of surreptitious glances by many of the females present.

As they continued down the corridor a slight young woman with dirty blond hair bustled into Atia seemingly by accident. The Apprentice Commander felt the woman's hand snake into the pocket of her jacket and emerge with the small disrupter weapon that, since her encounter with the Ripper, she always carried with her. With lightning speed Atia grabbed the woman's thin wrist and with her strong hand squeezed hard causing the female to cry out and drop the disrupter onto the carpeted floor. Ashto seeing what had happened and walking just behind his Apprentice Commander quickly bent down and retrieved the disrupter slipping it into his own coat pocket. Atia held on tightly to the woman who yelped, squawked and squealed pathetically and gave Atia a deeply black look as she did so.

'Excuse me madam; let me take hold of this person. I saw exactly what happened. This female was attempting to rob you,' said a balding man as he grabbed the woman's other arm and also laid a firm grip on to the collar of her somewhat grubby dress. He called out: 'Oh, Mr Stoker, would you be so good as to call for the police please.'

'Of course, Mr Terry,' replied a tall, burly, red-bearded man who emerged from a room that was obviously his office.

By now there was a large group of theatregoers observing with interest the fracas that was going on in the corridor. The young woman, still loudly squealing her innocence, tried to wriggle free of the grip the man had on her as someone in the crowd suggested that they had seen the woman earlier with a man acting most suspiciously. Mr Terry easily manhandled the complaining woman into Mr Stoker's office and Ashto and Atia, always keen to see Earth humans in various forms of stressful situations, followed them eager to see what would transpire.

Mr Stoker's office was on the small size but was full of dark polished wood paneling and an oak desk and two chairs. On the walls were a number of theatrical posters detailing some of the recent plays performed at the Lyceum, including Richard Mansfield's recent triumphant production of *Dr Jekyll and Mr Hyde*.

'I've sent young Murray for the police, Mr Terry and I'm sure they'll be here promptly,' said Mr Stoker. Mr Terry still had a firm grip on the young woman who occasionally whined that he was hurting her arm and neck. 'I hope, dear madam that you were not hurt in any way as a result of this individual's attempt to rob you?' inquired Mr Stoker looking at Atia. 'Did she actually take anything from your person?'

Atia glanced at Ashto who responded by tapping the pocket of his jacket and indicating that he had safely retrieved the disrupter.

'No, luckily she did not, Mr…'

'Oh, please forgive me I should have introduced myself. My name is Mr Stoker, the business manager of the Lyceum theatre and this is Mr Terry who is the theatre's treasurer.' The Jaran pair shook hands with Stoker and introduced themselves. They were both pleased that they were visually recording the events that had unfolded since they had arrived at the theatre – this was all valuable data on Earth human behaviour.

Atia said: 'Mr Terry, please ensure that you are not actually hurting the young female you are currently holding on to.'

'Be assured dear lady,' said Mr Stoker, 'Mr Terry is a gentleman in all senses of the word. No harm at all shall come to this woman.' The young woman seeing that Atia might be an unlikely ally continued to squeal and proclaim her innocence.

At that moment there was a brief knock on the door. It opened and a head, along with the policeman's helmet it was wearing, appeared round it. "Excuse me,' said the police officer, 'I'll take this female off your hands now, Sir, if I may,' said the constable to the treasurer, Mr Terry, who proceeded to hand over the woman to the law officer. The constable firmly gripped the woman who continued to grumble loudly about how she had been mistreated in the room. The policeman studiously ignored her. 'Oh, by the way,' the police officer added, 'we've also arrested her male accomplice, an individual called Norris, who was lurking around at the front of the theatre waiting for her to emerge. We've been after this pair for a while – they've regularly been seen pickpocketing around the West End over the last few weeks.'

'Thank you, Constable, most efficient I must say,' said Mr Stoker who looked relieved when the policeman had departed and the problem had been solved. 'We don't get this sort of thing happening very often but when it does it can be very upsetting for all those involved,' said Mr Stoker addressing Ashto and Atia. 'I do hope that this unfortunate occurrence will not put you off visiting our theatre in the future.'

Atia who had taken an interest in the various accents she came across since first coming to London had noticed that the distinguished looking, red-haired business manager of the theatre, who Atia estimated was in his early forties and who was almost as tall as the First Commander, had the same sort of softly attractive Irish accent as poor Marie Jeanette Kelly had had before her life was so cruelly snuffed out by Jack the Ripper.

'Think nothing further about it, Mr Stoker, these

unfortunate things sometimes happen,' said Ashto, 'Mrs Ashton and myself are very much looking forward to tonight's play. Oh, and we would be very grateful if our names were not mentioned in any newspaper report pertaining to tonight's incident.'

'I'm so very pleased to hear you say that, Mr Ashton. And we will certainly make no mention of your names if that is what you so wish. And of course, Mr and Mrs Ashton, the next time you visit the Lyceum your tickets will be completely free of any charge.'

The Jaran pair smiled at the two men and thanked them. Mr Terry held open the door and as the Jarans left the office Atia noticed that on the outside of the door, in gold lettering, was inscribed the full name of the Lyceum's business manager *Mr Abraham Stoker*. What an interesting name, she thought.

Later that evening, back at their guesthouse room Ashto and Atia were reflecting on the play they had seen.

'I thought that the actors playing the roles of Macbeth and his wife were very convincing, Margot,' said First Commander Ashto.

'I agree, Trevor. Henry Irving and Ellen Terry were extremely skilled at portraying the ambitious nature of the pair as they plotted and planned,' replied Apprentice Commander Atia.

'Yes, Margot, Miss Terry in particular I thought had a magnificent presence about her on the stage of the theatre. That long, red hair, her beautiful but conniving visage as she persuaded her husband to kill the old king was very compelling.'

'Do you think Ellen Terry is any relation to Mr Terry, the Lyceum Theatre's treasurer, Trevor?'

'I'm not sure, Margot. It would be an easy enough task to find out though. Why do you ask?'

'Oh, no particular reason, Trevor I was just wondering. It will be very gratifying to return to the theatre to watch another of their plays in the near future.'

'Certainly, Margot, we must keep up to date with the productions due to be presented at the Lyceum.'

'That would be very pleasant, Trevor. In the meantime would you say that observing the play Macbeth by Mr Shakespeare has added anything to our understanding of the psychological make-up of Earth humans?'

'Hmm interesting, Margot, I believe that it definitely has. The play is about the destructive aspects of unbridled ambition and Earth people's capacity for committing acts of evil and it seems to me that it also contains an inherent warning against individuals obtaining political power no matter what harm their actions do to other humans. In the end Macbeth's desire for power does not only destroy a number of other individuals, some of whom at one time were his friends and colleagues, but also leads to his and his wife's destruction as well. There seems to be plenty of examples of this sort of behaviour and consequent outcomes in Earth's history.'

'That is true, Trevor. Although it must be said that, as far as ordinary humans are concerned, the quest for self-aggrandisment is usually at a much lower level of involvement than that of kings and queens in the distant past. In the world of today petty theft, as we have borne witness to tonight, is a much more common method of realising one's ambition to improve one's quality of life by the acquisition of relatively small amounts of money or goods. Perhaps the writer William Shakespeare uses the case of the Macbeths in a more generalized way as an illustration that naked ambition that is totally lacking in any moderation and personal responsibility is, by its very nature, a detrimental aspect of the human condition.'

'When the Macduff character appeared on stage brandishing the head of the tyrant Macbeth, I noticed that you gripped my hand tightly and appeared to be somewhat shocked. Are you fully recovered now, Margot? I was a little concerned that the violent nature of the play had brought back unfortunate memories that you could best do without.'

'I am fine now, Trevor.' Atia grasped Ashto's hand and smiled at him. 'It was seeing the severed head of Macbeth who, while to some extent, he deserved his fate that he had very much brought upon himself, the incident reminded me somewhat of that terrible night at 13, Miller's Court. It also caused me to remember that there is now another killer out there and on the loose who might go on to do further harm to others.'

'Well, Margot, let us hope that this latest murder is simply a one-off atrocity and not the beginning of a new series of outrages. I'm not sure that the people of Whitechapel could put up with another Jack the Ripper style rampage.'

'I hope very much that you are correct, Trevor.' Atia's face, as she considered what Ashto had said, looked far from optimistic.

4

Number 19, Cleveland Street.

He had heard whispers about the private club for some time and he felt full of restrained excitement as he arrived at the large Georgian building in Cleveland Street. After supplying the password to the burly and taciturn attendant who opened the front door and once he had provided the requisite amount of subscription money to a more friendly, bespectacled receptionist he was led into a large drawing room.

The lights in the room were dimmed and the atmosphere was sultry, smoky and fragrant. It seemed to him at once to be so full of excitement, opportunity and promise. Quiet music was playing from one of those phonograph machines he had recently heard so much about. Around the room, seated on sumptuous settees draped with eastern-style fabrics, were pairs of men, some young, some elderly, some engaged in conversation, often with arms entwined around each other, while others caressed and kissed. He smiled. This was very promising indeed, he told himself. The information the young man had recently supplied him with, prior to his succumbing to extreme loss of blood of course, had been invaluable. He had graphically described the activities that went on behind the seemingly respectable façade of this house in Cleveland Street. He had told him about the little cabal of individuals working for the General Post Office who flitted from their usual jobs into the dark goings on in this molly house, rather like the moths they wore as tattoos on their backs and which marked them out as willing members of their covert society. The extra money the members of the secret club were able to earn supplemented their rather meagre wages. None of that was any of his business of course. If these young men wanted to carry out their disgusting actions for money who was he to want to stop them?

So having recently tasted the joys of giving into his deepest desires, desires that had been swimming around in his mind since his childhood, he was now ready to indulge once more and utilise another mercenary young man's body in order to enjoy himself fully to the hilt again.

A waiter appeared at his side with a silver tray on which had been placed a glass of champagne; he took the drink and sipped it appreciatively. It was a nice wine certainly but nothing as satisfying as the warm life-giving liquid he would taste later. The waiter led him to a plush red settee in the furthest corner of the darkened room. There he sat enjoying his champagne, looking around, knowing that another would soon join him. He felt relaxed in spite of the knot of excitement that curled around his insides. Nervousness and excitement were such similar feelings he thought as he sipped some more of his sparkling wine.

And then suddenly, standing in front of him, was his companion for the evening. He gestured for him to sit down and then looked at him as he relaxed back into the plush settee. He was young, no more than sixteen or seventeen he estimated, fresh faced, fair haired, bright-eyed and giving every sign of being willing to fully take part in tonight's games. Just right, he thought. He smiled and the boy smiled back. He looked smart in his bright blue telegraph messenger boy jacket and his black bowler hat and appeared ready and eager to please, in return for a financial reward of course. The boy smiled again, removed his hat, smoothed his dark hair and put his hand on the man's knee and squeezed gently. He felt a thrill go through his body, not from the boy's touch, that totally disgusted him, but from the knowledge of what he would be able to do to this young individual later in the evening.

Soon they would discuss the price and he would hand over some money to the mercenary young man. Then they would walk back to his home. They would drink wine and exchange meaningful looks and then he would take the young man to the basement where it would all happen. He was hungry and he was sure that everything would happen just as he wanted and expected it to. The drugged drink he would give the boy would act on him by the time they entered the basement room. Then the young man would be unable to resist, as the drug would make it impossible for his arms and legs to respond to his brain. He had previously been assured that his fellow participant would remain fully conscious even though "the young lady would not be able to move an inch" whatever was done to her. The loathsome rat-like individual that had supplied the drug had told him this. A young lady! He smiled – not so far from the truth he thought – young certainly but he didn't want to be with a young lady on this particular night, he could wait for that particular pleasure. No, tonight this boy in his General Post Office uniform suited him down to the ground and, like the previous time, would provide him with a wonderful night's entertainment. The only part of the evening's activities he hadn't decided upon yet was where to leave his victim's remains once he had divested the young man of his clothes, slowly taken his fill and removed his fine, handsome looking head from the rest of his young body.

His mouth watered at the thought. The taste of blood was still in his mouth from the last time. It had been a divine, even a spiritual experience and tonight he was going to repeat it.

He grinned, gave the boy the money he asked for – a few coins, so little to provide him with so much enjoyment – and then led the way out into the cold and misty January night. It was only a short walk from the house in Cleveland Street to his own residence in Fitzroy Street and although the weather was bitterly cold he was warmed by the thought of what would soon take place. The boy smiled back at him as they walked along the street lit only dimly by the yellow glow of gas-lamps. Soon, he told himself; it would all happen so very soon.

5

A Body of Evidence

'They've found another one, Inspector.'

'Another what?' replied Reid, fearing for a moment that Bill Thick was going to inform him that another Ripper victim had been discovered horribly torn and mangled in some dark alleyway or, God help him, in another gore-filled room where some poor prossie had plied her trade before being ripped apart.

'Another headless body, Sir.'

Edmund Reid had been sitting at his desk reading the various reports of counterfeit gold sovereigns that had been turning up all over Whitechapel and further afield in other areas of London. He was puzzled. Apparently the coins had been examined by an expert who had called them the most skillful examples of counterfeiting he had ever seen with only one very obvious flaw apparent: the date. Usually counterfeiters were unskilled chancers whose efforts were crude and easily discovered but these sovereigns had been expertly produced by someone who knew what they were doing to the ultimate degree and then seemed to forget that having the correct year on the coin was actually important. All of the counterfeited gold coins that had turned up so far had been stamped with the year 1988 on the reverse side, beneath the depiction of St George killing the dragon, rather than 1888, or any other year in the past; a strange and unfathomable mistake indeed.

Reid feeling baffled, sighed, scratched his cheek and then shaking his head, closed the report and stood up. He reached for his bowler hat, scarf and overcoat as his sergeant informed him that the body minus its head again had, this time, been found floating in the Thames at Wapping. The strangely flawed, counterfeit coins would have to wait for another day.

At the same time Inspector Reid and Sergeant Thick departed from Leman Street Police Station, Ashto and Atia were also leaving Mrs Smith's Select Guesthouse in Bell Lane ready to begin another day of data collection. Wrapped up against the early morning cold the Jaran pair walked down Goulston Street and onto Whitechapel High Street. As was usually the case the thoroughfare was busy with people and traffic. Horse-drawn omnibuses vied for space on the road with wagons piled with straw, livestock, bricks, and sacks of coal, fruit, vegetables and a myriad of other items. People crowded the pavement, many on their way to work in the offices, workshops, shops, market stalls and slaughterhouses of the East End. Others were already starting their day's shopping, carefully examining the meat and vegetable produce on offer from the street stalls and vendors, keen to make their meagre monetary resources stretch as far as possible. Ashto and Atia had never quite got used to the number of humans that were packed into this one relatively small area of London. On Jara careful urban planning and a more equally distributed population had led to a far less crowded and a much more pleasant environment. On the whole food and other commodities were supplied via replicators or delivered from labfarms and vegetable producers straight to people's homes. Outside areas were generally reserved for recreational activities such as sports of various kinds or for simply strolling in and appreciating the perfect temperature of the climate controlled atmosphere. Here on the Earth no one would be able to conceive of the joys of endless summer days with perfectly calibrated temperatures the people of Jara had come to take for granted. Here in London individuals had to put up with the cold of winter, the thick fogs of anytime in the year and the rain that seemed to fall every day no matter what time of year it was. And yet, there was something about the unpredictable nature of the weather of London that both Ashto and Atia secretly liked and appreciated. The fact that it could be pouring with rain one minute and the sun shining down from clear skies the next was somehow authentic and life affirming for the two Jaran explorers. The first time Atia had seen a rainbow her initial thought was not about how the phenomenon was caused by the refraction of light in the atmosphere but how struck she had been by the emergence of such sudden and sublime beauty from out of the gloom of dark rainclouds.

The Jaran pair smiled at each other, pleased to be out in the area that they had come to know so well.

'Where shall we go for breakfast today, Margot?'

'Hmm. Shall we go to the Jubilee tearooms on Commercial Street.'

'A very good idea,' smiled the First Commander.

'Same as before Inspector.'

Reid and Sergeant Thick looked down at the headless corpse that had recently been dragged out of the murky water and deposited on the muddy, grey and foul smelling foreshore of the River Thames.

'Looks very much like it,' replied Reid staring intently at the pale body that made an incongruous picture against the dark gravelly mud and detritus of the riverbank.

'Age?'

'Young. I'd guess at about fifteen or sixteen – fair-haired seemingly – he kept himself in trim too. Been in the river for a day or two by the look of it.'

'Hmm, looks much the same as the first fellow. Let's roll him over, Bill.'

Reid didn't much like the cold, clammy feel of the pale waterlogged flesh as the two men bent down and rolled the body onto its front. Reid pulled out his handkerchief and wiped away some gritty mud from the shoulder of the dead boy.

'There's the tattoo again, Sergeant. Same butterfly or moth design.'

'Odd,' said Bill Thick, 'why would both victims have the same tattoo?'

'Well, it's the only clue we have at the moment. Right, let's roll him back again.' After doing so Reid carefully examined the dead man's wrinkled hands. 'Not a manual worker, no ingrained ink stains on his fingers or under the nails this time, so this young man wasn't a junior clerk but something else.' Reid sighed loudly. 'Well, we'll do the same as before and check the lists of recently missing people and see if anyone stands out. Didn't do much good last time though did it, Bill?'

'No, Inspector, it didn't. Our murderer obviously doesn't want to leave too many clues as to who his victims are, which is why he removes the head I suppose.'

'Yes Bill, although he might have a another reason for doing that.'

'Why's that, Sir?'

'Trophies, Bill, trophies; he may keep the heads as souvenirs of what he's done, what he's feels he's achieved.'

The Sergeant grimaced. 'So there's going to be more of these then, Inspector.'

'I'm afraid so, Sergeant, I am very much afraid so.'

Atia sipped her tea. The Jubilee tearoom was not the nicest place in London but in terms of Whitechapel it was a cut above most other eating-places in the area. The Jaran explorers had breakfasted on tea and some rather tasty warm bread rolls and honey and felt ready to begin their daily research.

'I thought we might explore the Chelsea area of London today, Margot. What do you think?'

'That is fine as far as I'm concerned, Trevor. Shall we walk down to Whitechapel High Street, we'll be more likely to find a hansom cab there than on Commercial Street?'

'Certainly, Margot, that is a splendid idea.'

Ashto paid for their tea and rolls and the Jaran pair left

the Jubilee tearoom and turned toward Whitechapel High Street, the busiest thoroughfare in the area. As they reached the road junction their attention was drawn to a large crowd that had gathered on the opposite side of the road on the corner of Leman Street. Always on the lookout for unusual events and occurrences to document as part of their research Ashto and Atia crossed the busy street with care, avoiding not only the traffic but also the ubiquitous piles of horse dung that littered this and every other road in London. They joined the throng that was made up of a collection of local people and, in front, a group of newspaper reporters all with their notebooks and pencils in hand. At the centre of interest were the unmistakable figures of Inspector Reid and the equally imposing presence of his sergeant who, looking thoughtful, was stroking his large blond mustache. The newspapermen were firing questions at the police inspector.

'Do you think this is the work of the Ripper?'

'Do you know the identity of the dead man?'

'Is there another maniac on the loose?'

'Should the public be worried?'

'Gentlemen, gentlemen,' said the Inspector, 'we do not yet know who the latest deceased person is but we are doing our best to find that information out and no, these recent murders are definitely not the work of Jack the Ripper. These murders were committed in a totally different way and of course both of the victims have been males. I should not have to remind any of you that the Whitechapel murderer concentrated his murderous efforts on women. Now you must excuse me as I am heading back to the station to continue working on solving these latest crimes.'

There were one or two more shouted questions from the

group of reporters directed at Inspector Reid as he walked away but he studiously ignored them and continued to proceed with Sergeant Thick down Leman Street toward their police station.

Atia and Ashto having learned nothing particularly new about the recent crimes turned and started to look for a hansom cab to take them to the west of the city. Before they could hail a suitable vehicle, however, they were greeted warmly from behind. Turning they saw the familiar figure of Mr Rogers, notebook in hand and smile upon his face.

'We meet again Mr and Mrs Ashton, this time I can assure you completely by accident.'

'We'll take your word for that,' Atia said, smiling back at the newspaper reporter.'

Ashto and Atia shook hands with Rogers. 'Did you learn anything new about the recent killings from Inspector Reid, Mr Rogers?' said the First Commander.

'No, not particularly, although I always think that our esteemed Inspector secretes a few pertinent facts up his sleeve. I'm not sure that he completely trusts the men of the press.'

'That's hard to believe,' said Atia with an amused glint in her eye.

'Quite,' replied Rogers. 'However, there is one interesting fact that I have learned from sources other than the Inspector, Mr and Mrs Ashton.

'And what would that be?' said Atia.

'Well, just between ourselves it appears that the two dead young males knew each other and moved within in the same, rather illicit circles. The police have not released that information yet as they say that it might hamper their inquiries if the true facts emerged before they have had the chance to fully investigate the murders.'

'And what would those same illicit circles be, Mr Rogers?' asked Atia.

'Hmm, I'm not sure that I feel very comfortable broaching such matters with a member of the fair sex, Mrs Ashton, but let us simply say that both young men apparently frequented a demi-monde where various illegal practices of an intimate nature were conducted in an atmosphere of a great deal of secrecy. It is very possible, I have heard, that both of the victims had been involved in male prostitution prior to being killed.'

'That is very disturbing news, Mr Rogers,' said Ashto. 'If what you say is correct then we must presume that this new killer is targeting those individuals who indulge in such practices and that if recent events are repeated we could expect more horrific murders in the future.'

'It would certainly appear that way, Mr Ashton. Not a very welcome prospect for this area, which still hasn't recovered fully from the last series of dreadful crimes. If you have no objections I will now take my leave of you both and head back to my office where I shall write my article about this latest outrage for this evening's edition of the Standard. As always, Mr and Mrs Ashton, it has been a pleasure conversing with you.'

Rogers smiled his usual attractive smile and touched the brim of his bowler hat. Ashto and Atia watched him as he confidently hailed a cab and quickly got into the vehicle before being carried off along the busy road towards the west of the city.

'Well, Margot, what do you make of that?'

'It is very disturbing and distressing news indeed, Trevor. It looks very much as though there is another unbalanced individual on the loose who is targeting a certain type of victim. Sadly it seems that another series of murders has begun and presumably will continue until the person responsible is apprehended by the police, or dealt with by some other agency.'

Ashto felt a little uneasy as he noticed a glint in Atia's eye and a slight excited tone in her voice as she talked about this new outrage that appeared to have been committed in the local area. After they flagged down a hansom cab and were being carried through the streets of London Ashto and Atia were both unusually quiet as they watched the passing sights. The First Commander was concerned that his Apprentice Commander and erstwhile wife was keen to involve herself in another dangerous hunt for a persistent serial killer. He was not sure if that would be the wisest thing to do and was already considering the arguments he would use to stop her doing such a thing. Atia was, indeed, already thinking of ways in which she and the First Commander could help track down this killer of young men. The prospect of bringing another evil person to justice had indeed firmly gripped her interest.

At Leman Street police station Inspector Reid was reading the post mortem report on the first murder victim, now known to be a young man by the name of Charles Hobbs. As he already knew the victim's missing head had been cut off with a sharp, probably, surgical saw. What Reid had not known before, however, were two very disturbing facts. Firstly that some sort of chloral based drug found in the remains had been administered to the young man called Hobbs prior to his death and that, seemingly the body had been drained of most of its blood before the head was removed and the body transported to the building site at which it was found. Reid could see why a drug was used, probably to make the victim insensible before he was killed, unable to fight back against his attacker, but he could not think of any credible reason why the blood would be totally removed from the body. Reid had an unpleasant picture lodge unbidden in his mind. He saw a young man drugged but still alive, being hung up by his ankles, suspended from a beam in a factory or workshop perhaps while his throat was slit causing the blood to pump out of his body and his life to ebb away. And then the killer would take his sharp saw and take off the young man's head to keep as a souvenir of what he had done. Would he then place the head in a jar of preservative or perhaps he boiled it until all the flesh had fallen off leaving just a skull for him to keep as his prize?

Reid grimaced at the scene he had just conjured up inside his own head. Is that what happened, he asked himself? He needed to look at the bodies again and check for the marks of ropes or ligatures on the ankles of the victims.

The Inspector grabbed his coat and hat, opened the door of his office and shouted for Sergeant Thick. He didn't like going to the Whitechapel mortuary in Eagle Street at the best of times but if he had to attend that place of death he would prefer to do so in the company of Bill Thick. At least they could share the odd piece of gallows' humour, which, he had found in the past, often went some way to dispel the gloomy thoughts and depression that such awful places seemed to engender in his mind.

Report Number 0013 to the Glorious and Munificent Jaran Galactic Federation High Council (Planetary Exploration and Viable Exo-Planet Evaluation Committee – Sector 2007 Sub-Committee) by First Commander Treve Pacton Ashto.

My greetings and utmost felicitations to the esteemed members of the sub-committee.

Apprentice Commander Atia and myself have continued to explore London moving out from the area in the east of the city where we have based ourselves into the more wealthier western region. The amount of data we have been able to collect has been immense and as usual we have uploaded it to the ship's main computer, which sub-committee members are invited to access and examine at their leisure. Both Atia and I very much hope and presume that the information will be of great help in your eventual deliberations.

On one particular day our researches took as to a part of London called Chelsea, a much more overtly wealthier area than that of Whitechapel. There the houses are bigger and the people that we saw in our perambulations around its streets look decidedly healthier and are certainly much better dressed. The area, apparently, is the base for many artists and writers, many of whom are well known and popular amongst the more well off and those who have the leisure time and the wherewithal to be interested in the finer aspects of life.

The streets in the Chelsea area with names such as Tite Street, Flood Street and Cheyne Walk seem to contain many of these wealthy abodes and Apprentice Commander Atia, who has made a particular study of the area, informed me of the actual position of the residences of a number of these artists, poets and novelists who live in the area. One of them, a male by the name of Oscar Wilde is a young man who is very well thought of apparently. He has been responsible, so Atia informs me, for a number of works of fiction and also for clever journalism and is considered to be something of an intellectual and wit. I think Atia was secretly hoping that we might bump into this individual as we strolled around the area. We actually stopped outside his attractive, redbrick family home at 16, Tite Street for some considerable time in the hope that we might have accidentally met him but to no avail.

At the end of Cheyne Walk, which runs alongside the great river known as the Thames, is an interesting space of greenery called Cremorne Gardens. This location, until relatively recently, was a lively gathering spot for young, usually well off, individuals in search of excitement, recreation and fun. Inevitably the Gardens, as they are known locally, also gained something of a notorious reputation as a meeting spot for local prostitutes where alcohol and possibly other narcotic substances could be obtained and utilised. In recent times however local residents upset at the reputation engendered by the pleasure gardens have successfully had the area closed down and part of the gardens has already been built over. Atia and myself stood in what is left of the area looking out over the Thames trying to imagine what the gardens would have been like in their heyday: full of lights, music, dancing and merriment, and even the occasional flight of hot air balloons. I have to admit that we would both have liked to experience the excitement of the pleasure gardens at that time, purely for information purposes of course.

On the subject of prostitution, which came to the fore in my reports about the Jack the Ripper case, the practice still exists in this more well to do area of London but it is not quite so desperate as it is in the East End where, for many of the women involved, it is literally a matter of survival. Here in the West End of the city it seems to be much more clandestine and undercover. It is rare to see women soliciting for business on the streets but there are certain areas where those in the know can find the services provided by these rather unfortunate if resourceful women. High-class establishments known as brothels, frequented by wealthy males seeking sexual gratification are, by all accounts, ubiquitous and well used. Child prostitution I am afraid to say is also all too common. Underneath the veneer of respectability this society seems to possess there is an extremely rotten core where certain individuals, if they can afford to pay, can access any sort of illicit and illegal pleasures they may desire. Even members of the ruling royal family have been rumoured to take part in such criminal activities. The present British queen, Victoria, who is considered to be the doyen of respectability would not, I presume, be made very happy by such revelations.

Going back to the river Thames, the important waterway that runs through the heart of London, which is vital for transport and commerce in the city, it is obvious to Atia and me that an appreciation of its importance will be vital for any future Jaran involvement in this the largest city in the most important state on the planet Earth. However, as I have mentioned before in these reports, the river is highly polluted with human sewage and industrial waste products to the point where in the past serious epidemics of fatal diseases have been prevalent because of it. This is due to the fact that much of the population of London also obtains its drinking water from the river. One service that Jaran technology could provide for the inhabitants of the city, at some point in the future, would be the major clean up of the river and the installation of much more efficient fresh water and sewerage systems in the city thus leading to a healthier population and the ending of such waterborne diseases such as cholera. This would, I am sure, go some way to winning over the hearts and minds of the population of the capital city and make the task of integrating Earth humans into the Galactic Federation significantly easier.

Well, that is all I have to report for now. I will be in touch again very soon.

With my utmost loyalty to the glorious Jaran Galactic Federation,

First Commander Treve Pacton Ashto.

6

The Beefsteak Room

Mrs Smith, the eponymous proprietress of the Select Guest House, the accommodation where Ashto and Atia had been living for the last six months, knocked on the door of their room.

'Good morning, Mrs Smith, what can I do for you?' said the First Commander as he opened the door and acknowledged the somewhat breathless landlady who proceeded to hand him an envelope.

'Oh, Mr Ashton, this letter has just arrived by special courier – it's addressed to you and your good lady wife,' said Mrs Smith, obviously excited by the first special courier ever to call at her establishment.

'Thank you very much, Mrs Smith. I do hope the climb up the staircase has not tired you too much?' said Ashto.

'Well, to tell you the truth, Mr Ashton, this damp

weather is not good either for me chest or me arthritis,' she said while trying to look past the large figure of the First Commander and peer into the room.

'Well, I do hope you feel better very soon, Mrs Smith. Good day for now and thank you for delivering this letter so promptly,' said Ashto beginning to close the door. Mrs Smith, who had been hoping to discover the identity of the sender of the letter, looked disappointed that no more information about the communication would be forthcoming and momentarily thought about putting her foot in the doorway to stop its closure but reluctantly thought it best not to perform such an action.

'What is that, Trevor?' said Atia who sat at the desk reading one of the day's newspapers.

'A communication from Mr Stoker of the Lyceum theatre,' said Ashto quickly opening the letter and reading from it. 'It is an invitation for both of us to dine with him on Sunday evening.'

'How very pleasant,' said Atia. 'Where will this dinner take place, Trevor?'

'According to this letter actually at the theatre itself which has a bespoke dining room that is, according to Mr Stoker, very well regarded.'

'How thoughtful of Mr Stoker to invite us. He has done so, I imagine, to make up for our recent experience with the young female pickpocket. How did he know where to find us?'

'If you remember, Margot, I left one of my cards on his desk. I thought that having a contact such as a theatre manager in the West End could be quite valuable to us in terms of our continuing researches.'

Atia looked thoughtful. 'Trevor, in the light of this invitation I do believe I should purchase a new outfit of clothes to wear for the occasion. Can we visit Liberty's later today?'

Ashto smiled indulgently. 'Yes, Margot, I think that would be a very good idea. I will make sure that I replicate a large number of gold sovereigns before we go!'

That evening Ashto glanced around the large dining room he had just entered through an impressive gothic style doorway. Oak panelled and hung with many paintings and photographs, with a fire blazing away in a huge fireplace at one end of the room and a suit of medieval armour in one of its corners, it was much larger than either of the two Jaran explorers had expected.

'Welcome to the Beefsteak Room, Mr and Mrs Ashton, we are so pleased to see you again,' said Mr Stoker who had led them into the theatre's private dining room, 'you will not yet have met Mr Henry Irving I think.'

'No indeed,' said Ashto shaking the hand of the acclaimed actor, 'we were very pleased to see your wonderful performance as Shakespeare's Macbeth recently, Mr Irving.' Ashto looked at the tall figure (for an Earth human) of Britain's most famous and lauded actor; a gaunt and austere looking person who had the most piercing eyes that Ashto had seen in his time on this planet.

Irving smiled at the Jaran Commander before switching his attention to Apprentice Commander Atia. 'My dearest lady,' he said grasping her hand and kissing it in a gesture that Atia had not yet experienced on the planet Earth, or anywhere else for that matter. 'I do hope that you are now fully recovered from the terrible experience with the female thief recently. Mr Stoker told me all about the incident. All of us at the Lyceum theatre were mortified that something so dire should happen to one of our own patrons, particularly one so divinely beautiful as yourself.' Irving kissed Atia's hand again holding on to it for an extended period before finally letting go.

In spite of herself, Atia blushed. This man, this middle aged actor, was possibly the most charming, charismatic and theatrical man she had ever met. 'Please do not concern yourself with my welfare, Mr Irving, I am far too naturally resilient to have been affected to any great degree by the unfortunate incident.'

'I am very pleased to hear that and I'm so gratified that you have accepted our invitation to dine with us this evening in my inner sanctum as it were. Please, Mr and Mrs Ashton, come take your seats at the table.'

Atia and Ashto were directed to the long dining table that sat in the centre of the room. The three men waited for Atia to be seated before they themselves sat down. Atia was seated next to Henry Irving and opposite Ashto who sat next to Mr Stoker. Atia smiled and looked around at the room, which was situated in the backstage area of the theatre. Despite being windowless the dining room, with its many framed pictures on the wall did not have an oppressive atmosphere but like Fortescues' restaurant had a warm and friendly ambience that Atia appreciated. Henry Irving noticed that Atia was looking at a particular painting set in a recess on the wall opposite where she sat.

'Ah, dear lady, you have noticed the portrait of yours truly in my younger days.'

'I have indeed, Mr Irving. It is a very fine portrait. Who is the artist responsible for painting it?'

'Mrs Ashton, I am surprised that you do not recognise the style of Mr Whistler who I believe is one of your countrymen. I sat for him a number of years ago and that portrait is the result. I do cherish it; hopefully you do not think that too conceited of me?'

'Indeed not, Mr Irving, I must say it captures your inner energy very well.'

'Thank you, dear lady, that is so very kind of you to say so. May I offer you a glass of wine?'

Atia smiled and nodded and Irving called over the waiter who stood in the corner of the room. 'Champagne please James, the '79 I think.' The waiter nodded and brought over one of the bottles that had been standing in ice buckets on a small table in one of the room's recesses and proceeded to fill the glasses of the four at the table.

'A toast is called for I believe,' said Irving in his deep, stentorian voice. 'To Mr and Mrs Ashton, our guests from the United States, and to all their fellow patrons of theatres everywhere.'

The four lifted their glasses and drank. It was Atia and Ashto's first experience of drinking champagne. They caught each other's eyes across the table and smiled. Since arriving on the Earth the two Jarans had enjoyed wine on a number of occasions and had developed a certain tolerance for alcohol, which was not usually the case where Jaran physiology was concerned.

'Do you and your wife often attend the theatre when you are at home in America?' said Mr Stoker looking at First Commander Ashto who was a little taken aback by the question. Information about theatres in the United States had not been something he had researched. He looked a little lost for a second or two but Atia came to the rescue. 'We have to admit, Mr Stoker, that it has only since we have been residing in London that we have taken to visiting the theatre. We will doubtless continue to do so once we return to New York City, our place of residence in America.'

'That is very gratifying to hear for those of us in the theatrical world,' said Stoker, smiling. Mr Irving and I have toured your native country and we were extremely impressed by the high regard that theatres were held in New York and in other places in the United States.'

The conversation was interrupted by a second waiter who entered from a door that obviously led to the nearby kitchen and presented Henry Irving with a piece of paper. 'Ah, tonight's menu has arrived. I shall crave your indulgence, Mr and Mrs Ashton, and read it out. The soup course will be Consommé à la Brunoise. That will be followed by Filets de Soles frits au Buerre and Côtelette d'Agneau grille, served with Pommes de Terre and Champignons. Dessert will be Soufflé Glacé aux Fraises. Where on earth chef obtains strawberries from at this time of the year is anyone's guess,' said a chuckling Henry Irving. Ashto looked rather mystified and Atia hoped he was not going to comment on the unfamiliar sounding items read out by Mr Irving.

'That sounds marvelous, Mr Irving. You really are spoiling us,' said the First Commander.

'Think nothing of it,' replied Irving. 'After the events of the other day it is the very least we could do for you and your dear wife.'

'Do we know anything more about the woman who attempted to rob me?' said Apprentice Commander Atia.

'Only that the woman, who goes by the name of Kate Williams apparently, is an inveterate pickpocket and that she and her accomplice, John Norris the police informed us, have been doing this sort of thing for a number of months, targeting innocent patrons in theatres that is. We are all relieved that such ne'er-do-wells are now safely locked away, hopefully for a very long time,' said Irving.

'I find that it is a great pity that some people, due to poverty in most cases, are driven to such criminal behaviour. I feel that as a society we ought to attempt to rehabilitate such individuals and set them on a more constructive pathway rather than simply punish them as harshly as possible,' said Atia.

'It does you great credit, Mrs Ashton, to express such humanitarian feelings but I think you are letting your natural feminine sensitivity lead you to that erroneous conclusion. Believe me, dear lady, if the arm of the law does not come down as hard as possible on such errant criminal behaviour then we might as well bid adieu to any form of civilized society,' replied Irving.

'With all due respect, Henry, I believe that I agree wholeheartedly with Mrs Ashton. We should as a country give such criminals every chance for redemption,' said Mr Stoker.

'Ah, Bram, spoken like a true writer of fiction!' said Irving smiling benignly.

'You are a writer too?' inquired Ashto.

'Yes, Mr Ashton, in my own small way I am. I have had published a number of short stories and one novel to date. Nothing as ambitious as the voluminous travel guide

I believe you are currently in the process of researching, however. My work as the business manager at the Lyceum keeps me very busy and so I usually only write when I take some leave from my duties working for Mr Irving.'

'Tell me, Mr Stoker,' said Atia, 'do I detect an Irish lilt in your mode of speech? I once knew someone from that particular part of Britain who had a similar accent.'

'Indeed, Mrs Ashton, you are correct; I do come from Ireland. I was born in Dublin and attended Trinity College before moving to London with my wife, Florence. It was my great fortune to meet Mr Irving the owner of this theatre and to begin working with him here.'

'Mr Stoker underplays his importance to the running of the Lyceum,' interjected Henry Irving. 'He is invaluable to the smooth and efficient management of this theatre, which would not be half as successful as it is without his work here.'

The red bearded Bram Stoker smiled in a surprisingly shy manner. 'As always,' he replied, 'Henry overstates my contribution to the success of the Lyceum, but I am extremely grateful for his hyperbole.'

The conversation was interrupted by one of the waiters who appeared from the kitchen and who looked inquiringly at Henry Irving. 'Excuse my intrusion, Mr Irving, but chef would like to know if His Royal Highness is due to join you again this evening?'

'Not this evening, Morris, he has other duties apparently.'

'Thank you, sir, shall we begin to serve the soup course now?'

'Yes please, Morris, I am sure our guests are looking forward to sampling the fare that chef is going to provide for us this evening.'

'His Royal Highness?' inquired Atia her large eyes wider than ever as she addressed Henry Irving.

'The Prince of Wales does occasionally dine with us in the Beefsteak Room. Often he just turns up, to the chagrin of Mr Renfield, our chef,' said Irving, smiling.

'And the Princess of Wales accompanies him too I assume,' said Atia.

Irving turned a slight shade of red. 'Er no, Mrs Ashton, he is normally accompanied by one of … er, his special female friends.'

'Oh, I see,' replied Atia, smiling a little at Irving's uncharacteristic show of embarrassment.

'Ah, here comes the soup,' said Irving, pleased that the subject under discussion could now be changed.

The occupants of the dining room were eager to begin eating it now being late in the evening. Ashto and Atia were soon somewhat relieved that its French title had disguised the fact that in front of them was a superior tasting soup made with a number of different vegetables.

When the soup course was finished and after the waiters had collected bowls and cutlery Mr Stoker continued the conversation: 'As well as the Prince of Wales joining us from time to time we regularly entertain a number of other distinguished guests here.'

'It is unlikely that we as citizens of the United States will be au fait with them, Mr Stoker.' (Ashto was inwardly extremely pleased that he was able to use a French expression he had recently learned.)

'Well, some of those who regularly dine with us have international reputations I believe. Hall Caine the famous novelist is a regular guest of ours and I am sure that you must have heard of the writer Oscar Wilde, with whom I was acquainted with at Trinity College and who, I am pleased to say, remains a personal friend of mine to this day. Wilde's witty asides, as well as his insightful views on many subjects including the theatre, are most edifying and entertaining,' said Mr Stoker.

'We have indeed heard of Mr Wilde,' said Atia, 'and I would very much like to meet the gentlemen.'

'Well, in that case dear lady you must dine with us again and we will also invite Mr Wilde as well,' said Irving.

'I believe that Oscar actually toured your country several years ago. Were you, by chance, able to attend any of the lectures he gave there?' said Stoker.

'We did not, unfortunately,' said Atia. 'We have only become aware of Mr Wilde's reputation as a writer since arriving in London last summer. We would certainly be very keen to meet him.'

'Then, my dear lady I am sure that Mr Stoker will arrange it.' Stoker smiled and nodded in agreement at Irving's suggestion.

'I will certainly do that, just as soon as I return from a brief holiday my wife and I are due to embark upon in a few days' time,' said Mr Stoker.

'And where are you and your wife holidaying, Mr Stoker?' said Ashto.

'We have a number of favourite places where we endeavour to spend our leisure time, Mr Ashton. One of them is the Yorkshire coastal town of Whitby. We try to travel there two or three times each year. I find the town is extremely conducive to my writing and my wife, even in these winter months, likes to exercise by taking bracing walks along the town's promenade each morning. We also enjoy walking to Whitby's ruined abbey, which involves a rather long climb up some steps, all one hundred and ninety nine of them.'

'And you say you spend some of your time there engaged in writing?'

'Indeed, Mr Ashton I do. We usually stay at The Royal Hotel in Whitby in the West Cliff area of the town. I find the upstairs lounge at the hotel is a quiet place where I can settle down to several hours writing each morning as long I can draw myself away from the wonderful view one is provided with from that location.'

'It sounds very restful, Mr Stoker,' said Ashto.

'Indeed it is, Mr Ashton, a very pleasant place to visit away from the hustle and bustle of the capital. In fact it would very much be the ideal location for you and your dear lady wife to undertake some of your researches for a short time. Not everything that is of import in this country takes place in London you know.'

'If I were you,' said Henry Irving who had, along with Atia, been listening to the conversation of the two men, 'I would be very tempted to accompany Mr and Mrs Stoker on their trip north. They are extremely convivial company and your researches would, I believe, Mr Ashton, benefit from a change of scenery.'

'A capital idea,' said Mr Stoker, whose eyes had brightened at the prospect of showing the two *Americans* around one of his favourite places in the whole of the British Isles.

'I… we would be only too pleased to accompany you

and your wife on such a trip in the future, Mr Stoker,' said Atia.

'Well there's no need to put such a venture off, dear lady. The pair of you could come with my wife Florence and me in our upcoming journey. We will show you the sights of Whitby and you will also find plenty of occasions to write copious notes about what you observe. I can assure you that visitors from your fine country would find the coastal air of the town very bracing and healthy.'

Atia shared a quick glance at Ashto who smiled back at her. 'That is a very generous offer, Mr Stoker. My wife and I would be only too pleased to accompany you and Mrs Stoker to Whitby,' said Ashto.

'Wonderful. Let us drink to our forthcoming trip,' replied Bram Stoker as he raised his glass of wine to the two Jaran travellers. The business manager of the Lyceum smiled at Atia who became aware that he looked at her in what she could only describe as a somewhat lascivious way. It was a look and attitude that the Apprentice Commander had grown quite used to since she and the First Commander had begun to interact with Earth males. *I must remember to not in any way encourage that sort of thing*, thought Atia.

The remainder of the evening proceeded extremely convivially with Ashto and Atia enjoying the conversation and the fine food. The insights they gathered from the two, rather gossipy well-connected theatre men were invaluable to them and hopefully would be of great interest to their superiors back on Jara.

Later, back in their modest room at Mrs Smith's Select Guest House, the Jaran pair reflected on their evening.

'It will be an interesting experience to leave London for a while and explore another part of Great Britain,' said Atia.

'It certainly will, Margot. It will add a useful extra dimension to our researches.'

'What are your thoughts about Henry Irving, Trevor?'

'Hm, very charismatic, expressive and rather full of himself of course; he is obviously very well suited to his chosen theatrical profession.'

'Agreed, Trevor, and Mr Stoker?'

'He is a more approachable individual, friendly, devoted to Irving and obviously someone who is ambitious to be an established writer. Also, despite being married, he is someone the Earth humans would say has an eye for the ladies.'

'My thoughts exactly, Trevor; I do believe that when we are in this Whitby place I must be fully on my guard in case he declares his undying love for me!' Atia smiled broadly at Ashto before giving him a peck on the cheek.

The First Commander smiled back at his Apprentice Commander but his eyes did not show very much amusement at all.

7

Sovereigns, Slayings and Sedition

Inspector Reid shook his head. He put down the post-mortem report on the second headless body on his desk and sighed loudly. This year of 1889 was becoming even worse on the policing front than even the previous awful one had been. Not only had two murders taken place in quick succession but the police had been receiving reports from the intelligence services that a new bombing campaign was being planned by Fenian extremists who wanted home rule for Ireland and were prepared to blow people up in order to secure their aim. Added to that more counterfeit gold coins were turning up all over the city with that same strange flaw on them as before. A report showed that the latest of them had shown up at the well-to-do Regent Street store of Liberty's and because they had first been discovered in the East End the job of tracking down the counterfeiter had ended up on his plate. Reid sighed again as he tried to decide which of these problems he should attempt to tackle first.

The Inspector got up and walked to his office door, opened it and shouted for his Sergeant.

'Bill,' said Reid addressing his faithful Sergeant Thick who had quickly appeared, 'we're going to have to step up our investigations into these headless bodies that keep turning up before we get completely snowed under.'

'Right, Sir,' said Bill Thick.

'You've read the latest report on the second victim, any thoughts?' said Reid.

'Not really, Inspector, apart from the fact that the body was drained of blood like the first one and the rope marks around both the young men's ankles seems to show that they were hoisted up into an upside down position seemingly to enable their blood to drain away quicker.'

'Hmm, why on earth, Bill, would someone want to do that?'

'To keep the blood as a trophy, like they kept the head perhaps?'

'Hmm, that's an interesting idea. Could they have collected the blood to keep as a reminder of what they had done? There'd be bottles of the stuff! Pretty grisly though, eh Bill.'

'Yes Sir, but as we've seen before where these lunatics are concerned we have to expect all sorts of weird behaviour.'

'Hmm, you're right Bill. What about that part of the report that said on both men there may have been a bite mark on their necks that had been there before the head was removed. What do you make of that, Bill?'

'No ideas on that one I'm afraid, Inspector, it sounds even barmier than hanging the poor sods up and draining all their blood.'

'Well, it may be important, Bill. Something for us to consider I suppose. At least we now know a bit about the two. The first chap, Hobbs, was a office clerk as we surmised and the second was a telegraph boy by the name of Bell, William Bell.'

'That's right, Sir. According to some of their friends they were involved in various illicit practices for money.'

'Yes, Bill, they were prostituting themselves, let's not beat around the bush.'

'Yes, Sir, disgusting if you ask me.'

'Each to his own, Sergeant, each to his own. However, what is absolutely certain is that they were murdered in a particularly brutal way, perhaps as a direct consequence of their illegal activities. Have we got any further in finding out where they operated from?'

'Not yet, Inspector; We're trying to find out where they got their tattoos done as that might us find the link between the two.'

'Let's hope that something comes up soon in that regard. Anything else you need to tell me?'

'Sir, I've just got some more information on the Fenian bomb threats. Apparently some explosive material was found in the left luggage office of Mark Lane railway station last night. Looks like the warnings from the Special Irish Branch were correct.'

'Another headache to add to the ones we already have,

at least it's not on our patch. Thanks Bill, let me know once any more news comes in.'

'Will do, Sir.'

Inspector Reid went back to his desk. He had just had a thought regarding the counterfeit coins that had turned up at that posh Regent's Street store the other day. It may just be a coincidence but the report from Detective Constable Perkins who had been shadowing the Ashtons had mentioned that he had followed them around the Liberty's store on two occasions recently. If only we could tie their visit with the appearance of the counterfeit sovereigns. Reid scratched his head. Unlikely he thought, whatever the Ashtons were they didn't seem like counterfeiters, even if they were Americans. Still he would bear it in mind; you never know with foreigners. He and the Sergeant ought to go and interview the staff who served the Ashton couple, sooner rather than later. Rather more important investigations should come first though.

Reid sighed for the umpteenth time that morning and opened up the folder about the headless bodies. Definitely more serious things to worry about, he thought. Bloody murder and terrorist bombs always trump counterfeiting. He sighed yet again, rubbed his eyes and read the latest report on the headless murder victim for the third time.

The Inspector shook his head as he reached the end of the post mortem report on the latest of the headless bodies. He leaned back in his chair and stretched. His mouth was dry, time for a cup of tea. He was just about to stand up intending to leave his office and walk down the corridor to the staff room where he knew there would be a welcoming pot of tea on the go when there was a quick knock on the door and a returning and angry looking Sergeant Bill Thick bustled his way into the room.

'Sir, look at this!' said the enraged Sergeant brandishing a newspaper, the latest edition of The Evening Standard.

Reid grabbed the paper and quickly read the headline and front-page story before angrily throwing the offending newspaper onto the floor and looking, wide-eyed at his Sergeant. 'Bloody reporters! Do they have to do this every bloody time? We're going to go through the same thing again aren't we? It's just like the Ripper case all over again! Sensationalist newspapers stoking up people's fears! It won't be long before we have George Lusk's Whitechapel Vigilance Committee knocking on our doors again demanding action, with local Jews being threatened and beaten up all over the East End. Come on Bill, let's go to the pub, I'm in need of a drink.'

The newspaper lay on the floor, its front-page banner headline screamed out: "Vampire Killer Stalks the East End".

… 8

A Bloody Basement

He grinned as he gave the glass of champagne to the young man who quickly drank it. The boy probably thought he was outwardly happy because he was looking forward to the physical exertions that were soon going to take place between the two of them. How wrong could he be? The young man who had just been paid and who now sat feeling warm and comfortable in the drawing room of his home was also no doubt anticipating the various bodily activities he was fully expecting to soon be engaged in. This one who was fair-haired, no older than nineteen and, like the other two, obviously used to flaunting his youthful good looks would soon be very, very disappointed.

He grinned again. The disgusting activities that this boy was expecting to perform would not actually occur of course. Instead other interesting activities of his own devising would soon be taking place in the basement of the large house in which he lived alone. Soon the drug he had put in the boy's champagne would begin to work and he would become paralysed and unable to prevent that which would soon happen to him.

He had again met the young man at the house in Cleveland Street. Like the previous one he had appeared dressed in his blue telegraph messenger boy uniform, ready and willing to meet well-off men and earn an amount of money in return for certain services rendered. As before the boy didn't demur when it was suggested that they should adjourn to his house a few minutes walk away from Cleveland Street. The young man had been confident, full of himself, truculent even, as they had left the establishment. He had even whispered into his ear about one or two of the more arcane practices he could perform when they were comfortably settled in the man's home. He actually sounded enthusiastic about the prospect. The man had smiled back despite being inwardly disgusted by the boy's appalling offers. He would definitely increase the young man's suffering tonight to pay him back for those crude suggestions.

He let the boy fondle his knee while the drug took its effect. The boy's hand was in the process of moving up his thigh towards his crotch when it suddenly stopped. His eyes had widened as the paralysis had begun to set in. His newly refilled glass of champagne fell from his grasp and a look of shock showed on his face, now set in stone. It would be the last expression he would ever wear on his face the man thought, satisfied with how the events of the evening had played out so far. He licked his lips before removing the shiny metallic device of his own design from its box. He fitted it into his mouth and grinned at the young man before clamping his mouth with its metal enhancement onto the boy's neck. He bit into the soft skin until he felt the warm iron flavored liquid come into contact with his taste buds. He sucked hard and with his hands squeezed the neck in order to increase the blood flow. Not too much he thought, careful not to take in a debilitating amount of the drug that was currently coursing around the young man's body. He moved his head away from the boy's neck. He felt some blood run down his chin and quickly gathered it up and transferred it to his mouth licking his lips with appreciation.

The boy still stared at him with wide, unblinking eyes that clearly registered everything that was happening to him. It must be very frustrating, the man thought, smiling broadly. He chuckled as he started to undress the boy. He made a pile of the clothes on the drawing room floor. When the young man was naked the man grabbed him under each arm and dragged him across the room and out into the hallway. Once there he opened the door to the cellar and, puffing slightly with the effort continued to drag the boy's naked body with the staring, horrified eyes down the steps. The body made soft thudding noises as it bounced down the steps, causing the man to chuckle again.

Once at the bottom the man stretched out the still conscious body and tied the end of the already prepared rope around the boy's ankles. From then it was a simple job, using the pulley system of his own devising, to hoist the body up so that it hung, upside down from the wooden framework he had installed in the basement. Tonight's activities, he thought, would be the third occasion that the equipment had been used. He smiled with great satisfaction and looked at the boy's face, now the wrong way up, and yet again chuckled at the look of absolute horror that was fixed upon the young man's face.

'Now the amusement begins,' said the man speaking aloud as he gazed in wonder at his excellent work so far. He opened a drawer in his workbench and took out one of the razor sharp knives he kept there. He smiled again as he moved it slowly and deliberately towards the young man's neck.

9

Whitby

As she looked out of the railway carriage window at the passing scenery, Atia felt pleased that she and Ashto had agreed to accompany the Stokers to Whitby. It was the first occasion that the Jaran couple had travelled outside London since arriving on the planet the previous August and Atia was excited by the prospect of visiting the coastal town that Bram Stoker had waxed so lyrically about. The journey so far had fascinated the Jaran pair. Travelling north from London up to the county of Yorkshire they were able to get their first glimpse of the diversity of the towns and the countryside they passed through on this primitive but charming method of steam transport. At Rillington railway station they had changed trains and were now travelling on the Whitby branch line through the attractive looking towns of Pickering and Grosmont as they approached the east coast and Whitby.

Atia looked across to Ashto who sat opposite her in the carriage. She smiled at him and he smiled back and she noted that he too seemed fascinated by the passing countryside. Then Atia saw the sea in the far distance, it's blueness on this fine February day suddenly reminding her that this was the first time she had seen the ocean from ground level. Her only previous sighting of the sea that covered two-thirds of this planet's surface had been from space as she and the First Commander had orbited the Earth prior to leaving their ship to make the descent in their shuttle craft. The small blue/green planet Earth had certainly been quite beautiful from space but looked even more attractive now as the steam powered locomotive chuffed ever closer to the coast.

'It will not be long now until we reach the town,' said Mr Stoker addressing his Jaran travelling companions.

'We are very fortunate that the weather today is so very clement,' said Mrs Stoker. 'Sometimes the winter rain and wind can be far from pleasant here.'

Atia smiled and nodded at Mrs Stoker. Today had been the first time the Jarans had met Bram's, extremely good-looking wife, Florence. Atia and Ashto found her to be very quiet and reserved and somewhat difficult to converse with but Atia in particular realised that generally speaking women in this so-called Victorian age were expected to keep their opinions largely to themselves and defer to their husband in all instances. Atia smiled to herself as she looked out of the carriage window again at the fast-approaching Whitby railway station; thankfully that was not the Jaran way at all, she thought.

'I have arranged for a carriage to take us to the hotel,' said Bram Stoker. 'It's the Royal Hotel's own carriage and will only take a few minutes for it to transport us there. I'm sure the two ladies will need to refresh themselves in their rooms before dining this evening. I thought in the meantime, Mr Ashton, that you and I could enjoy a preprandial whiskey in the hotel's lounge.'

'Erm, yes of course Mr Stoker, although I might only drink water; whiskey is not something I enjoy to be perfectly honest.' Ashto still had memories of being very drunk on a succession of beer and whiskies in a Whitechapel public house not very long after arriving on Earth; it wasn't a very pleasant memory.

'Of course, Mr Ashton we are here to relax and to luxuriate in the fine sea air, although I must say I myself find that a whiskey or a brandy accompanied by a good cigar is one of the best ways to relax known to mortal man.'

'I'm afraid I do not smoke either Mr Stoker,' Ashto replied smiling.

'Well, each to his own, Mr Ashton. Ah, here we are,' said Mr Stoker as the train slowly pulled into Whitby railway station in a veil of smoke and hissing steam.

The four occupants of the carriage compartment rose and the two men lifted down the luggage from the overhead shelf before waiting for a porter to open the door of the first class compartment and to carry the baggage belonging to the four travellers to the waiting horse-drawn carriage.

Later that day Ashto joined Mr Stoker in the hotel lounge. The First Commander stood for a while appreciating the view through the windows across the harbour to the eastern side of the town with its church and abbey still just visible atop the cliff against a darkening sky.

Stoker put down his newspaper as he gestured for Ashto to sit down in the armchair next to his. 'I've just been reading today's copy of the Times, Mr Ashton. The series of murders apparently continues apace with another headless body being recently discovered by the police in the East End of the city.'

Ashto nodded. "It does seem that the police authorities have again another challenge to test their skills and resources. One can only hope that the perpetrator of these foul crimes is soon brought to justice,' Ashto said.

'Indeed,' replied Stoker. 'Apparently, according to the report, the bodies were completely drained of blood before being transported to the places where they were eventually found by the police. That is most odd. Why would anyone do such a thing, Mr Ashton? The newspapers are saying that these new outrages are the work of "The Vampire Killer," as they have dubbed him.'

'It is beyond my understanding,' said Ashto shaking his head, telling himself that later he must use the handheld computer that was linked to the main computer onboard the spacecraft currently orbiting the Earth to look up the meaning of the word *Vampire*. His thoughts immediately went back to the aftermath following the murder of Mary Kelly, Marie Jeanette as Atia had called her. It took a considerable time for Atia to get over the horror of that night injured, as she had been both physically and mentally. On many nights First Commander Ashto had needed to hold Atia tightly, comforting her after she had awoken from an unbidden graphic dream sobbing. Even now, several weeks after that terrible night the previous November, when Atia had finally ended the reign of terror imposed in Whitechapel by the man the newspapers had christened Jack the Ripper, she was still deeply affected by the experience. She had reluctantly used her disrupter weapon to take a life reducing the crazed murderer to his component atoms but not before he had plunged his blood-soaked knife into her side. The police would never know the true story of why the Ripper murders had ceased that night.

'Mr Ashton, are you all right?' Stoker looked concerned.

Ashto realised that Stoker had said something to him that he hadn't heard, wrapped up as he was in the memory of Atia's suffering since those awful and bloody events. 'I'm very well, Mr Stoker, I was simply carried away for a moment by the interesting view.'

'If you are sure,' said Stoker; still looking worried that Ashto appeared to have been in quite a different world for a short period. 'By the way, Mr Ashton, please call me by my Christian name. As you know most of my friends call me Bram, although my wife refers to me as Abraham whenever she is displeased with me!' Stoker gave a hearty laugh and Ashto smiled back.

'Of course, Bram, and you must call me Trevor from now on.'

'I will certainly do so, Trevor. Now I will stop talking about the dead bodies drained of their blood that have been discovered in various parts of London. Soon our wives will be joining us and I do not think such macabre matters need concern those fair creatures!

'No, of course not,' said Ashto, not without feeling a sense of irony. The macabre sight of Mary Kelly's bloody remains would no doubt stay with Atia for the rest of her life.

'Ah, Mr Stoker, I was told you and your party had arrived. How was your journey?'

'It was tolerably good,' replied Stoker addressing the short, rather rotund figure of the man who had greeted him. 'Trevor, let me have the pleasure of introducing Mr George Swailes who is the manager of the Royal Hotel. Mr Swailes, this is Mr Trevor Ashton who is a visitor to our shores from the United States of America.'

'Mr Ashton, I'm very pleased to meet you. You have decided then to sample the many delights we have to offer in Whitby. I hope we live up to the introduction Mr Stoker has doubtless provided you with.' Mr Swailes beamed as he shook Ashto's hand.

'I am very pleased to be here, Mr Swailes, and I am sure that Whitby will prove to be everything that Mr Stoker has promised,' replied the First Commander.

'I do hope so, Mr Ashton. Tell me, how long have you been in our country and as an alien visitor have you been surprised by anything that you have come across so far.'

Ashto was momentarily wrong-footed by Mr Swailes' terminology and it was a second or two before he was able to answer his question. 'Erm... I, we... my wife and I, that is, have been surprised by many things in your country. We have, up to now concentrated on discovering as much as we can about London, where we have been based since arriving in Britain last August, but we are very keen to visit other places and Whitby seemed a very good place to begin and we have Mr Stoker to thank for recommending it to us.'

'Well, that is very good news, Mr Ashton, and I am overjoyed to hear it. Will you two gentlemen and your good lady wives be joining us for dinner this evening?'

'Indeed we will, Mr Swailes. We are looking forward to sampling some of your culinary delights, particularly your locally caught dressed crab' replied Bram Stoker.

The four companions sat drinking port after they had enjoyed the dinner provided by the Royal Hotel. Both the Jarans were careful about how much they drank, their physiology not being quite as attuned to alcohol as Earth humans were, as they had both discovered in the past few months. However, Ashto and Atia had definitely become rather fond of the various types of wine they had sampled at Fortescues' restaurant in recent times.

'I hope that you will find plenty to write about in Whitby for your book, Mr Ashton,' said Mrs Stoker.

'I am sure we will, Mrs Stoker,' Ashto replied, 'I am particularly intrigued by the buildings on top of the hill at the other side of the harbour.'

'The church and abbey,' interjected Bram Stoker. 'We must visit them tomorrow, Trevor. I think you will find it an interesting walk. I suppose the one thing the United States lacks are examples of buildings that are many centuries old?'

'Indeed, Bram, that is true. The United States is a relatively new country, as you know, and for visitors like Margot and me it is always fascinating to be able to commune with places of such antiquity.'

'Well, parts of the Church of St Mary date back to the 12th century, I believe, although there was a great many additions to the building made in the early years of the present century. The Abbey itself dates from its establishment in the 7th century and was victim of the dissolution of the monasteries in around 1538, an act that was ordered by King Henry VIII of course.'

Atia, who had researched a little of Whitby's history before setting off for the town, said: 'He was not a man to be trifled with by all accounts.'

'Indeed not, dear lady, definitely a tyrant of the first degree.' Stoker patted Atia's arm before giving it a gentle squeeze.

'Do you plan to spend some time writing tomorrow, my dear,' said a not very amused Florence Stoker who had noticed her husband's hand had lingered a little too long on Atia's arm. She was quite aware that he was a man who often took far too much interest in other women and was sure that he'd had a number of brief affairs in the past.

'Yes, I believe I shall,' said Bram Stoker smiling. I will rise early I think and spend the morning engaged in some research in the library of the Whitby Literary and Philosophical Society, which is situated on the quay and of which I am a member.'

'Into what subject are your researches directed, Mr Stoker?' said Atia.

'Call me Bram, please, and I shall call you Margot if that is not too forward of me?' the big Irishmen said with a twinkle in his eye as he smiled at Atia. 'I have been looking forward to examining in detail a book by Miss Emily Gerard that has recently been obtained by the library. It is entitled *Essays on Roumanian Superstitions* and is, by all accounts absolutely fascinating.'

'My dear husband is always interested in researching such arcane subjects to use in his short stories,' explained Florence Stoker.

'Actually my dear, I am hoping to use some of the material in Miss Gerard's book when I write my second novel. How I will use those researches I am not yet too clear but I believe the ancient folklore and legends from faraway Eastern Europe, with their strange beliefs about men that change into wolves and bats and suchlike, will spark a few literary ideas in my mind. Perhaps a story involving mysterious lords, dark castles and even darker dungeons' said the large Irishman, chuckling.

'That sounds fascinating,' said Atia.

'Indeed it does, said Ashto.

'Yes, I believe that the reading public enjoy stories that excite or even shock and I expect Miss Gerard's work will contain plenty of examples of weird and strange practices and beliefs that are followed by folk in that rather primitive area of the world. Apparently the people in that Balkan region have many tales of humans transmogrifying into such creatures of the night.'

'It all sounds terrifying! I much prefer it when my husband turns his mind to more believable matters in his stories,' said Florence.

'Well, my dear we live in such peculiar times, what with the Jack the Ripper murders last year and these recent headless bodies that have been found by the police in London. Only the other day at the Lyceum a doctor of my acquaintance, who works at a mental asylum in the capital, was telling me about a patient he deals with who refuses to eat proper food but insists on catching spiders, flies and other insects and eating them! No one is very sure why he does that.'

'How disgusting,' said Florence Stoker, 'perhaps we could change the subject to matters more normal.'

'Of course, my dear,' replied Bram Stoker.

'Well, "There are more things in heaven and earth Horatio,"' said Atia smiling, pleased to have remembered a quote from the famous writer Shakespeare.

'Ah, the Bard indeed, and as with most things he was completely correct!' said Stoker, smiling longingly at Atia who was hoping that she wasn't blushing as a result of his overt attention.

'After your researches,' interrupted a rather annoyed Florence Stoker, 'will we be showing the Ashtons some of our favourite places around the town?'

'Yes, of course, my dear, I am very much looking forward to directing our American friends around Whitby.' Turning to the Ashtons he continued, 'I would suggest that you wear some particularly warm apparel tomorrow. Up at the church and abbey the wind can be very fierce, especially at this time of the year and there is always the possibility of rain.'

The Jaran explorers nodded and smiled. Even though they had been on Earth for only a relatively brief period of time they were certainly fully cognizant of the vicissitudes of the British weather.

10

A visit to Scotland Yard

'Sergeant, what's this about the Ashtons leaving London?'

Edmund Reid had finished reading the latest report from Perkins, the police constable given the job of following Ashto and Atia and now had called for Detective Sergeant Bill Thick to join him in his office.

'Yes, Inspector, they appear to have gone on holiday with another couple to somewhere in Yorkshire.'

'A holiday, in February?'

'Well, Sir, you know what these foreigners are like and the couple they are with are theatrical types and they're even odder of course.'

'Is Perkins still keeping his eye on them?'

'Yes, Inspector, he's following them to wherever they're bound for. He'll send us a telegram when he knows where they end up. He's a good lad.'

'Well, let's hope so. I don't want that pair running around without us knowing what they're up to. Any more news of the Fenian bomb threat?'

'No, Sir; the Special Irish Branch has said they'll let us know if they get any more information.'

'Hmm. I'm not sure we can totally rely on their good offices. They only let us know what's happening if or when it suits them.'

'Yes, Sir.'

'Any more about the counterfeited sovereigns?'

'None have turned up for a few days, Inspector.'

Reid was aware that he was stalling for time with his sergeant, as he didn't relish the thought of hearing the details about the latest murder victim.

'Right, Bill, let's have the report.'

Sergeant Thick passed the brown cardboard folder he had been holding to the Detective Inspector.

'Tell me about what I'm going to read in here, Bill.'

'Third victim's name is Albert Jameson, aged eighteen. Worked for the Post Office as a telegram boy, like the previous victim and has got the same moth design tattoo on his shoulder. As before the body had been drained of blood and there was evidence of bite marks on his neck, again like the others.'

'Has the family been contacted?'

'Yes Sir, that was done yesterday. Jameson lived with his mother in Camden, there's no father around. His mum didn't know anything about the tattoo or what the lad got up to at night. Didn't know where he got his money from too, seems like he gave most of it to her though to spend down the pub.'

'Wonderful. Do these people have no control over their benighted offspring? Was he involved in prostitution too?'

'Seems like it. According to his friends he used to frequent various places where such transactions take place. Lots of money to be made from rich, bent toffs apparently.'

'Any particular location where these... activities take place?'

'Yes, Sir; there is a particular house that keeps being mentioned by some of the acquaintances of these murdered young men, a place in Cleveland Street, number 19,' said Sergeant Thick checking his notebook.

'Is that so? Well, Bill that sounds as if it would be a very good place for us to pay a visit to. I think we'll set about getting a warrant that will let us have a look inside, see what these toffs and swells get up to in their spare time.'

'I think that's all they have, Sir.'

'What's that, Bill?'

'Spare time,' answered the Sergeant.

Reid looked up from the report he had started to flick through. 'True, very true. Well, let's give them something else to do, Bill eh? Spare time! I'll give 'em spare time! Let's get started by going to see Fred Abberline at the Yard.'

'It can't be done, Edmund, I'm very sorry.'

'What do you mean, Fred?'

Detective Chief Inspector Frederick Abberline scratched the side of his face and pulled at his gingery whiskers that grew in profusion from his cheeks. A tall man he looked down at the much shorter Edmund Reid. 'We can't have you poking around in Cleveland Street I'm afraid.'

'For goodness sake, Fred, why not?'

'Because there is a current investigation under way into a property in Cleveland Street and we can't have you, or anyone else, muddying the water there. I'm sorry, Edmund.'

'What sort of an investigation?'

'I can't tell you that, I'm afraid.'

'But the house at 19, Cleveland Street has come up in our investigation into the deaths of three young men whose bodies have turned up in the East End. It could be vital to the case.'

'Ah, the Vampire Killer! Don't the Press come up with some sensational names for these sad, murderous individuals?'

'They do, Fred and in the process they frighten people. So we need to get this individual off the street and into a gaol cell. You know the East End better than anyone else alive, people in the area are scared… again!'

'Well, Detective Inspector Reid, we still haven't caught the previous maniac yet. Any further clues on the Ripper?'

'I think you know the answer to that, Fred. There's been not a peep from him since November. It's all gone quiet. He's either given up or he's dead. Possibly topped himself in a fit of remorse. It looks very much like that young lawyer we fished out of the Thames in December could have been the killer after all.'

'Montague Druitt? No I don't think so, Edmund. The only evidence we had on him was that he did himself in soon after the last murder. That was all we had to go on; we needed more.'

'Well, wouldn't it be better then if we got this latest one behind bars? The boys that were killed were all participants in male prostitution and it looks very much they all visited the house in Cleveland Street. If we had a warrant to search the building it could well lead to us to arrest whoever was responsible for their murders.'

'I agree with you, Edmund but it just isn't going to happen.'

'But Fred, why on Earth not?'

'Orders from above?'

'The Commissioner?'

'Yes… and higher still?'

'What's higher than the Commissioner of the Metropolitan Police? Oh…the Government you mean?'

'That's right Edmund. We've known about number 19, Cleveland Street for some time. If I had had my way we'd have been in there with force ages ago but we have had specific instructions from Downing Street to steer clear of the place for the time being at least. It's a great shame but there's nothing I can do about it.'

'Is it because of the toffs who go there?'

'I think we both know the answer to that.'

'Members of the House of Commons use the place?'

'Probably, and their Lordships too for that matter; it may go even higher than that!'

'There isn't anywhere higher than… you don't mean… the Palace?'

'If that's the conclusion you have reached, Edmund I could not possibly comment on the matter.' Abberline gave Reid a large wink.

A shocked looking Edmund Reid picked up his bowler

hat from Abberline's desk. 'Look Fred, will you let me know if anything changes?'

'I will, Edmund, I will.'

Detective Inspector Reid left Scotland Yard and headed back to Leman Street with a great many more questions in his head than he had answers.

11

One Hundred and Ninety-Nine steps

The steps leading up to Whitby Abbey and the Church of St Mary the Virgin were an exacting climb despite First Commander Ashto and Apprentice Commander Atia being in good physical condition. Bram and Florence Stoker found the ascent much more difficult and both had to stop several times to rest. Although the manager of the London's Lyceum theatre was only forty-one and had been, in his university days, an enthusiastic athlete and sportsman he was now a little on the overweight side and partial to a number of fine cigars each day; his breathlessness reflecting those vices. Atia thought that had she been wearing her one piece, flexible Jaran uniform, clothing that allowed her perfect freedom of movement, instead of the layers of heavy cloth that she was forced to wear as a fashionable well-to-do Earth woman, she would have bounded up the steps two at a time. Instead she, along with Ashto, occasionally had to wait while the Stokers caught their breath before continuing to huff and puff their way up the stone staircase that had been built into the side of the cliff.

At the top of the steps a breathless Bram Stoker turned around to look at Whitby harbour. 'Now that… Mr and Mrs Ashton… is a view to behold… do you not agree?' he spluttered.

'It's a fine sight, Mr Stoker… er, Bram,' said Ashto.

Ashto and Atia were genuinely impressed with the vista that stretched out before them. Of course, the array of tall-masted sailing ships, busy dockworkers, steam powered cranes, lifting gear and ramshackle buildings looked extremely primitive to them but both were now so attuned to life on the planet Earth that they were able to appreciate the charming nature of all they could see.

As the four walked towards it the Church of St Mary looked stark against the dark and threatening looking clouds that had gathered while they had been climbing the steps. 'Looks like we're going to have some rain soon. It's not entirely unknown on this coast,' said Stoker, amusement in his voice. The Jaran pair who now found the use of irony by the inhabitants of the Earth fairly easy to recognise both smiled.

'Can we have a stroll around inside the church?' asked Atia.

'Of course, my dear lady, it has a very peaceful and quiet interior that is well worth experiencing,' replied Stoker.

The London theatre manager enjoyed showing his new

friends around the church pointing out interesting features as they progressed through the building. The Jarans had so far not carried out much research into the various religions of Earth and were pleased to be able to give some thought to the subject. Religion on Jara was generally considered to be a somewhat outmoded and a rarely considered vestige of the past. The populations of Jara and its sister planets that made up the Galactic Federation were on the whole agnostic about spiritual matters. Many years before most of the inhabitants of the Federation had decided that such beliefs were an entirely individual matter and bespoke buildings for the purpose of expressing a religious belief had long since been abandoned. Those people who liked to practise their beliefs in an overt manner often had shrines in their homes or gardens where they could worship in any way and to any personal or household deity they thought fit. First Commander Ashto, who considered himself to be a practical male of science, had generally eschewed such religious observances but he was nevertheless fascinated by the multifarious belief systems that had grown up on the planet Earth. Both he and the Apprentice Commander had realised that this was an important area of life that they would need to investigate and research in the five years they were due to stay on the Earth. Living in the East End of London had certainly made them aware of the important nature of religious observances with its population drawn from many areas and cultures of the world.

Atia in particular was interested in the quiet and peaceful nature of the church's interior with its wooden box pews and unusual triple-decker pulpit. Although she was, as usual, surreptitiously filming her experiences, she also ensured that she made copious notes in her notebook for the benefit of the Stokers who had come to expect no less of the couple purportedly from the United States who were in Britain to research a travel book for consumption back in their presumed homeland.

As the four completed their tour of the inside of the church and made their way out of the building's porch intending to head for the ruins of Whitby Abbey, a strange occurrence took place. A large black dog, mouth drawn back, sharp teeth exposed in a threatening manner and dribbling copious amounts of drool, stood on the path before them. As the four came closer to the hound it began to bark and emit low throaty growls, its main attention seemingly levelled at the two Jaran explorers. Bram Stoker moved ahead of his wife and held out his hand to the dog and spoke what he obviously believed were calming sounds in the hound's direction. The dog ignored him and stood still, focusing all his belligerent attention on Ashto and Atia. The Jarans, generally unused to such animals as this aggressive canine creature, were taken aback by the threatening, predatory way it stared wide-eyed at them and they backed away a few steps. Atia instinctively felt for the disrupter weapon that she kept in a pocket in the voluminous folds of her dress. If this animal attacked her as seemed more than likely it would she would have no alternative but to vaporise the creature before it got a chance to rip out her or Ashto's throat. How she would explain her action to the Stokers she had no idea. Bram Stoker continued in his attempt to make soothing noises in the dog's direction as the dog, still looking fixedly at the Jaran pair, barked even louder. Just as it seemed likely the hound was about to leap onto them a loud voice from behind the space travellers shouted.

'Prince, come here sir! Heel now sir!' The dog looked round, reluctantly stopped barking, and growling quietly in a guttural way and with its bloodshot eyes still focused on Ashto and Atia, moved in a sideways fashion to the place where the voice had come from. The Jarans and the Stokers watched the dog as it moved past them and then turned to look at the owner of the stentorian voice.

'I'm sorry sirs and ladies. I ain't certain as to what's got in him today, he's usually the quiet sort, nowt normally fashes him, but he's bin unsettled ever since his brekkast,' said the man. His dog stood beside him still growling in menacing fashion and with teeth bared and a resentful look in his eyes that seemed to convey his belief that his freedom to bark and threaten had been unfairly curtailed.

Atia looked the man up and down. She found his ancient, gnarled and weather-beaten, white-whiskered face quite fascinating. 'Tell me, is your dog normally placid?' she asked.

'Aye miss, my dearie, that he is. I've had Prince masel ever since he was a pup an' walked him round this kirk-garth ev'ry day an' this is first time he's ever behoved in such a way. Norm'ly he's as placid and calm a beast as a person could ever meet. I begs all of your pardons I do.'

'Well, take care then my good man and make sure your dog does not get into the habit of barking at those going about their private and lawful business,' said Stoker.

The man touched his forehead with the knuckles of his right hand, in naval fashion. 'Ye can be assured sir that I will be mekin' sure he toes the line from now on,' the old man replied.

'Ah, I see that you are an ex-seaman?' said Stoker.

'That I am sir. I be forty year afore the mast, both man and bairn.'

'Sir, what is your name?' interjected First Commander Ashto?'

'Me name's Steward, sir, Alfred Steward. An' I apologise again to thee all for Prince's behaviour, sirs and madams. He mebbe lacks a bit o' belly-timber so I'd better gang home'ards an' feed him.'

Ashto smiled back at the man, whose dog continued to emit a soft rumbling growl.

'Well, Mr Steward, good day to you, I think we must be on our way before the coming rainstorm. By the way do you think the sudden change in the weather has anything to do with your dogs aberrant behaviour?' said the First Commander looking up at the deeply black storm clouds that had gathered above. As he spoke the dog's growl got a little louder and the old seaman was forced to tighten his grip on its rope collar as it made an abortive attempt to move in Ashto's direction.

The old man, looking abashed, did not reply but simply saluted again as he held on to his dog. The Jaran pair and the Stokers left him and walked away down the churchyard path past the many gravestones and crosses of the long and not so long dead. Atia whispered to her First Commander as they walked behind Mr and Mrs Stoker: 'do you think the canine creature sensed that we were not inhabitants of this planet?'

'I do not know, Margot. It has never happened before. It's decidedly odd in any case," Ashto replied.

Bram Stoker turned to the Jaran pair. 'I believe we should endeavour to find shelter, the rain is likely to be very heavy.' As he spoke large drops started to fall on the gravel path and the quartet quickened their pace and headed towards a white marquee that had been set up next to the Abbey ruins.

There they sat down and listened to the heavy rain beat down on the canvas above them while being served tea and cakes by one of the many black and white clad waitresses employed inside the tent.

'This weather is dashed odd; rain was not in the forecast in today's Times. I'm beginning to wonder whether the experts that produce such predictions actually know what they are talking about,' said Bram Stoker

Ashto and Atia could have given Stoker a very accurate and highly detailed weather forecast of anywhere in the world by using one of their computer terminals to link up with their spacecraft that was currently in orbit around the earth along with a number of small satellites they utilised to obtain information about the Earth. It was with the help of their ship's computer and the orbiting satellites that a few months before they had been able to track down the criminal known as Jack the Ripper by isolating traces of his DNA as he made his murderous way about the East End of London.

'I suppose that close proximity to the sea may have something to do with the changeable nature of the weather,' said Atia.

'That may be indeed the case, dear lady,' replied Stoker, 'but it is still rather annoying. Would you like some more madeira cake?'

'No thank you, Mr Stoker.'

'On the subject of the weather have you told Mr and Mrs Ashton about the shipwreck we were able to view from this vantage point some years ago?' said Florence Stoker.

'No I haven't, my dear,' said Bram Stoker. Turning to the Jaran pair he continued, 'yes, we were here five years ago, October I think it was, when there was a terrible and ferocious storm. Florence and I watched as a ship attempted to get into the harbour but was beached on the sands near Tate Hill Pier. It turned out that the ship was a Russian schooner called the Dimetry, which was out of the port of Narva; thankfully all seven of the crew were brought ashore alive.'

'That must have been quite a sight?' said the First Commander.

'Indeed it was,' said Florence Stoker, 'it was perhaps the most dramatic event, outside of the theatre, I have ever witnessed.'

'It was a timely reminder of the terrible forces that nature sometimes bring to bear on the world, particularly in coastal regions such as this. And now,' said Bram Stoker addressing his wife and the Jaran pair, 'it very much looks that today's rain has abated somewhat and we will now be able to have a closer look at the abbey ruins.'

That evening, back at the Royal Hotel the four visitors were having dinner seated in the hotel's glass fronted dining room and listening to the rain, which had returned, pattering on the windows.

'Are you enjoying your dinner, my dear?' said Florence Stoker to her husband, who was eating his way through some locally caught, dressed crabs.

'I am, very much,' replied her husband his mouth full of crabmeat and brown bread.

'Well, be careful you don't overeat, you know how sometimes you have tummy troubles after a large meal, this late in the evening.'

'Thank you, my dear, I shall be very careful,' said Bram Stoker smiling at his wife through slightly gritted teeth.

'Tell me, Mr Stoker,' said Atia, 'how did your morning's researches go. You were planning to look at a book about eastern European myths, I believe.'

'That is correct, Mrs Ashton… Margot. Miss Gerard's book was indeed absolutely fascinating. Her examination of such legends and superstitions that have grown up in the Styria and Transylvania regions are most compelling. Do you know that she writes how the peasant population of those areas often attaches garlic flowers to the door of their abodes to protect their occupants from the assault of undead vampires? She says these creatures are called Nosferatu in the local language?'

'This word vampire, which the newspapers back in London have begun to use in connection with the recent murders that have been taking place, I have to admit is a term with which I am not very familiar,' said Atia.

'Ah, well it is interesting how that particular word has been taken up by newspaper editors. It is not an unfamiliar word to those who have, for example, followed the work of my fellow Dublin born writer Sheridan Le Fanu. A few years ago he wrote a novel called *Carmilla* which tells a story of a wealthy European countess who has the ability to change into an animal and attack people, feeding on their blood and sometimes passing on her undying vampire's' attributes to her victims.'

'A fascinating narrative,' said Atia.

'Indeed,' replied Bram Stoker. 'In fact the vampire motif has also been used by a number of others over the years such as Polidori, the erstwhile friend of the poet Lord Byron; Sir Richard Burton, the explorer and a close friend of mine; as well as by cheap sensational penny dreadful pamphleteers such as the writer of *Varney the Vampire*, another story about a fearsome bloodsucking creature.'

'I think we've had quite enough about such ridiculous tales for now, my dear. You will be giving us all nightmares,' said Florence Stoker.

'I'm sorry, my dear, forgive me if I become carried away. It's just that today I have decided to write a story, perhaps even a novel, based around such mythical creatures. At the moment I have only a few vague ideas but the stories related in Miss Gerard's book have given me a great deal of food for thought.'

'That sounds very interesting, Mr Stoker. Do you have an idea how the narrative of such a story would develop?' asked Atia.

'Not at the moment, dear lady, but I fancy that the events would take place in London and would involve a nobleman from eastern Europe who has devilish traits and who has decided to attack the inhabitants of the capital for, as yet, some undecided motive. I'm thinking of calling the villain of the piece the Count de Ville.'

'Perhaps we might see your proposed story one day depicted on the stage of the Lyceum,' said Atia smiling.

'That is an interesting thought, Mrs Ashton... Margot. I am sure that Henry Irving could play the role of the Count with his usual skill. I believe his gentlemanly mannerisms allied with his expertise at portraying villainous characters on the stage would fit very well with my proposed fictional evil aristocrat,' answered Bram Stoker with a chuckle.

'I read that we already have a murderous individual predating individuals in London and seemingly drinking the blood of his unfortunate victims. It was referred to in this morning's edition of The Times so I presume the events depicted there must be accurate,' said Mrs Stoker

'The truth is sometimes even stranger than fiction, my dear,' replied her husband. 'Changing the subject completely,' Stoker continued and addressing the Jaran pair, 'it appears that the weather may be a little more clement tomorrow, without too much rain and wind, so hopefully we can spend time looking around Whitby town as well as the surrounding countryside, perhaps even walking out to a beautiful little spot called Robin Hood's Bay. Would that appeal to you both?'

'It would indeed,' said Ashto. Atia nodded her agreement.

'Then it is settled,' said the ebullient Irishman.

'And perhaps we could avoid discussing such gruesome topics as devilish counts and bloodsucking murderers,' said Florence Stoker, only half joking.

'We will, my dear,' said her husband winking at his wife, 'I shall not breathe another word of such matters.'

Report Number 0014 to the Glorious and Munificent Jaran Galactic Federation High Council (Planetary Exploration and Viable Exo-Planet Evaluation Committee – Sector 2007 Sub-Committee) by First Commander Treve Pacton Ashto.

My greetings and utmost felicitations to the esteemed members of the sub-committee.

Apprentice Commander Atia and I have left London for the first time since arriving on this planet. We have travelled by steam locomotive transport to a region of Britain known as Yorkshire and are now in the coastal town of Whitby on the east coast of this small island that is, as you know, the most powerful state on this planet.

Whitby is a most interesting place and, in its own way, a very beautiful one. Fundamentally it is a settlement where the main industry is the harvesting of sea creatures on a large scale carried out mainly by wind-powered ships. The resulting catches of fish and shellfish are then processed and the majority is sent to other spots in the British Isles, most importantly the large cities, including London itself. Whitby harbour, the site where seagoing vessels of various types sail or steam into, is the most fascinating of places. While the ships and boats themselves are very primitive the expertise in the building, maintenance and sailing of them are very well developed, a consequence of the importance of the oceans on this uniquely watery planet.

The area around Whitby is equally attractive. We have been escorted around the area by a human couple who have visited the town many times before and today led us on a longish walk to a very beautiful bay area further down the coast, which has been given the name Robin Hood's Bay. (Robin Hood is apparently a legendary figure from Britain's distant past known for his struggle against the tyranny of its rulers and championing the poorer elements of society against the rich vested interests of the time. This story, while perhaps apocryphal, does point out the innate romantism of the people of these islands.) At the village that nestles in the bay we had refreshments at an ancient looking inn and sat near a large window, which looked out over the ocean, sand and seaweed covered rocks. It was a very beautiful and picturesque sight.

While we were on our walk we were able to experience at first hand the very attractive countryside in this part of Britain. The high level of precipitation this area experiences has led to a wonderfully green and diverse ecological system that contains many different sorts of wild plants, animals and birdlife even in these winter months of the year. There are some indications however that the increased population growth of these islands in the far future could lead to an inevitable increase in agricultural food production and an imbalance in the relationship between farming and the natural ecology of the countryside. This is something that was experienced and subsequently dealt with in the far distant past on Jara, of course, and would be an area of expertise that our diplomats would definitely be able to give advice on in any possible future visits to, and interactions with, the humans on the planet Earth. The wealth of information that we have gathered on this our first excursion outside the main city of Britain is in the process of being sent to the sub-committee and will, I hope, prove as fascinating to you as it was to us.

Soon we will be returning to London and our adoptive home in the East End of the city. Atia and I are very much looking forward to continuing with our collection of data about other areas of London and its indigenous population. It is a big city by Earth standards (and Jaran standards for that matter) and there many aspects we have yet to discover which we will pass on to the sub-committee as efficiently and as quickly as possible knowing how crucial you consider our mission to be.

With my utmost loyalty to the glorious Jaran Galactic Federation,

First Commander Treve Pacton Ashto.

12

A Stranger in a Strange Land

'Good morning, Mrs Stoker, is Mr Stoker not joining you for breakfast?' said the First Commander as Florence Stoker sat down with the Jaran pair at a table.

'No, I'm afraid not. He had something of an upset stomach and as a consequence has had a very troubled night. He woke me up in the early hours shouting out and complaining of a nightmare he had been having. I did tell him that dining on shellfish so late in the evening would not be a good idea, but, as is often the case, he did not listen to my advice,' said the Earth woman somewhat huffily.

'That is a great pity,' said Atia. 'I hope he feels better for the journey back to London.'

Ashto and Atia had just finished their plates of bacon

and eggs and were now eating toast with marmalade and enjoying cups of coffee.

'Yes, I do hope so,' said Florence Stoker. 'He was looking a little green around the gills early on but I'm sure he will improve soon.'

The Jaran pair quickly referenced Mrs Stoker's idiom by way of consulting their implanted neural chips that enabled them to converse in English. There were still many aspects of the complicated language that was spoken on these islands that Ashto and Atia would have had trouble translating were it not for the implants in their brains which connected directly to their handheld computers, which in turn were in constant communication with the main computer that was aboard their orbiting Explorer-class spacecraft.

Before the Jarans could think of a suitable reply Mr Swailes, the hotel manager, interrupted them. ' Good morning to you all,' he said. 'Mr Stoker is not having breakfast this fine morning?'

Mrs Stoker explained to Mr Swailes about the cause for her husband's absence.

'That is so unfortunate,' replied Mr Swailes, 'I have heard it said that shellfish suppers such as crab do not suit everyone's digestion. I do hope he feels well enough to travel today. What time is your train due to depart Whitby, Mrs Stoker?'

'We are due to leave at 11 o'clock this morning. I take it that we will again be able to avail ourselves of the hotel's carriage,' said Florence Stoker.

'My dear lady, of course you shall. I will have it ready and waiting for your party's departure from 10.30 this morning,' replied the manager.

On the way to the railway station an almost totally recovered Bram Stoker was regaling the Jaran pair with detailed information about his bad dream of the night before.

'It was all very odd. I found myself wandering alone in a strange and foreign location; a stranger in a strange land you might say. It was a dark, foggy and forested place. I could hear wolves howling in the distance. A mysterious black carriage drove past me at great speed through the mist, the horses steaming as if on fire. Of course I am in no doubt these… visions were a consequence of my evening's crab meal as well as my researches into the myths of Eastern Europe, with my subconscious mind conjuring up these images, but it was all so vivid… so real. And in my dream I wanted to awaken but was unable to do so. In the swirling mist I saw a figure of a man who was tall and dressed all in a long black cloak and who was standing with his back to me. I did not want to approach him but my legs acted without my consent as it were. It was as if I simply glided forward towards the figure and as I drew near to him he slowly turned around until he faced me. And there to my surprise was the face of Henry Irving! Gaunt, white faced, cadaverous almost. He opened his mouth and exposed long and prominent fangs in the place of his teeth, fangs that glowed even in the darkness of the forest. Around his mouth there was blood, some of which dribbled down the side of his mouth and… '

'Bram! My dear, that is quite enough. We will all be suffering from perpetual night horrors at this rate. We have had enough of such disturbing nonsense. You must endeavour to forget such things otherwise such awful images will return this evening.'

'You are quite correct, Florence my dear,' said a flushed

looking Bram Stoker. 'I will put the dream behind me and endeavour to forget all about it. After all it appears the real world is disturbing enough.'

'What do you mean, my dear?'

'Well, Mr Swailes told me before we left the hotel that the old mariner we spoke to the other day outside St Mary's church had been found dead in the churchyard. He was sitting in one of the benches, his eyes wide open as if he was staring out to sea.'

'Mr Steward, the elderly man?' said Atia.

'Yes, dear lady, he was sat there quite peacefully and had simply expired, it seems.'

'That is a great pity,' said Ashto.

'Indeed it is,' replied Bram Stoker.

'Was his dog with him?' asked Atia.

'No, it wasn't but several onlookers reported seeing a large, black dog running down the steps from the church and abbey as though it were pursued by a pack of wolves.'

'That is all very odd,' said Atia. 'Has the poor creature been apprehended?'

'Apparently not, according to Mr Swailes the dog kept running through the town and disappeared into the surrounding countryside. No doubt a farmer will shoot it at some point, particularly if it begins to worry the local sheep population.'

'What a tragic situation,' said Atia.

'It certainly is,' said Florence Stoker. 'One can only hope that the poor, elderly man's dog is captured very soon before it is shot.'

'Indeed so, my dear,' replied her husband. 'It is true that in the midst of life there is always death.' Bram Stoker looked out of the horse drawn carriage at the morning street scenes, a wistful expression on his face.

As the carriage arrived at Whitby railway station the four travellers disembarked and headed for the platform and the train that would take them on their journey back to London. All were in a sombre mood after hearing of the demise of the old sailor. None spoke of the man's death on the way back but all were rather more thoughtfully quiet than usual, Atia and Ashto were content to look out at the passing scenery, taking account of the beauty of the varying countryside, and ostentatiously making notes in their respective notebooks. Every so often they looked at each other with fondness in their eyes and smiled.

Later, back in their room at Mrs Smith's Select Guesthouse, as they lay in bed together, they reflected on their trip to Whitby.

'It is strange having seen this world from orbit and still being surprised at how green and how beautiful this small island is, outside the confines of this large city,' said the Apprentice Commander.

'How true that is, Margot. It may seem odd but our journey has made me feel a great deal of fondness for this area of the planet Earth, this place that is known as Britain. I do believe that we should very soon organise many more journeys to other locations in these islands and experience the beauty of as many other places as we can fit in.'

'I was thinking very much the same thing, Trevor. Our mission is to collect as much information about this planet as possible and so we most branch out from London even though there is still much to discover in this city.'

'Very true, Margot, and of course we must also, during the next four or so years, visit as many of the other countries on this world as possible. I have read that Paris, in the nation state known as France is a very attractive, vibrant and romantic place for couples to visit.'

Atia turned her head and gave Ashto a kiss. 'Yes, Trevor we must. I have also heard that.' They smiled and kissed again.

13

Counterfeit

'Any news about the Ashtons in Yorkshire?' Inspector Reid sat on the edge of his desk looking at the latest report about the counterfeit sovereigns.

Sergeant William Thick stroked his large, luxurious moustache before consulting his notebook and nodded: 'Yes sir, Perkins telegraphed yesterday afternoon. The Ashtons caught the train back from Whitby and should be back in their Whitechapel guesthouse by now.'

'That's handy. Now that it looks as if we might have a link between them and the counterfeit sovereigns at Liberty's it may be a good idea to have them in for questioning. What was the name of the shop assistant who served them?'

Bill Thick turned over a couple of pages of his notebook. 'Mary Parks is her name. She was reasonably sure about her description: a well-dressed couple, slightly strange accents, the tall, striking looking woman bought a dress and paid for it with gold sovereigns. Later on Miss Parks' manager spotted that some of the sovereigns the store had taken during the day were our counterfeited ones, which could have been those that Mrs Ashton handed over. Not certain but definitely possible.'

'We may have them, Bill, we may have them. I don't know *how* they counterfeit the sovereigns but I'm almost sure it's them that's doing it!'

'Maybe they've got an accomplice and they just supply the funds.'

'Possibly, Bill, but the only person that Perkins has seen them talking to is that newspaperman... what's his name?'

'William Rogers, sir, works for the Standard. He's unlikely to be a counterfeiter though.'

'I'm not so sure, Sergeant. Reporters, I don't trust them one little bit. Slimy individuals. Wasn't it him that came up with the name The Vampire Killer?'

'The very same, sir.'

'Pity we can't arrest him for hindering our investigations. It's got Whitechapel all in turmoil again and the Standard keeps reminding us that we still haven't caught the Ripper yet. The Ripper! That's another nickname that was almost certainly invented by a blasted journalist. They'll soon be telling us that Spring Heeled Jack is on the loose again!'

'Shall I go and get the Ashtons and bring them to the station?'

'No, not yet, Sergeant; let's get Perkins back on them and let's see if we can catch 'em in the act of passing on those dodgy sovereigns.'

'Right, Sir I'll let him know – he's probably caught up on his sleep by now.'

'Tell him I'm not allowing him to sleep until we've caught whoever it is making these counterfeit coins.'

Inspector Reid put down the file on the counterfeit sovereigns and picked up the weightier file about the recent murders. He looked again at the photographs of the three headless corpses that that been found around the East End. He sighed. Why wasn't life simple any more? In the past blokes just strangled their wives in drunken temper tantrums on a Saturday night. It was all very straightforward. Once they had sobered up and admitted their guilt they cried all the way to the hangman's noose. Things then were nice and uncomplicated. Now it seems murders are committed by deranged individuals doing people in for motives that are impossible to fathom. For some reason the Ripper targeted local women, some of who were involved in casual prostitution. This latest maniac seems to have taken a dislike to certain young men and drains them of their blood before cutting off their heads and leaving their bodies lying around the local area. Why? What makes this one tick? He sighed again. On his desk was another file that he was reluctant to pick up. Irish Fenians making bomb threats again according to the Special Irish Branch. He just didn't have the time to look into that one just yet. No doubt officers from the Special Branch will be paying him a visit soon and asking him what he was doing about the supposed bombers. If there was anyone he hated more than maniac killers carrying out a series of motiveless murders it was the overbearing blokes from the Special Branch who believed they had the right to ride roughshod over him and order him about. Well, I'll cross that bridge when I come to it, he thought and sighed loudly again.

At that precise moment, back in Mrs Smith's Select Guesthouse, an annoyed First Commander Ashto was banging the top of the portable replicator in an increasingly determined manner. The replicator had been malfunctioning for the past few weeks and Ashto usually found that a quick tap was enough to get it working again. He wasn't an expert on replicator technology and was becoming increasing frustrated at the machine's hit or miss performance where it would stop halfway through a production programme or sometimes not even switch on at all.

Apprentice Commander Atia looked up from reading the morning's copy of the Times, disturbed by the muttering and banging coming from the direction of her mission commander. 'Would you like me to have a look at the replicator, Trevor?'

'If you could, Margot, that might be a very good idea.'

Atia smiled and left the desk where she had been reading the newspaper. 'Do we require some more gold coins, Trevor?'

'Yes, Margot, we do. We have used our supply up in our recent trip to Yorkshire. Do you have the expertise to get this infernal device to work again?'

'I do not know, Trevor but I can run a diagnostic on it.' Atia pressed a few of the raised areas on her handheld computer. She looked at the screen, a puzzled look on her face. 'Hmm, that is interesting. There are one or two faults with the replicator that I think I can put right but looking at the machine's production history since we arrived on this planet it appears that there has been an error in the design details of the gold sovereigns the device has been producing.'

'Oh, what error is that, Margot?'

'Well, Trevor it appears that the replicator has been putting the wrong date on the gold coins since we programmed it to produce them.'

'Really? What date has been put on the coins?'

'1988.'

'But that's ninety-nine years in the future.'

'True, Trevor, an error we have failed to notice in the last seven months!'

'Perhaps no one will else will notice, Margot.'

'I think we can assume that someone eventually will, Trevor and that would cause us a problem if their usage is traced back to us.'

The First Commander frowned. 'That is correct, Margot. How can we have let that mistake occur?' He looked at the replicator and considered smashing it beyond repair.

Atia used her computer to reconfigure the machine and after a few minutes she was able to announce that the error had been fixed. She programmed the machine to produce a number of sovereigns and examined them carefully.

'Trevor these sovereigns seem to be correct in every detail.'

'Well done Margot,' said Ashto having a good look at the coins. '1888 – that makes rather more sense.'

'Let us hope, Trevor, that the talented Inspector Reid does not connect us with the erroneous coins we have been using for the past seven months.'

Ashto frowned again. We will need to consider our response very carefully if the inspector decides to question us about the matter.'

'Indeed we will, Trevor, indeed we will.'

At Leman Street Police Station Detective Inspector Reid and Detective Sergeant Bill Thick were discussing information they had received regarding the three murdered young men.

'So that's definite then?' said Reid.

'Yes sir,' replied the sergeant. 'All three have been loosely connected with the building in Cleveland Street. They were all known to be working as male prossies and would occasionally meet their clients at the address in Cleveland Street. Each one had the same tattoo, which was apparently to designate they were all members of the same group that offered to do certain things with certain men for money. It should be a fairly simple matter to find out who the person is they met in the house.'

'Yes, Bill, you would think so wouldn't you? Trouble is Detective Chief Inspector Abberline has warned us off the place. Hmm, maybe we could get someone into the building just to see what's going on there.'

'We could pull Perkins away from the Ashton case and get him to go undercover into Cleveland Street. He looks young enough to pass scrutiny; he's only just started shaving! Two of the murdered men…' Sergeant Thick looked at his notebook, 'Jameson and Bell, worked for the Post Office as telegram boys so if we got Perkins a uniform he would look right at home there.'

'We don't need to ask Abberline for permission to do this I think; I hope that's the case anyway,' Reid sounded a little unsure. 'Tell Perkins he'll need to get the same tattoo that all three victims had on their shoulders as well,' he added.

'I'm not sure he'll be happy doing that, Sir.'

'Well, that's very hard luck on him, Sergeant. If he

wants to get on in the Metropolitan Police Service tell him he'll do as he's told. Get someone else to follow the Ashton couple.'

'Right, Sir.'

'And, Bill.'

'Yes, Sir?'

'Tell young Perkins to be careful. There's a murderer on the loose.'

'Will do, Sir.' Sergeant Bill Thick smiled to himself as he left Inspector Reid's office.

'So your plan is to go shopping in Liberty's, spend some of the new sovereigns and ensure that Reid's man Perkins sees us doing that so that he can examine the coins and report back to Inspector Reid that it is not us who have been responsible for using the original coins with the erroneous dates on them?'

'That is correct, Trevor.'

'That is inspired, Margot. Shall we do that right away?'

'I think we should, Trevor. I could do with a new hat.'

Ashto smiled. 'We must ensure that constable Perkins is following us before we hand over the coins.'

'Indeed we should, Trevor. But the young man has been following us all over the country so there is little reason to believe he will not do so this afternoon.'

'Yes, I have to admit I felt a little sorry for him when we saw him caught in the rain in Whitby. He does need to try a little bit harder at making himself rather more inconspicuous.'

'Yes, Trevor, the poor young man was soaked and I'm sure that he was watching our hotel every evening. Goodness only knows when he was allowed to sleep. Inspector Reid certainly likes his officers to work hard.'

'That he does, Margot.' Ashto went to the window and looked out to the street below. 'That's very curious.'

'What is, Trevor?'

'Well, young Mr Perkins is not in his usual place. Since we returned from Whitby he has been posing as a street beggar just opposite the guesthouse but he is not there at present.'

'He is taking a break to see to his bodily needs perhaps?'

'That is possible, Margot but he usually has a colleague who comes along every couple of hours to enable him to leave his post temporarily. There is no member of the police there at the moment.'

'That is curious. Perkins has been most assiduous in carrying the task he has been set by his superiors. I sometimes think we should contact Inspector Reid and advise him how well his young Detective Constable has been following orders and how skilled he is at his job.'

Ashto chuckled: 'although he is not quite skilled enough to avoid being seen by us. In any case I'm not sure Reid or Perkins would welcome our comments, Margot. Well, shall we leave for Liberty's now? Perhaps we could call into somewhere in the West End for tea and cream cakes?'

'That is a splendid notion, Trevor,' said Atia beaming at Ashto's suggestion.

The First Commander and his Apprentice Commander paused outside Liberty's department store in Regent Street looking into the windows and carefully scanning the surrounding area for signs of Perkins.

'Most peculiar,' said Ashto, 'Perkins in normally so very easy to spot.'

'That is true, Trevor, I think we have another one of Reid's men following us. I do hope nothing has happened to poor Mr Perkins.'

'Ah yes, Margot, I have just spotted him. Short, stocky, moustache, bowler hat.'

'Yes, Trevor, that will be young Perkin's replacement I should think. Well, let's lead him into the store and enable him to witness us in the process of spending some of the newly made and correctly dated sovereigns.' The Jaran pair smiled at each other and entered the store they had grown to know so well.

14

Another Victim

'And what is your name my young friend?'

'It's Sid to me mates, although me muvver calls me some other fings from time to time.'

'I imagine she would.' He smiled at the young man who sat with him on the plush, red velvet settee. Sid had just wandered over to him and had touched his knee as he sat down. The young man's touch disgusted him as usual but he made certain his distain did not show on his face. He sipped from his glass of champagne as he assessed this individual. Fair-haired, young, of course, he seems even younger than the other three had, hardly begun to shave. The telegram boy uniform fitted him very well and definitely suited him, the man thought, although he's no more than a boy. His mother will certainly miss him terribly. He smiled at the thought, and the young man smiled back at him.

'So what shall I call *you* then?' said the boy.

'Call me... Jack, that will do.'

'Just as long as you ain't Jack the Ripper!' chuckled the boy

He smiled. 'There is absolutely nothing to worry about in that particular department I can assure you,' he said.

No, he wouldn't want to be confused with that disturbed, frenzied individual – the maniac who rips and mutilates the bodies of poor unfortunates for no discernable reason. He, on the other hand, is an artist as well as a scientist. An artist who shows proper respect when he takes the lifeblood of these boys, just like the Aztec priests of old with their blood sacrifices. He really didn't like being compared to that animal they call Jack the Ripper. He would make sure he mentioned that fact to the young man, when the time came.

'So are we goin' to your 'ouse then?'

'I thought we might. There is plenty of champagne there and we could make ourselves extremely comfortable.'

'That sounds very nice. So what *is* yer name? Your real 'un not the code name you use for this place.'

'Oh, I think Jack Varney will suffice for now, at least until later when we've got to know each other a little bit better.' The man smiled at his use of the epithet Varney, the name of a vampire in a penny dreadful pamphlet that was popular a few years ago. It seemed to fit with the nickname the newspapers had given him: "The Vampire Killer" – very appropriate he thought.

This young man was inquisitive. He liked that. Usually the ones he picked up at this establishment, this brothel, were not actually interested in him, all they were bothered about was the money he handed over to them once they had left the building. There was something different about this one. He wondered why. Never mind, he thought, I'll find out later perhaps once he had given him something to drink at the house. He smiled, drained his champagne glass and stood. The young man followed him like a faithful hound. At the cloakroom he retrieved his cane, coat and hat and the two left number 19, Cleveland Street and headed for his residence. Once outside he had handed the boy his money and asked him about the sorts of activities he liked doing. The young man was quite reticent unlike the others who were only too willing to go into disgusting detail about their particular skills in that area. He liked this one's shyness. He obviously had not done this sort of thing too many times before and still found it difficult to talk about such *personal* matters. Well, after the special drink his tongue will loosen a little – until it eventually becomes paralysed like the rest of his body of course – and then he will be able to find out a little more about this one and why he seems so different to the others. He smiled to himself as he and the young man walked along. Not long now, he thought. As he anticipated the taste of this boy's blood his mouth began to water. Not long now.

The headless body had been found by a member of the public under a railway arch in Pinchin Street in Whitechapel. Inspector Reid and Sergeant Thick stood looking down at the ghastly pale remains; both had tears in their eyes.

'Any chance it's not him?' said Reid.

'It's definitely him, sir. No doubt about it. He once showed me that scar on his leg he got when he was a nipper and had boiling water tipped on him by his drunken father,' replied the Sergeant.

Reid found it difficult to speak. He swallowed hard to try and rid himself of the large lump that had formed in his throat. 'He was one of ours Bill... this lad... one of ours. I'm going to get the bastard that did this... if it's the last thing I ever do.' Reid paused as he tried to gather himself. 'Erm, his mother needs to be told... '

'I'll do it, Sir. I've known the family ever since we locked the father up a few years back. I suppose I'm the reason Perkins... Philip... joined the force. It was almost like a thank-you for saving his Ma from taking any more beatings at the hands of her husband.'

'Brothers and sisters?'

'Yes Sir, there are three sisters; they're all older than him. I'll make sure they're told too.'

'Thanks Bill, I appreciate it.' Inspector Reid was grateful that he didn't have to inform the Perkins' family about what had happened. He often had nightmares about having to do that sort of thing.

'Any clues on the body?' Reid found it difficult to even look at the dead headless body of Perkins let alone touch it. Reluctantly he bent down to examine what was left of the neck. 'Same teeth marks, Bill; the poor lad!'

'Let's hope he wasn't conscious when that happened, Sir.'

Reid wiped his eyes. 'Let's turn him over then.'

'No other marks on his back, just the tattoo we ordered him to get,' said Sergeant Thick as the two men looked down at the young man's back with the small butterfly or moth tattoo on his shoulder. They stood with their heads bowed, almost as if in prayer. Both of the senior police officers looked and felt utterly forlorn.

Reid broke the silence with a heartfelt sigh: 'Right, let's get this body to the coroner and see what he can find out.'

'My guess it'll be the same story as before, Sir.'

'Yes, I know. We can only try though, Bill.'

'Yes, Sir.'

'Perkins went to the house in Cleveland Street twice before *this* happened?'

'Yes, that's right Sir, he reported back that there were various individuals in the building, mostly toffs of one sort or another. He said he had spoken to a couple of them who were acting somewhat suspiciously – or more suspiciously than most of 'em were anyway. Neither had offered to leave with him so he had ruled them out. He was going back for a final go at finding the murderer but wasn't very hopeful at discovering anything.'

Reid frowned. 'We know that some of the victims definitely frequented that den of iniquity. I've asked Abberline again if I can mount a full-scale raid on the place. He has refused and reprimanded me for sending Perkins in there undercover. Apparently there are too many well-known toffs with vested interests in that bloody place. And now this has happened!' Reid looked down again at the headless body of Perkins and shook his head slowly before gesturing to nearby uniformed officers to bring over the handcart to remove the body and take it to the mortuary. 'Let's go Bill. We've got work to do.'

'What is the matter, Margot? You looked shocked.' The First Commander was lying on the bed reading the latest short story by Oscar Wilde in Blackwood's Magazine and the Apprentice Commander had just returned from her journey to buy the day's copy of the Times newspaper.

'I've just bumped into Mr Rogers.'

'That is something of a coincidence. Do you think he's watching us again, Margot?'

'It is possible, but more importantly he told me about some very grave news.'

'Really, Margot, what exactly?'

'Our Constable Perkins, he has become the latest victim of the Vampire Killer!'

'No. That is terrible. Is he sure?'

'Yes, Trevor, he had just been to Leman Street Police Station and was coming to inform us. It seems young Perkins was investigating the recent murders and has himself fallen victim to the murderer.' Atia was close to tears. Ashto went over to her and put his arm around her leading to the chair by the desk where Atia normally sat.

'Trevor.'

'Yes, Margot.'

'I strongly believe we must do something about this so-called Vampire killer. Constable Perkins seemed such a nice young man and I do not think any others should suffer his fate.'

'Do you mean we should attempt to track down the murderer as we did with Jack the Ripper?'

'Yes, Trevor, I mean exactly that. We have the resources to do so. We can help the police apprehend this heartless killer or, as we did with the Ripper, deal with him ourselves.'

'Margot, it could be dangerous. When you found the Ripper, you almost… died. I could not face that possibility again.'

Atia looked up at her Mission Commander and smiled. 'We… I will be very careful but I sincerely believe that this person, this murderer, needs to be stopped and we could help to do that. I do not intend to confront the murderous individual myself again but we must help the police in some way and aid them in bringing the killer to justice. I think we owe it to poor Constable Perkins.'

Ashto nodded. He bent down and kissed Atia on her cheek. 'If that is what you believe to be the correct course of action, Margot, then that is what we shall do.' He smiled at her but deep inside he was full of misgivings.

At Leman Street police station Inspector Reid was reading through the Coroner's report on Constable Philip Perkins. As in the previous murders the body had shown evidence of a strong chloral based drug that had obviously been used to render the young man paralysed, powerless to fight back as the killer had dealt with him. Sadly there was also evidence that Perkin's death had not been a quick one. Rope marks around his ankles showed that like the other young men he had been hoisted up while he was powerless to prevent what was happening and while in an upside down position had experienced a bite on his neck from which most of the blood in his body had been slowly drained. His eventual death was due to a massive loss of blood and Perkins' head had been removed post-mortem as in the previous murders. The only slightly unusual aspect about the body was that in the clenched fist of Perkins' right hand a small piece of purple cotton thread had been found. What was the significance, if any, of that one stray item, thought Reid?

Reid shrugged, sighed and waved away a fly that had

been buzzing around his head for the last few minutes. The Inspector was too preoccupied by the Coroner's report to wonder why it was that so early in the year a house-fly would be bothering him.

In their room at Mrs Smith's Select Guesthouse Ashto and Atia sat at the desk looking intently at their computer screen.

'Did we get the entire report downloaded?' asked Atia.

'We did, Margot, although it does not, at first sight, seem to convey anything we do not already know,' replied the First Commander.

'If we leave the fly drone in Inspector Reid's office, Trevor, we will be able to listen in to any conversations he has about the horrible circumstances of the murder with his colleague, Sergeant Thick.'

'Very true, Margot,' said Ashto as he maneuvered the small drone disguised as a flying insect so it nestled on the wall in the Detective Inspector's office, its camera and microphone transmitting everything that was occurring back to the Jaran's computer.

'Do you think the small cotton thread Perkins was clutching in his right hand has any significance?' said Ashto.

'I do not know, Trevor. It would be useful if we were able to examine it.'

'True, Margot, although there is little chance that we will be able to do that.'

'Perhaps, Trevor,' replied Atia, 'although there is one possibility we might want to explore. Ah, Sergeant Thick has entered Inspector Reid's office.'

'Bill, have we got the piece of cotton thread that was found in Perkins' hand?'

'Yes Sir, it's in the evidence box.'

'Go and get it, please Bill. I'd like to have another good look at it.'

'Will do sir.'

'So, please explain your thinking, Margot.'

'Well, Trevor, the cotton thread seems to be the only piece of evidence, other than the victim's body, the police have. If we could somehow obtain the thread and examine it using our own resources it might provide us with a clue as to the possible whereabouts and identity of the killer.'

'I suppose there is a small possibility it could be useful to us but how would we obtain the thread?'

'Well Trevor, in a minute or two Sergeant Thick is going to bring it to Inspector Reid's office, and I am thinking that it might be possible to use the fly drone to pick up the thread and bring it back to us.'

'That is an idea, Margot. Let's see if we can do that. We'll have to wait for the exact moment and then hope that I can control the fly drone as deftly as possible.'

Back in Inspector Reid's office Sergeant Thick presented a small brown envelope to the Inspector. Reid took the envelope and carefully using a pair of tweezers removed the small piece of purple cotton thread and then looked at it using a magnifying glass he had taken from his desk drawer.

'Anything unusual about it, Sir?'

'Not that I can see but there must be a reason why Perkins thought it might be significant. Let's think about it Bill. When he knew he had been drugged, as a good policeman, he looked around to see if there was anything in the room he was in that would provide us with a clue as to where he was when he was… you know, murdered.'

'He knew what was about to happen to him?'

'Yes, Bill I think he did. He knew he had been drugged in some way and he wanted to provide us with some sort of clue. So before he became completely paralysed he picked a thread in… what?'

'Something purple, the chair he was sitting in? A tablecloth?'

'Perhaps, Bill.'

'Well, if that's all we have sir, that's not very much.'

The Inspector sighed. 'True. I don't think there's anything else this cotton thread can tell us. Just the colour, perhaps.' Reid swatted at the fly that had decided to bother him again. 'Blasted thing, it's been flying around my head all morning.' The Inspector swore as the fly landed on his ear. 'Bloody hell!' In trying to wave away the insect on the lobe of his ear Reid let go of the purple thread. 'Damn it!' he exclaimed as he bent down to retrieve it from the floor. 'Where the hell has it gone?' said Inspector Reid as he got down on his hands and knees to look for the small strand of material.

'I can't seem to see it anywhere,' replied Sergeant Thick as he too got down on the floor to search for the elusive thread.

'Have you managed to pick it up, Trevor?'

'Yes, Margot, it was quite a tricky operation but I've been able to get the drone to hang on to the thread. I'll now fly it out of the Inspector's office and bring it back here.'

'Well done, Trevor. It is obvious that the police would

not be able to get any forensic information from the strand of material but we just might.'

'Hopefully that will be the case, Margot,' said the First Commander as he carefully used the computer to guide the fly drone out of Leman Street Police Station and back towards Bell Lane and Mrs Smith's Select Guesthouse.

15

Another Day, Another Police Interview

'Well, Mr and Mrs Ashton, thank you for coming to the station today.'

'It is always a pleasure to talk with you, Inspector Reid. What can we do to help you on this occasion?' said Ashto, hoping he looked calm and collected while on the inside feeling extremely apprehensive. Why had Reid asked him and Atia to come and speak to him at his office in Leman Street police station?

Edmund Reid looked carefully at the Ashton couple as they sat on the other side of his office desk. They both wore very annoying smiles but he could also see a feint look of concern on their faces. There *was* something they felt guilty about and he was determined he wouldn't let them leave the station this time without trying to get some sort of a confession from them.

'The other day, Mr and Mrs Ashton, you were in the female garment section of the Liberty's department store on Regent Street. Is that correct?'

'It is indeed, Inspector Reid, we often shop there,' said First Commander Ashto, who now had a puzzled expression on his face.

'And at that time did you, Mrs Ashton, purchase a dress from the store?'

'The last time we shopped at Liberty's I actually purchased a new hat, Inspector Reid. It was on the previous occasion that I purchased an evening gown,' said Apprentice Commander Atia, smiling her most beatific smile at the Inspector who quickly looked down at his notes.

'Yes, I apologise, Mrs Ashton. On the previous shopping expedition, when you bought the dress how did you pay for it?'

'Why, we purchased the gown with gold sovereigns,' said Atia still smiling warmly at Inspector Reid.

'Do you always use sovereigns to pay for your purchases at Liberty's, Mrs Ashton?'

'Yes Inspector, why do you ask?' said Atia who also now looked puzzled.

'Mrs Ashton, can I ask you where you obtained the gold coins from?'

'Of course, Inspector Reid, we obtained them from a bank.'

'And which bank would that be, Mrs Ashton?'

'The transaction was, as you would expect, carried out by my husband, Inspector.'

'Mr Ashton?'

'Inspector, we obtained the sovereigns from the branch of the Westminster bank which is situated at 41, Lothbury Street.'

'And by what means did you pay for the sovereigns?'

'We presented a banker's draft which we had brought with us from our bank in New York City.'

'And what is the name of the bank in the United States?'

'Inspector, it is called The Bank of New York and I can assure you it is a very safe and financially secure bank as well as always being very efficient and completely honest. Inspector Reid, can I inquire why you are asking these questions?'

'Mr and Mrs Ashton over the last few months a large number of counterfeit gold sovereigns have been appearing in various places throughout London and we are endeavouring to discover the origin of those fraudulent coins.'

'Do you suspect Mrs Ashton and me? I would be very surprised by such an accusation. Do you really suppose that we would be capable of producing counterfeit coins, Inspector? With the greatest respect, Inspector Reid, I think your investigations would be more likely to bear fruit if they were directed elsewhere.'

'That may be so, Mr Ashton. My conversation with you and your good lady wife is only a very small part of our overall investigation into this very serious crime, a crime, I hasten to add, that can lead to a very long prison sentence.'

'Well of course, Inspector, Margot and I are only too willing to assist your investigation in every way we can but I really do think that you are wasting your very valuable time in talking to us.'

'I understand Mr Ashton.' Inspector Reid looked at Ashto to see if he could read any further uncertainty or guilt in the man's eyes before softly sighing. For today, at least, he would have to admit failure where the Ashtons were concerned, but his day of reckoning would come, he was sure of it.

'Can I thank you again, Mr Ashton, and Mrs Ashton of course, for coming to the station today and answering my questions. I hope it has not caused you too much inconvenience. We will get in touch with you again if we have any further questions for you.'

'We will only be too pleased to answer any questions you have for us,' said the First Commander.

'Inspector,' said Atia, 'can I say how sorry we were to hear that one of your officers was murdered in the course of his duty recently. When we read about the incident in the newspaper both Mr Ashton and myself were so very sad that one so young could have been a victim of a crazed killer. We can only hope that you will capture Constable Perkins' murderer very soon.'

'Thank you very much for those kind words, Mrs Ashton, I can assure you that no stone will remain unturned in our determination to apprehend the villain who did the deed.'

Ashto and Atia stood up smiled at Inspector Reid and waited for him to move to the door and open it for them. After shaking hands with the Inspector they headed to the entrance of the police station. Reid as usual stood and watched them leave. It was his turn to look a little puzzled. The Ashtons seemed confident enough when answering his questions but there was still something there, in their eyes perhaps, that showed him they were worried or felt guilty. He shrugged. Oh well, he thought, it will be a relatively easy matter to check out the veracity of their story. I'll try to find time later in the week to visit the bank in Lothbury Street and talk to the manager, although from past experience he knew that getting information from banks about their customers was well nigh impossible. In the meantime, he thought, there are much more important matters to deal with.

The Jaran pair smiled with relief as they walked down the steps outside Leman Street police station and began to head back towards their guesthouse on Bell Lane.

'You do know that Inspector Reid will check the details of our story with the bank you mentioned, Trevor.'

'Yes, of course, Margot, but it will give us a little time to decide what we will do next. In the worst case scenario it may be that we have to adopt different identities and move away from the Whitechapel area to a region of Britain where we would be unlikely to bump into the Inspector.'

'That would be a great pity, Trevor, but you are correct that it may well be necessary.'

'Margot, in the meantime we will need to decide how we shall inform Inspector Reid about what we have discovered with regard to the cotton thread,' said Ashto.

'Oh I should think that an anonymous letter to the Inspector should suffice, Trevor.'

'A sensible idea, Margot, and then we can only hope that the limited information we are able to provide will help in the police investigation.'

'Hopefully so, Trevor, for now I think we can begin our

own investigation into this so-called Vampire Killer. The brief amount of information we were able to glean from the thread will perhaps provide us with a means of tracking down the murderer.'

Ashto nodded but deep down he was wary of the little note of excitement that was present in Atia's voice. There was no doubt in his mind that his Apprentice Commander, the object of his love, was again going to enjoy endeavouring to be a real life Sherlock Holmes and try her utmost to bring a dangerous murderer to justice.

Report Number 0015 to the Glorious and Munificent Jaran Galactic Federation High Council (Planetary Exploration and Viable Exo-Planet Evaluation Committee – Sector 2007 Sub-Committee) by First Commander Treve Pacton Ashto.

My greetings and utmost felicitations to the esteemed members of the sub-committee.

Our mission on this smallish planet on the edge of the galaxy continues apace. I very much hope that the members of the sub-committee have found the wealth of information Apprentice Commander Atia and myself have sent so far to be both interesting and informative. We further hope the fruits of our researches will provide a great amount of helpful detail for the sub-committee in its discussions about the Earth and its possible future incorporation into the Galactic Federation.

On a rather depressing note the Whitechapel area in which we reside has again been shocked by another series of murders. The victims this time are all young men and their headless bodies have been found in a number of places in the East End of London. Regretfully it seems that Earth people, or at least a small proportion of them, are somewhat prone to violent behaviour and the brutal slaying of their fellow human beings. It is to hoped that in the future Galactic Federation personnel will be able to give Earth humans advice and support on the identification and the psychiatric treatment of sociopathic individuals of the kind that currently seem to plague this city. Meanwhile the local police authorities seem just as baffled by this new series of killings as they were with the Jack the Ripper murders last year. As a result of their inability to find the killer, Apprentice Commander Atia and I have decided to surreptitiously provide the police with some help and assistance. In my next report I will hopefully be able to inform the members of the sub-committee whether our efforts have borne fruit.

In my past reports I have commented on the incredibly wide gap there exists between rich and poor in this country which is the richest and most powerful state on this planet. The wealth of Britain is largely due to its vast empire that extends around the globe and which is exploited for its raw materials, mineral deposits and trade. However, this wealth has almost exclusively benefited the already rich minority of individuals and has not trickled down to the general public who remain poor and in many cases literally poverty stricken. As I have said before in London, the richest city in the richest country on the planet, it is possible to witness unfortunate individuals starving to death on the streets. In every walk of life in this place the class or caste system means that an impenetrable barrier exists between people who in geographical terms actually live close to each other. This difference in these social classes is perceivable in most aspects of life. For example, allow me to mention transport. Following our train journey to an area of the country's northern region recently, Apprentice Commander Atia and I have made a study of the different forms of transportation in the sprawling city of London. The most obvious technological achievement in this area is the underground railway, which contrary to its name only runs underground for part of its network. Although limited in its scope at present it will no doubt develop further in the future and will perhaps become a model for similar mass transport systems in other parts of this planet. Apart from railways, above ground transport is, of course, mostly drawn by equine quadrupeds known as horses. Various forms of wheeled carriages can be seen in London from simple carts or wagons used to move goods around the city to omnibuses designed to carry large number of passengers. Wealthy members of the London society often have their own private carriages to transport them about the city, usually vehicles called locally as broughams, landaus or barouches. The ubiquitous two wheeled hansom cabs, which can be hailed on the streets, are the swiftest method to negotiate the London thoroughfares although the weight of traffic in the city often makes getting from one place to another relatively slow. One of the many improvements representatives from the Galactic Federation could make in the event of the Earth being admitted to the organisation would be the installation of a properly integrated transport system with the introduction of electric powered vehicles which would be a great boon to the city and obviate the need for horses which produce vast amounts of waste which has to be dealt with at present. Electric vehicles would also mean that the combustion engine technology, which is at the moment in its infancy on this planet, could be abandoned and the inevitable future polluting effects of that technology totally avoided.

Of course all of that is mere speculation at present so Apprentice Commander Atia and I will continue in our task to gain as much intelligence as possible about the planet Earth, which of course will be passed on to the subcommittee using the usual channels. I will submit my next report as soon as possible.

With my utmost loyalty to the glorious Jaran Galactic Federation,

First Commander Treve Pacton Ashto.

16

A Letter

'What's that, Bill?' Inspector Reid pointed at the envelope his Detective Sergeant held in his hand.

'It's yet another bloomin' anonymous letter about the Vampire Killer, Sir.'

'Oh for God's sake, Bill, please don't use the bloody name the papers are calling him. What does the letter say?'

'I haven't read it, Sir; I'm assuming it's the usual nonsense. I'll just put it with the others.' Sergeant Thick opened the large box file that sat on his desk and dropped the latest letter in among the many others that were contained there. 'And of course we're still getting letters about the Ripper murders with all sorts of barmy ideas about who the killer is. I still laugh about that letter that accused me of being the Ripper. Damn cheek! There are even some that say a member of the Royal Family is responsible! Do you remember those ones addressed to "Dear Boss" that were sent to Chief Inspector Abberline? There are boxes and boxes of them and some other ones in the evidence room. I pity the poor souls who are going to have to read 'em all at some point.'

'I don't think anyone has enough time to do that at present, there's too much going on. I'm sure some amateur sleuth will one day go through them all and probably write a book and come up with all sorts of lunatic theories about who the Ripper is… or was.'

'Was, Sir?'

'Well, we haven't seen any poor dead women with all their guts hanging out for several months now so maybe he's gone for good.'

'That young bloke who was pulled out of the Thames on the last day of last year perhaps? What was he, a lawyer?'

'Druitt? He was a schoolmaster I think. But no, Abberline has ruled him out of the picture; there's no evidence at all he was the Whitechapel murderer. The Yard's investigations have shown that he wasn't even in London when some of the murders happened apparently. No, the Ripper has stopped because either he's also dead or he's biding his time before he starts up again. Meanwhile we've got this other charmer to deal with.' Reid was about to walk back to his office, when he stopped and turned back to his sergeant: 'Bill, let me have a look at that letter.'

'The latest one?'

'Yes, Bill. Give it here.'

Reid took from the envelope the single sheet of writing paper, unfolded it and stood reading it. 'Hey, Bill, listen to this: "Dear Inspector Reid, with reference to the small piece of purple thread that was found on the body of

Constable Perkins I can inform you that the cotton strand contained very small amounts of certain chemicals including formaldehyde and arsenic. These are substances used in various industries including taxidermy and embalming. It is possible therefore that the individuals murdered by the so-called Vampire Killer met their end in locations where bodies of humans or animals are preserved for anatomical study, embalming processes or for aesthetic or decorative reasons. Therefore you might want to look for the killer in hospital medical research laboratories or mortuaries, the workshops of taxidermists or museum conservators or the workplaces of undertakers who regularly embalm the bodies of the recently dead to enable relatives and friends to view their deceased loved ones prior to burial. Good luck!" What do you think of that, Sergeant?'

'Sir, sounds like nonsense to me.'

'Perhaps Bill, but it's a bit different than most of the letters we get sent.'

'In what way, Sir?'

'Well Sergeant, for a start it's well written, there aren't all the spelling mistakes we usually get with such letters. The ones we normally receive sound like they've been penned by madmen, but this one sounds almost… normal.'

'But Sir, our people couldn't find anything on that piece of thread when they examined it before it erm, got mislaid.'

Inspector Reid winced at the memory. He'd dropped the cotton strand when he'd waved away a fly that had been bothering him and, despite the best efforts of Sergeant Thick and himself to find it again it had seemingly disappeared for good.

'More to the point, Bill how did anyone outside this

station even get to hear about the thread, let alone conduct tests on it?'

Sergeant William Thick looked puzzled and shook his head. 'It doesn't make much sense, Sir.'

'No, Bill, it doesn't. But if this letter somehow is right, and we're looking for some sort of workshop or laboratory, where would we start?'

'The London Hospital on Whitechapel Road is a teaching hospital – it'll have those sorts of places'

'As good a place to start as any I should think, Bill. Get your hat and coat, Sergeant, let's see if we can find someone there to tell us about arsenic and formaldehyde.'

'It's a very long list, Margot.'

'It is, Trevor but at least it gives us a starting point.'

First Commander Ashto and Apprentice Commander Atia looked down the list of names and locations of potential places in London where the chemicals they had discovered on the small strand of material they had stolen from under the noses of the police might well be used. There were a great many of them. Using the computer aboard their ship in orbit about the Earth, as well as the network of satellites that were constantly passing information back to them they had been able to compile this very lengthy list of possible places where the Vampire Murderer could have dealt with his victims.

'Yes, Margot but *where* do we start?'

'A good question, Trevor, at the top of the list I suppose.'

'The local hospital?'

'I think so,' said Atia enthusiastically, 'and I believe that we have a valid reason for revisiting that particular place.'

Ashto smiled at the way his Apprentice Commander was so obviously energised by their plan to track down this latest killer. He was reminded of something the fictional detective Sherlock Holmes had said in a story that he had enjoyed reading: "The game is afoot." However, what he and Atia were planning to do was real life and not a story. He felt more than a little concerned at the potential danger their plan might lead them into.

17

The Undertaker

The widow of the recently deceased man sat in his parlour frequently dabbing her eyes with her small lace handkerchief. The undertaker had taken part in this scene so many times before that he was secretly amazed at how he could still pretend to show sympathy and interest in the grief of those who came to his establishment in order to plan their loved one's interment. He nodded with feigned empathy and understanding at the elderly woman opposite, dressed as she was in regulation black mourning clothes and veil and who kept sniffing frequently and so very annoyingly. The undertaker's face was arranged in such a practised way as to convey his mock concern and sympathy for the grieving widow and the middle aged son who stood beside his mother, his hand resting supportively on her left shoulder.

It's always the same he thought as he briefly paused in his unctuous recital of the whys and wherefores of the coffins and embalming services he offered as the widow sniffed again and then proceeded to loudly blow her nose. Most of those who came along to see him about such funereal matters were not, his intuition told him, actually very interested in which coffin would be best or how the departed person should appear in it when on show but in truth only wanted to get the whole process over and done with as quickly as possible so they could concentrate on the most important matter in hand – the last Will and Testament of the deceased. The bearded son, standing there stiffly, trying hard to look concerned for his poor mother, hand still on her shoulder in what he imagined was a consoling way, was extremely easy to read. What he was thinking about involved detailed assessments and calculations about how much money he would be getting from the estate of his *dear* departed father and how much more he deserved compared to his uncaring siblings who hadn't even bothered to come along to the undertaker's with their recently widowed mother. Inwardly the undertaker scoffed, while keeping his face fixed in a well-practised mask of sympathy.

'I am terribly sorry,' sniffed the widow drying her eyes for the umpteenth time, 'it has all been such a shock with poor Reginald being taken so suddenly without any warning at all.'

'Do not concern yourself, Mrs Wright, do take your time, there is no need to rush our deliberations in the slightest way.' The undertaker wanted to check his pocket watch as he had already been sitting with the widow Wright for what seemed like hours. He had things to do and plans to make and could really do with her quickly making a few decisions about her husband's funeral details.

'Oh, Mr Pell, you are so very kind. How fortunate we are that someone so caring, reassuring and understanding will be in charge of sending poor Reginald off on his final journey.' At which point she began to weep copiously again. Mr Pell, the undertaker, almost tutted aloud but was able to stop himself in time. Oh, come on you stupid old bitch, he thought, make some decisions for God's sake! However, his mask of grave concern remained firmly fixed in place.

The son, also called Reginald apparently, with his mother so overcome by her grief, decided it was time for him to make an intervention. 'Mr Pell, can you inform us just how much your services will cost in total?'

If the father was as pompously stiff and taciturn as the son, Mr Pell thought, then the old man wouldn't be missed for very long; probably only until the reading of the Will had taken place. Pell smiled broadly inside his head.

'Well, Mr Wright, that is very much dependent on the type of casket that is chosen by your dear mother, as well as the many extra services we can provide pursuant to her eventual instructions.' The son nodded solemnly, puffed out his chest and took a sly look at his pocket watch that nestled in his well-filled waistcoat. He was bored now, the undertaker thought, and was so obviously keen to go for his lunch and a few glasses of claret at his club. It was so very evident that he now wanted his mother to quickly decide on the funeral details, as long as they didn't cost *too* much and reduce the amount he would inherit from the old man. With just a hint of impatience in his voice he quietly spoke to his still weeping mother: 'Mama, I believe that you need to express your final wishes regarding the details of father's funeral to Mr Pell.'

'Of course,' replied the woman, giving one last heartfelt sob before dabbing at her eyes again.

I do dislike all these ostentatious shows of feigned emotions, thought the undertaker, while smiling benevolently at the elderly widow. 'Perhaps you would both like to follow me and view the caskets we have on show,' said the undertaker offering his hand to the widow. As soon as we get this over with, he thought, the sooner I can start planning the more important aspects of my life.

Mr Pell stood at the front door to what he described as his studio that adjoined his house in Fitzroy Street. He watched as Mrs Wright, who was still dabbing her nose, and her son departed in the steady rain as they looked for a cab to take them home. Pell breathed a sigh of relief. It had been an infuriating last hour trying to get any decisions out of the stupid old widow amidst her annoying and continual sobbing. How he disliked the people he was forced to deal with. How he hated their self-centered shows of emotion. In the end Mrs Wright had proved completely unable to make any choices at all and the son had decided everything for her, opting for a cheaper coffin than Pell had originally hoped he would sell to the pair. Oh well, he thought, he was sure that he could add one or two little extras to the Wright's eventual bill that would make up for any loss in that area. He smiled. He felt in charge of things and had already begun to look forward to his forthcoming visit to the house in Cleveland Street where his next exquisite entertainment was likely to be found. The joy of expectation tingled through his body. Soon, very, very soon he thought excitedly.

18

Another Meeting

First Commander Ashto and Apprentice Commander Atia had visited the London Hospital in the Whitechapel Road a few months before. On that occasion they had spoken to Frederick Treves, one of the eminent doctors who worked there, and had been introduced by him to the hospital's most famous patient, Joseph Merrick, also known by the press and public as the Elephant Man. This morning, as they re-entered the impressive entrance of the hospital on their way to meet Mr Treves again, they were surprised to bump into Detective Inspector Reid and Sergeant Thick who were in the process of leaving the building.

'Ah, Mr and Mrs Ashton, good morning, we meet yet again. I hope your visit to this hospital is not to do with any medical issue,' said Inspector Reid, doffing his bowler hat to the pair.

'A very good morning to you, Inspector Reid and to you, Sergeant Thick. In fact we are here today to visit a particular friend of ours, Mr Merrick, whom we first got to know last year and who resides at the hospital as you are aware.'

'The Elephant Man, you mean,' said the sergeant.

'Sergeant Thick, we do not call Joseph by that name, an appellation that was invented by a newspaper journalist who I believe was more interested in sensationalism rather than he was in the truth. We think that cruel nickname greatly demeans a person who is an intelligent and sensitive young man.'

'Apologies, Miss,' said the somewhat abashed Sergeant Thick, tipping his bowler hat in deference to the forthright Mrs Ashton.

'Is your visit connected with one of your current investigations, Inspector?' said First Commander Ashto.

'I'm sorry Mr Ashton, but I cannot reveal the reason for our visit. Police business, as you know, needs to be kept completely confidential.'

'Of course, Inspector, pardon me for inquiring.'

'That is quite all right, Mr Ashton, we live and learn as they say,' said the Inspector, 'but however interesting and informative as it always is to chat with you both my sergeant and I must leave as we have urgent business to attend to; so goodbye for now, I am sure we shall soon meet again,' continued the Inspector doffing his hat once more and smiling at the Ashtons.

'Yes, goodbye Inspector, Sergeant, I'm sure we shall,' said the First Commander.

At the bottom of the steps Reid stopped and looked back at the Ashtons as they entered the hospital. He shook his head and Sergeant Thick looked quizzically at him.

'That pair, Bill. I can't work them out at all. Always popping up when you least expect them. Something's not right, you know. Is Gibbs still keeping tabs on them?'

'Yes Sir, I saw him follow them into the building just now.'

'Get his report to me later today. I want to know what those two are really up to at the hospital as soon as possible.'

'Will do, Sir.'

Reid shrugged resignedly and shook his head again. He realised he had been performing those actions on a very regular basis recently. 'Back to the station, Bill, lets examine that list again.'

Inside the hospital the Ashtons waited for Frederick Treves to appear. He was the surgeon who had saved the life of Joseph Merrick by rescuing him from the freak show in the Whitechapel Road where he and his dreadful deformities were being displayed for paying customers to gawp at and mock. Treves had provided the so-called Elephant Man with rooms in the hospital where he could be well treated and cared for. It was only after the Jarans had met the unfortunate Mr Merrick and had realised that despite his terrible fate he had nevertheless displayed such humanity, fortitude and optimism that Atia had vowed that she and Ashto would help track down the killer, Jack the Ripper, who was as evil as Joseph Merrick, the Elephant Man, was good.

'What do you suppose Inspector Reid and the Sergeant were doing here at the hospital, Margot?'

'Impossible to say of course but I'm rather hoping, Trevor, that his visit was connected to the letter we sent to him regarding the piece of cotton thread. After all this place was top of our list, so maybe it was on the police's too.'

'Hmm, my thoughts exactly, Margot.'

At that moment the Jaran pair's conversation was interrupted by Mr Treves who walked quickly towards them smiling, hand outraised in friendly and welcoming fashion. Short in stature, slightly balding and with a fine and well-groomed mustache and who, Atia estimated, was in his mid-30s, he shook their hands enthusiastically. 'How very pleasing it is to see you both again; how are your researches coming along?' Treves asked in his slightly high-pitched voice.

'They are coming along very well, Mr Treves, and keeping us both very busy,' said Ashto.

'Good, good, I'm so very pleased. Would you both like to come to my office? It's not too far away as you know.'

In Frederick Treves' office Ashto and Atia sat facing the surgeon across his desk.

'You are here to visit John I presume?' (For some reason that neither of the Jaran visitors could ever fathom, Treves always referred to Joseph Merrick as John).

'That is correct, Mr Treves, as our recent telegram requested. How is he progressing?'

'Not very well I'm afraid. I have to say that despite him being cared for very well here there is little doubt that John's condition is quickly deteriorating. The deformities around his cranium are getting worse day by day and that is causing his head, which as you know was already terribly enlarged, to become progressively and significantly heavier. It is more and more of a struggle for him to keep his head held in an upright position and that situation is beginning to lead to breathing difficulties. At present too he is suffering from pneumonia brought about by a chest infection and is in a very bad way generally. As a consequence I am afraid to say that I am, temporarily at least, not allowing him to have any visitors. I apologise profusely therefore that you will not be able to see John today. It may be possible perhaps in a week's time, but I cannot promise you.'

'Mr Treves, that is such bad news. Can I inquire as to the long-term prognosis for Mr Merrick? Is there any cause for optimism?' As Atia spoke a tear ran down her cheek, which she was forced to wipe away.

'I fear that the answer is no, Mrs Ashton. Although John is a young man, not yet twenty-seven years old, I'm afraid the prospect of his survival, even in the short term, is unfortunately not very hopeful. In my opinion it will be surprising if John even sees the end of this current year; it is very likely that another winter will lead to his demise. As his dear friend I find it is a terribly difficult conclusion to have to come to.' Frederick Treves, the Jaran pair noticed, also had tears in his eyes as he finished speaking.

'That is very sad news indeed, Mr Treves,' said the First Commander. Apprentice Commander Atia was, Ashto noticed, unable to speak so upset was she by what the doctor had said. 'We will contact you in a week's time, Mr Treves and see whether Mr Merrick's condition has improved at that point.' Treves nodded but did not look very optimistic. 'Mr Treves, before we leave here we were wondering if you could help us on a small point regarding our researches?'

'Of course, Mr Ashton, I'll certainly try,' replied Treves.

'It is a very small matter indeed but we were wondering if any of the staff members at this hospital would, in the course of their work, use the chemical substances arsenic and formaldehyde in combination?'

Treves looked surprised. 'That is extraordinary, Mr Ashton.'

'Why is that, Mr Treves?'

'Well, less than half-an-hour ago, Inspector Reid of the Metropolitan Police was here, in this very room, asking exactly the same question!'

'Oh... what a strange coincidence.'

'Indeed, Mr Ashton; can I enquire why you ask such a question?'

'Well... I... we... were...'

'Mr Treves, we were looking at the uses of a number a different substances in manufacturing industries in this country and comparing them to the similar ways they are utilised in the United States where, as you know, we come from. These two chemicals, we discovered are used in a number of areas that were quite new to us and we were interested in following them up to try to give a complete picture of the ways in which life here in Great Britain is very different to that of America,' said Atia having quickly recovered enough from her sadness to speak.

'I think I understand,' said the surgeon looking somewhat unconvinced. 'Well, as I told the Detective Inspector a short while ago,' he continued, 'such chemicals together would have been used in our laboratories in the past to preserve examples of human tissue and organs used by medical students at various stages in their training.

These days, however, other chemicals, less hazardous to the individuals using them, are more often used in the preservation process in hospital laboratories. The chemicals you have mentioned are perhaps more likely to be utilised in smaller scale situations such as by taxidermists when they are preserving animal carcasses for display purposes in museums or private households, or by undertakers in the embalming process when they are preparing recently deceased corpses for viewing prior to burials. I am sorry that I can't be any more specific, but it is exactly the same the answer I gave to Inspector Reid and his sergeant.'

'Thank you, Mr Treves, that is very helpful to our general researches,' said Atia, now fully in charge of her emotions again.

'Your researches are certainly taking in a wealth of detail, Mrs Ashton. I am very much looking forward to reading your finished work. Will the volume be published in this country as well as in the United States, Mr Ashton?'

'That is something we are not yet quite certain about, Mr Treves, publishing is, as you probably know, not always a straightforward business. We can honestly say, however, that if or when our book is published we will certainly ensure that you will receive a signed copy,' said Ashto.

'Oh, that is most kind, Mr Ashton. In turn I will keep you fully appraised about John's condition and will inform you if or when you may pay a visit to him again.'

A little later the Jaran pair stood outside the main entrance of the London Hospital. Saddened by the news of Joseph Merrick's illness they nevertheless were encouraged by the information they had gained from Treves.

'It looks very much that based on Mr Treves' information we can shorten the list of locations where the Vampire Killer may be operating from,' said Atia.

'Indeed, Margot.' I suggest that we could target small-scale taxidermy practitioners in the first instance,' replied Ashto.

'Agreed, Trevor. I think we should endeavour to pay our first visits right away.'

'Yes, Margot, perhaps after we have had a cup of tea first.'

Atia smiled, 'of course we shall, Trevor.'

19

A Fenian Outrage?

He was pleased to have finished his footslogging round the streets of Whitechapel; it had been another cold and wet March night and he was really looking forward to a nice warming cup of tea and a bit of a sit down. Nothing of any importance had happened during his shift; he had moved on a couple of rowdy drunks and told them to go home and he had threatened a noisy married couple who were having a loud argument standing outside their house just after midnight with arrest if they didn't shut up and stop annoying their neighbours. It had been a fairly typical Whitechapel night in fact. Still it was quite an improvement on what it had all been like towards the end of last year during the height of the Ripper murders when everyone, especially the 'unfortunates' as the papers called them – the women who plied their trade on the streets – were terrified at what horror was going to take place next.

Certainly things had seemed to have calmed down since then despite some headless bodies being discovered about the area recently, Constable Edwin Leadbeater thought, although he was still on his guard and, as he walked around the area, half expecting to come across the dead and mutilated body of some poor woman. Ever since the Jack the Ripper outrages it had been impressed on all police constables that they should always pay attention to anything at all unusual they noticed while they were on their beat so when Constable Leadbeater walked down Leman Street and saw three men acting suspiciously in the shadows at the rear of the police station he thought it best to investigate and see what they were up to. Taking out his truncheon from its leather holder fastened to his belt and with his whistle handy, just in case he needed to summon other officers to back him up, he shone his bullseye lamp at the three who were gathered in a doorway that was no longer used by the occupants of the large, three storey, wedge shaped police building.

' 'Ere what are you lot up to?'

One of the men smiled at the policeman as he walked nearer.

'Evenin' officer, we're doin' nothin' wrong; just 'avin' a bit of a chat wiv me two chinas 'ere.'

The two men to either side of the man who spoke nodded, forced smiles on their faces.

'What's that behind where you're standing?' said Constable Leadbeater noticing that a parcel wrapped in brown paper lay to the rear of the men next just inside the disused doorway.

The constable's question obviously caused a certain amount of confusion among the men as they looked down at the package, then at each other and then mumbled a few incoherent words.

P.C. Leadbeater held up his bull's-eye lamp in his left hand and walked towards the three men his truncheon raised in his right. However, at that point the three men decided to act, quickly moving to push the policeman backwards, causing him to fall to the ground. As he fell he instinctively picked up his whistle that had been dangling from his neck ready to blow. Unfortunately for Constable Leadbeater the whistle never reached his lips as two of the men began to set about him with thick leather coshes filled with lead that they had pulled from their coat pockets. The third man then walked up to the prone policeman and let fly with a hefty kick into the Constable's stomach.

'Take that yer interferin' mutton shunter,' said the man who preceded to kick him several times more in the ribs before the three men ran from the scene leaving the brown paper parcel lying in the doorway.

Constable Leadbeater groaned. He could taste blood in his mouth and feel it dribbling out of his mouth and nose. His stomach and chest hurt every time he drew breath. He would have preferred to stay where he was lying on the pavement and quietly go to sleep, perhaps then the pains in his chest and abdomen would stop. However, he realised he should get up and go into the police station on the outside of which he now lay and let his H Division colleagues know about what had happened.

And then he heard the ticking sound loud and clear. Was it in his head? Was it something to do with the blood that was running copiously from his mouth and nose and was now pooling on the cold, damp pavement? And then he realised the ticking was coming from the parcel the men had left. A ticking package could mean a bomb – he had remembered that fact from his training when he had first joined the police force two years before. As a young man he had tended to disbelieve some of the stories the older time-hardened police officers had told him, they were always full of doom and gloom. They had said that if you heard a ticking box like this then you should get away from it as quickly as you can.

P.C. Leadbeater slowly and with great difficulty raised himself from the ground onto his knees; every bit of his body hurting. His head throbbed where the men had hit him with their coshes and there was a fearful pain in both his chest and his abdomen.

And then the ticking stopped. What did that mean? Was he now safe? What had fellow officers told him to do when the ticking stopped? What had they said? He couldn't quite remember.

The young police constable was still wondering what the answers to these questions were when suddenly there was a blinding flash of bright, white light, and an eardrum bursting crash followed by merciful blackness.

20

Abberline and Reid Talk and Atia Comes Up With a Plan

'What the bloody hell is going on, Edmund? I've had the Special Irish Branch round my neck for the last 24 hours. I've had no sleep, I've had nothing to eat and the missus will forget who I am if I don't make an appearance at home in the very near future.'

'I'm sorry, Fred, but as you know we're snowed under here. We've had no leads or whispers at all about possible Fenian activity in the Whitechapel area otherwise we'd have been on to them. This explosion has come out of the blue as far as this area's concerned. Luckily there was not much damage done to the building and the only person injured was the constable who found the bomb in the first place.'

'Well, Edmund that may be so, that may be so, but I do need something to throw the Special Branch's way. The last Fenian bombing was four years ago and we don't want to go through all that again do we? What about the injured constable… Leadbeater wasn't it? Has he been able to shed any light on it?'

'Still too ill to speak, I'm afraid, so it'll be a while before he can tell us anything. Most likely it wasn't Fenians at all that planted the bomb. It may have been anarchists. Plenty of those around the East End, mostly Russian Jews I would think.'

'Whoever did explode a bomb outside the back door of a police station knows that it's going to make us look like a laughing stock with the public, another blow to people's trust in the police. And God knows what the press is saying about it. I've deliberately not looked at a newspaper for two days. I can't stand it Edmund, I can't stand it!'

'No, sir, I've put some of our best men on the case but there are so many other things going on at the moment we're very thinly stretched.'

'All right, Edmund, all right, have you made any headway with this Vampire Murderer?'

Reid winced at Abberline's use of the newspapers' sensationalist name for the killer. 'We could, Sir, if we were allowed to raid the molly house in Cleveland Street and investigate all its visitors and occupants.'

'I've told you before, Edmund, that place is out of bounds for the time being. I will let you know when we're ready to go in there but for now you've got to keep well away from 19, Cleveland Street.' Detective Chief Inspector Abberline swatted away a fly that had been bothering him ever since Inspector Reid had arrived in his office. 'What about the General Post Office? Two out of the four victims were telegraph boys, what have they told you?'

'They seem to know very little. We've questioned a number of their telegraph boys in Leman Street and they're all very tight-lipped about the goings on at 19, Cleveland Street.'

'Well, Inspector, put some more pressure on them; we need to show the public we've got the situation under control. If we have another murder in the East End the whole place is likely to blow up and we'll have another "Bloody Sunday" public disorder on our hands.'

'Yes, Sir.' Reid draw himself up to his full height, which in fact was not very tall, before realising it would be best to withdraw from Abberline's office before he said something in anger that he later would regret. 'Anything else, Sir?'

Abberline looked sad: 'No, Edmund, not at the moment, just keep me fully apprised as to the situation. That's all.'

'Sir,' said Reid who turned on his heels and left the room.

In Mrs Smith's Select Guesthouse in Whitechapel's Bell Lane Ashto and Atia had been looking intently at their small computer screen as they had listened in on the conversation between the two police detectives in Chief Inspector Abberline's office. Now Ashto was carefully controlling the fly drone that had been spying on the two men out of the Metropolitan Police headquarters at Scotland Yard and maneuvering it back towards their room.

'Well, Trevor, that was very interesting,' said Atia.

'Indeed it was, Margot. Inspector Abberline did not sound very happy at all.'

'No, Trevor, he did not. What is particularly interesting is the information that there seems to be a connection between the victims of the Vampire Killer and a house in Cleveland Street, which, according to the police reports we've seen is a male brothel of some repute. I think that that helps us in deciding what we can do to help the police track down the killer of those four young men.'

'What do you propose we should do, Margot?' said Ashto as he concentrated on guiding the drone through the streets of the East End.

'Well, Trevor, you know that I am relatively skillful where disguises are concerned?'

'Yes, Margot,' Ashto said with a slight concern in his voice.

'What if I, dressed as a young man, offered myself up as bait while visiting the house in Cleveland Street and attempted to attract the killer. I could then overpower the individual before delivering him, anonymously of course, to the police authorities in Leman Street. Inspector Reid would doubtless be very pleased, a murderer would be off the streets and the police could turn their attention to the bombing campaign that seems to have started in the city.'

'And leave him more time to investigate the counterfeited coins we somewhat inadvertently spread around the area. No, Margot, the whole thing sounds far too dangerous. Need I remind you what happened last time you confronted a crazed murderer? You were almost killed.'

'I know Trevor and I realise that as my Mission

Commander you would have the ultimate say in whether my plan goes ahead so all I would ask is that you think about it for a time and do not come to an immediate decision.'

'That is fair, Margot. However, do you actually think it is at all possible for you to disguise yourself as a young man? I would somehow doubt it.'

'Well, we'll see. I would first need to find out a little more about these telegraph boys and what exactly their actual function is and then replicate a facsimile of the type of uniform I believe they are attired in. That shouldn't be too difficult. I will also need to study the speech patterns of the young men who perform the role of telegraph boys and then of course I will have to work out what one says and does in a male brothel, the fly drone should be able to supply us with that information and…'

'Wait, Margot! You are presuming that I will allow you to go ahead with this mission and place yourself in danger again. This is truly something I will need time to consider; I cannot be rushed.'

'No, Trevor, of course, I apologise for getting carried away. Let us concentrate on returning the drone.'

'Yes, Margot, that is exactly what I am doing,' said Ashto a little more sharply than he had intended.

First Commander Ashto, these days, rarely sounded concerned but Atia realised that her plan had provided him with something very real to worry about. She would have to be extremely careful not to cause him to bar her from helping to track down the Vampire Killer. However, since the awful death of poor Constable Perkins and then hearing about the illness that had recently afflicted poor Joseph Merrick she had felt more determined than ever that she would do something to make people's life in Whitechapel better. She would not admit it to the First Commander but she had grown very fond of the people of planet Earth and the various quirks of living on this small, insignificant lump of rock on the edge of the galaxy. More and more Earth, and particularly London, was becoming to seem very much like a home from home where she felt happy and fulfilled.

21

Atia Adopts Another Disguise

'So, how do I look, Trevor?'

'You look very good, Margot, but I'm not totally convinced that you will pass scrutiny as a young Earth male.'

'Really, Trevor, I thought that I fitted the part perfectly.'

'Well, outwardly you do, I suppose, although you'll be quite a lot taller than most of the young men on this planet but don't you think your speech and general demeanor will be a little more difficult to portray in an accurate way?'

Atia walked up and down and peered at herself squinting into the old, rust speckled mirror that hung on the wall of their room at Mrs Smith's Select Guesthouse. 'Yes, that is true, Trevor, but I have been working hard on those particular aspects, so how does this sound to you?' Atia sniffed loudly and ran the sleeve of her blue telegraph boy jacket across her nose and mouth: 'Well, me ole china plate, I'm just off to the boozer to 'ave a few pints on the slate an' a bit of a chinwag with a few blokes I know. Course, I tol' me mum I'd be poppin' into the Holy Ghost shop to confess all me sins but she'll believe anythink, the old dear. On the way I'll prob'ly 'ave a butchers at the howlers an' toffs an' proper bits o' frock in the street, all done out in their finest klobber. After I come outa the pub I'll stroll down pros' avenue, past the Gaiety Bar in the Strand an' see what's brewin' an' if there's anythink what tickles me fancy. An' if I gets the chance I'll nip into the nearest hug centre with one of the wagtails, gawblimy if I don't!'

Ashto realised that his mouth was gaping wide open with surprise at what he'd just heard. Atia smiled broadly at him, pleased with herself. 'Margot, you never cease to amaze me! I did not comprehend any of what you've just said but it sounds exactly like the way young men speak when you overhear them on the street or in the local markets. How did you learn all that?'

'Like you said, Trevor, I just listen to what certain people are saying in the street. The neural implant helps too of course,' said Atia tapping the side of her head. 'By the way what do you think I should do with my "barnet" as my imagined young man might refer to his hair?'

'Well, please do not cut it short, Margot. If you tuck it up into your telegraph boy headwear that should suffice.'

'Just as long as I don't take my cap off.' Atia fiddled with her long, dark hair and made sure that the pins and grips she used to keep it in place were secure. 'I think that will do just as long as I don't have to exert myself too much.'

'So, Margot, what exactly is your plan?'

'Well, Trevor, I intend to go to the house in Cleveland Street and bluff my way inside somehow. From that point I will need to look out for anyone acting suspiciously and with murderous intent and endeavour to win his confidence until I get the chance to overpower him and deliver him safely to the police.'

'How will you do that, Margot, without compromising your elaborate disguise?'

'Ah, I haven't quite worked that out as yet. I will certainly need to improvise as the occasion arises. Do not look so worried, Trevor,' Atia smiled fondly, reaching out to hold Ashto's hand, 'and thank you for allowing me to undertake this task.'

'Well, Margot, I am still unsure that this is the correct action to take but you were right of course, you should be given the chance, as part of our overall mission, to look into all aspects of human behaviour.'

'Thank you, Trevor; I think we were right to go ahead with this plan and you must not worry too much about me.'

'But I do worry, Margot. Again you are placing yourself in terrible danger and the chance that you may be injured again is extremely high.'

'I will be perfectly safe, Trevor. Besides I will be maintaining constant communication with you by means of my concealed camera. You will, I presume, be in a nearby strategic position which will enable you to come to my aid if at all necessary.'

'I certainly will be, Margot. At the first sign of danger I will be at your side.'

'That is very reassuring, Trevor but you must let me first ascertain that I am actually in the presence of the killer before you come to my assistance. That is very important of course if this ruse is to work.'

'I totally understand, Margot.' Ashto nevertheless looked concerned and downcast.

'Please do not worry, Trevor. I feel perfectly confident that I will be able to manage any situation that may arise.'

Ashto nodded, but inside was feeling skeptical. He knew that Atia, his Apprentice Commander on this mission, was adept in various self-defensive martial techniques but could not stop thinking about the injury she had sustained when dealing with Jack the Ripper, an injury that could easily have resulted in her death. He smiled at Atia and hoped that his smile looked reassuring to her and would convince her that he was happy with her plan of action even though, deep down, he felt anything but reassured.

'When do you propose to initiate your plan, Margot?'

'Well, Trevor I think we should strike while the iron is hot, as the Earth humans say, and begin this evening.'

'Very well, Margot I will attach the hidden camera to your telegraph boy apparel but also a microphone in case there is a systemic failure with the optical device.'

'A good idea, Trevor, one can never be too prepared,' said Atia, knowing that the words she used in this conversation with Ashto would either reassure him or make him worry to an even greater extent. 'I will make my way to Cleveland Street and see what will happen when I knock on the door and try to seek an entrance to the establishment.'

'And I will follow at a discrete distance. We must bear in mind that one of Inspector Reid's officers will doubtless follow me but I will ensure he loses me in the first crowded street we come to.'

'Of course, Trevor.'
'And, Margot.'
'Yes, Trevor?'
'Do be very careful.'

22

A Confrontation

Atia made sure she was not followed as she left Mrs Smith's Select Guest House. There was no reason at all why Reid's man would follow a telegraph boy although he may have been confused as to why he hadn't noticed him go into Mrs Smith's premises in the first place.

She felt good as she swaggered down Bell Lane, Goulston Street and into Whitechapel High Street. Atia was pleased with her disguise that made her feel much less encumbered than she did when wearing the many-layered female clothes she usually had to endure. She also held a lighted cigarette in her hand, which she occasionally placed to her mouth and pretended to smoke: 'An authentic look for a young Earth male,' she had explained to Ashto. She had also decided that every time she passed a young female in the street she would smile in as lascivious a way as possible and in return she received a variety of responses ranging from utter distain to reciprocal smiles.

Once she reached Whitechapel High Street she planned to hail a hansom cab to Oxford Street and then walk the short distance from there to Cleveland Street where she would try to work out a method that would enable her to enter the house mentioned in the police report the Jarans had spied upon. Somewhere behind her, First Commander Ashto would be following to ensure that she came to no danger. He would have to be careful not to let Reid's undercover officer discover that he was following her. Hopefully he would have his notebook to hand and would be making occasional notes in it in order to fool his follower he was doing his usual research activity. Reid's man would doubtless think it was strange that Mr Ashton was on his own but would perhaps assume that his wife was not feeling well and was staying in bed back at the guesthouse in Bell Lane.

By the time Atia's hansom cab stopped in Oxford Street and she had paid the driver it was early evening and the streets were crowded. That would make it easy for the First Commander to lose the police officer who would have followed him all the way from the East End. Meanwhile she would make her way up Newman Street, across Mortimer Street and into Cleveland Street where she would locate number 19 before working out the best way to get inside the building.

First Commander Ashto had to admit to himself that he really enjoyed thwarting the Metropolitan Police officer who had been given the task of following him. He had stopped occasionally to make notes in his notebook while checking he was still being tailed before quickly entering a large store and finding his way out of a side door and emerging into a large group in the crowded street. Checking carefully that he had lost the undercover policeman in the busy and darkening Oxford Street he could now make his way north to where Atia would soon be attempting to enter number 19, Cleveland Street. It was important to their plan that he was to be on hand to go to her aid if required. It was a matter of chance that as he proceeded down the street he was bundled into by someone running at speed along the pavement. Both Ashto and the running man ended up in a heap on the ground and the First Commander was just about to address the man and ensure he was not hurt when cries of "stop that thief!" rang in his ear. Instinctively he caught hold of the man who was small, wiry and rat-like and who was in the process of getting to his feet in order to dash away. Ashto put him into an arm lock to stop him from leaving the scene.

'Ow, that 'urts! Leggo of me, I ain't done noffink!' shouted the man. Ashto increased his restraining grip and ensured that the man was about to go nowhere.

'Thank you, sir, I hope you are not hurt,' said a voice.

'I am fine, thank you.' A young woman in a green coat and elaborate brown hat was smiling at him.

'Oh, I am so grateful to you for stopping that individual who had just stolen my handbag,' she said.

Ashto looked at the woman noticing how her attractive green eyes matched the colour of her outfit. He smiled back at her as a growing crowd of bystanders had formed around the scene and handed the handbag back to her.

'What's all this then?' said a uniformed policeman who elbowed his way through the throng.

'Officer, this rogue,' (the woman pointed at the man Ashto clung onto) 'stole my handbag and took off with it down the street. Bravely this gentleman,' (she now pointed at Ashto) 'apprehended him and retrieved my bag.'

'I'll take care of this villain now, Sir, if you don't mind,' said the burly, mustachioed policeman grabbing the man by the collar in a practised fashion. 'Miss, I will have to ask you and this gentleman to accompany me to the station so that I can complete the charge sheet against this 'ere thieving scoundrel,' said the police constable looking at the woman in green.

'Oh, is that totally necessary, officer? I do have an important appointment to fulfill,' said Ashto.

'I'm afraid it is necessary, Sir,' said the policeman in his most dominating voice while still holding on to the would-be robber, who continued to wriggle, complain and express his innocence. 'If you and the young lady would like to follow me, sir, I've had dealings with this particular rogue before so it won't take long.'

'Oh, very well,' said Ashto, looking at his pocket watch. 'Is the police station very far, officer?'

'No, Sir, not far away at all, so if you and the young lady would like to come this way.' The constable, still holding firmly to his captive, pushed his way through the crowd while looking askance at a young man who had shouted some abuse at him and led the way towards Charing Cross police station. Somewhat reluctantly Ashto and the young woman followed him.

'May I inquire as to your name?' said the woman, smiling at Ashto.

'I am so sorry; I should have already introduced myself. My name is Trevor Ashton,' said Ashto shaking the woman's gloved hand.

'I am very pleased to meet you, Mr Ashton. I am Isabel Wells and I will be eternally grateful to you for stopping that man from stealing my bag.'

'That is quite all right, Miss Wells, think nothing of it.' Ashto smiled at the young lady as she walked alongside him.

'Mr Ashton, please forgive my impertinence, but do I detect a slight foreign accent in your mode of speech?'

'That is very perceptive of you, Miss Wells. I am from the United States of America. My wife and I are in Great Britain carrying out research for a travellers' guide that will be aimed at other visitors from our country.'

'How fascinating, Mr Ashton, my fiancé is also an aspiring writer; it must be so comforting having your wife with you when you are so far from home?'

'It is indeed and we *are* a very long way from home. Miss Wells, do you reside in London?'

'No, I live in Bromley in Kent, Mr Ashton. I am currently in the West End shopping in preparation for my marriage which is due to take place in a few month's time.'

'Then you must be very busy, Miss Wells. Hopefully we will not be detained for any length of time.' Ashto looked worried and glanced at his pocket watch again.

'You look very concerned, Mr Ashton. The appointment you mentioned, it is important?'

'It is indeed, Miss Wells. I am due to rendezvous with my wife and I do not want her to worry unduly.'

'Well, Mr Ashton, when we reach the police station I

will endeavour to impress upon the police officers that they must not delay you for very long.'

'That is very kind of you, Miss Wells,' said Ashto looking at his watch again and feeling extremely worried.

As Atia made her way along Cleveland Street looking for number 19 she noticed four individuals standing on the pavement ahead of her. As she got nearer to the group she could see that they, like her, were dressed in telegraph boy uniforms. One of the young men, who she took to be the leader of the group, slowly approached her smiling in a sinister fashion.

'An' who the hell are you me ol' matey I've not seen you before? We 'opes you ain't looking for one of them Mary Ann's what mince about round 'ere so's you can do a bit of gobblin' on 'im.' The young man popped out his tongue and wiggled it around suggestively. His young friends sniggered.

Atia decided that an overtly belligerent attitude was needed in this situation. 'So what if I am, I don't fink it's none of yer business? Now if you'd like to shut yer big saucebox and let me by I'd be most 'appy.'

The leader of the group smiled again, cracked his knuckles and the three other individuals began to surround Atia, who looked around at them and quickly assessed the situation. There was no sign of the First Commander arriving to support her so Atia decided it would be wise to get the first blows in before they did and so moved quickly on to the attack. She hoped that her telegraph boy cap would stay on her head during the activities of the next few seconds.

At Charing Cross police station a police sergeant was speaking to Ashto and Isabel Wells: 'Well, Miss Wells and Mr Ashton, I very much hope that you haven't been inconvenienced too much. Thank you for coming to the station and giving your statements. You can be assured that the scoundrel who tried to rob you, Miss Wells, will be spending some considerable time in gaol at Her Majesty's pleasure.'

'Thank you Sergeant, hopefully he'll learn his lesson in the process.'

'That's very unlikely, Miss. He's already spent most of his useless life so far behind bars. That type never really learns anything except new ways to rob law-abiding people.'

'How terrible,' said Isabel Wells.

'Yes,' said Ashto; 'if only poverty could be eradicated so there was no need for individuals like him to turn to criminal behaviour.'

'A worthy sentiment, Mr Ashton, but a vain hope I'm afraid. Crime and criminals will always be with us,' said the policeman as he showed the pair out of the door that led to the street outside.

'Well, Miss Wells, I hope that your interrupted shopping expedition is a fruitful one. Can I hail a cab for you?' said Ashto.

'That is not necessary, Mr Ashton. It has been very pleasant to meet you and I hope your wife will understand the reason for your lateness. I thank you again for preventing the robbery.'

"That is quite all right, Miss Wells. Good luck with the planning of your wedding, by the way.'

'Goodbye then, Mr Ashton,' smiled Isabel Wells who

went on her way. The First Commander hurried towards Cleveland Street as quickly as he could.

Atia looked at the four young men as they lay on the ground groaning. Having quickly examined each one and ensuring that none had broken bones or serious injuries she prepared to leave the scene and make her way to the house at number 19. Before she did so she again knelt by the leader of the group who sat against a garden wall moaning and cradling his right elbow that Atia had recently twisted in a painful and disabling maneuver. 'What is your name?' said Atia.

'Me name's Bob, Bobby. Who are you?'

'It doesn't matter who I am. Tell me what you know about number 19,' said Atia indicating the house that was situated a short distance away.

'It's where all the fairies and Mary Anns go. A couple of our mates have gone there to earn some extra money and 'ave wound up bein' killed. You don't wanna go in there, you really don't.'

'Don't worry about me. How does someone get inside the house?'

'I went in once with me mate – it was 'orrible, blokes slobbering over each other – some with no clothes on – mostly toffs too. Some of 'em were in dresses and fings! I got outa there quick an' tried to get the mutton shunters to go in there but they weren't interested. An' then me mate ends up dead with 'is 'ead cut off. I told the police again but they wouldn't listen; not interested in the likes of me.'

Atia reached down and examined the young man's arm. He looked puzzled as she did so before pulling his arm away. 'Hey, you've done enough damage, I fink me arm's broke.'

'No it's not. At worse there is some ligament damage and some bruising but it will be fine again in a few days' time.' She took a sovereign from her pocket and gave it to the young man who looked carefully at it. 'Do you know what the password is to get into number 19?'

'Me mate just tol' the big bloke on the door *bull cabinet* or somefing like that an' they let us in. I wish they 'adn't… it was bloomin' 'orrible.'

'Yes, so you've already said.' Atia again briefly examined the other young telegraph boys for the cuts and bruises she had inflicted on them before helping them on to their feet and ushering them off down the street, well away from the house at number 19. She was ready.

Number 19, Cleveland Street

The First Commander walked quickly towards Cleveland Street, pausing only in a shop doorway to furtively view the optical footage of Atia dealing with four young men who had stopped her in the street. He saw that his Apprentice Commander had been able to deal quickly with the limited threat offered by the four and had sent them on their way with just a few bruises and battered egos to complain about. He saw her walk up to the impressive doorway of number 19, Cleveland Street and pull at the doorbell chain.

The door opened and a large, stocky man completely filled the doorway. He greeted Atia in her telegraph boy uniform with a grimace-like smile and gruff invitation to inform him of the password that would allow her access to the house.

Atia who had quickly checked with her neural implant the information the erstwhile belligerent young man had provided her with replied 'boulle cabinet' which she had discovered was an expensive piece of ornate French furniture. Why it had been chosen as a password to get into this house remained a mystery to her, however.

The man nodded and stood to one side allowing Atia to just squeeze past his huge frame and enter the house and its wide hallway.

The first thing she noticed once she had entered the dimly lit reception room were the fragrant smells of jasmine and sandalwood that hung in the air combined with a great amount of tobacco smoke. Around the large room were plush couches and sofas many of which were adorned with males some dressed in formal evening wear along with others more exotically attired in silk kimono style robes and colourful kaftans. Scratchy music was playing quietly on a phonograph machine in one of the corners of the room while waiters dashed to and fro ferrying drinks to their customers. Atia was just beginning to wonder what she should do when she was approached by a man who was obviously a maître d' of some sort.

'You been here before?' said the man.

'Nah. It's me first time,' replied Atia.

'Well, if you want to earn some ready money I would suggest you stop just staring and go and introduce yourself to one of the seated gentlemen and begin a conversation. And be polite too; we don't want none of your street talking here; our gentlemen are very refined in their tastes.'

Atia glanced around the room. She had no idea the sort of person she was looking for. The Vampire Murderer may not even be here of course. In fact he may never have even frequented this establishment and simply picked up the unfortunate murdered telegraph boys somewhere else, even the police were not sure about that. She had been so convinced about her plan beforehand but now she wasn't so sure. There was nothing else for her to do but approach one of the men so she headed for a middle aged, plump gentleman who was seated on a plush red settee and who was holding a glass of sparkling wine while smoking a large cigar. 'My, my, you're a tall one,' he said, winking at her.

Atia sat next to the man who was dressed in an evening suit and was smiling broadly at her. He placed his hand on her knee and Atia, momentarily slipping back into her Victorian woman mode, thought about slapping him across the face before remembering it would not be a particularly sensible thing to do in the present circumstances.

'And what can I call you, my young man?'

'Er, Stevie, but you can call me whatever you like as long as you pay me.'

The man laughed. 'Of course, Stevie.' He reached into his waistcoat pocket and pulled out three crowns, 'Will this do?'

Atia had no idea what the rate would be for the services the man required, whatever those services might turn out to be. 'Yeah, mate that'll be fine ta,' said Atia taking the coins and slipping them into her jacket pocket.

'Well, my tall friend, shall we adjourn to the private room I have reserved where we can be alone and have some quiet fun?'

The man stood, picked up a champagne bottle that lay on the nearby table and swaying unsteadily from side to side led the way down a corridor where he stopped at a door and turned a key that protruded from the lock. Directing Atia into the room he locked the door and dropped the key into his trouser pocket.

Atia glanced around the small room, which had an ornate day bed in it along with a couple of armchairs and velvet drapery at the window. She watched the man as he began to take off his clothes, his cigar still firmly stuck in his mouth. She began to wonder what the best strategy to deal with this situation would be. Soon he would expect some sort of intimate sexual behaviour on her part and that would mean the end to her well-planned disguise. Could this man be the Vampire Killer? It was unlikely she thought. The killer's modus operandi would surely entail him taking his victims away from this place and murdering them elsewhere, probably in a nearby house or other building he owned. Whatever this man was planning to do with her it was not going to involve murder and bloodletting she surmised.

Quickly deciding what to do she moved over to the man who looked up expectantly. Atia took the cigar out of his mouth before grabbing the man's neck and expertly pressing on his occipital and phrenic nerves, which resulted in him quickly losing consciousness. After laying him down on the bed in the recovery position she examined the contents of his wallet. A business card told her that this man, Charles East, was a barrister, a Queen's Counsel no less. Replacing his wallet Atia then extracted the door key from the man's trousers, which now lay around his ankles, and opened the door before locking it again and slipping the key into her pocket. He'll be unconscious for the next thirty minutes or so thought Atia, which would give her a bit of time to check out this establishment a little more thoroughly.

Wandering back down the corridor she was able to stand behind a large aspidistra pot plant and survey the reception room. How could she even begin to spot someone who was a potential murderer? All the men in the room seemed to be enjoying themselves, no one looked full of obvious murderous intent, all seemed focused on enjoying the chatter and bodily delights of the other men they were with. She was mentally chastising herself for not having a proper plan to actually find the Vampire Killer. It had all seemed so straightforward in the outside world and now, in this secret den where homosexual men could act in a completely free and easy way, she was bereft of ideas about what to do next. She was just about to head for the front door and leave the building when she heard a gruff voice from behind her.

'Hey, what are yer doin'?'

She looked around. One of the waiters who had been delivering drinks to a private room was looking quizzically at her. Atia made a swift decision. Quickly looking around to ensure she was not being observed she grabbed the waiter by his lapels and, almost lifting him off his feet, propelled him back to the door of the room she had recently emerged from. She reached into her pocket, retrieved the door key and pushed the man, who could only splutter his objections, into the room where Charles East still lay on the day bed snoring peacefully.

'Do not shout for help,' said Atia in her most threatening tone. The waiter seeing Atia's determined face quickly nodded. 'I want to ask you some questions. Answer them and you will come to no harm.' The man, with a frightened look on his face, nodded enthusiastically. 'Are you aware that two telegraph boys were recently found murdered?' The man nodded. 'Do you know if one or both of them had ever visited this establishment?'

The man hesitated before shaking his head. Atia scowled and took a threatening step towards him. 'I ain't sure,' said the man quickly, 'we get a lot of you telegraph boys 'ere an' I don't know if those two ever came 'ere. They probably did, but I don't know for certain.'

'What about the guests that frequent this place, any suspicious ones?'

The man laughed nervously. 'You've got to be joking. They're all a bit suspicious ain't they? None of 'em are supposed to be 'ere, they're all breakin' the law and they all act as shifty as 'ell.'

Atia decided that the man was speaking truthfully and so there was little point questioning him any further. She gently grabbed the waiter's neck and pressed down on the same pressure points as she had with the first man before laying his unconscious form on the day bed next to Charles East QC. She smiled as she imagined the conversation that might take place when the two men woke up and found themselves in such a strange position. Atia let herself out of the room before locking it and pushing the key under the door for the men to eventually discover.

On the way out she nodded at the large doorkeeper. As he opened the front door for her she stopped and said: 'Them two telegraph boys what got topped recently, did they ever come 'ere?' The large man smiled threateningly and Atia noticed how a scar, which ran diagonally across the whole of his face made his smile look particularly twisted and cruel. He didn't say a word in answer to her question but simply indicated with his thumb that she should be on her way pretty sharpish. Atia shrugged, nodded again and exited number 19, Cleveland Street and stepped out onto the pavement outside. Speaking aloud into her microphone as she stood in the deserted street she contacted Ashto and arranged to meet with him down the road at the corner of Mortimer Street. She felt disappointed and deflated that she had not been able to find out anything useful in her little adventure this evening.

The undertaker watched Atia leave. He had thought about approaching the striking looking telegraph boy when he had first entered the reception room but decided he was much too tall for him; not his type at all. The boy looked about eighteen years old, fresh faced with almost feminine features and was, at five feet eleven inches tall, well above the average height for a young man. He smiled and congratulated himself, as he always did, on his uncanny ability to assess the height of someone from a distance. He was able to do the same with those individuals who were going to occupy one of his coffins without having to get out a measuring tape. But no, the lad was far too tall despite having the most attractive head on his shoulders than he had ever seen before on an adolescent youth. He would certainly remember that face and its handsome features if he ever met up with him again. However, he liked them much smaller. Smaller ones are much easier to deal with and, he smiled to himself again, they contain almost as much blood as the bigger ones. Sadly the very tall telegraph boy had been the only one of his kind to visit this disgusting house tonight. A great shame he thought as he had been in just the right mood for it all to happen again this evening. Oh well, there was no rush, best to get it right rather than to take a risk. There was always tomorrow evening.

He finished his glass of champagne, shrugged off the entreaties of the appalling degenerate person he had been sharing his sofa with, retrieved his coat and left. He was disappointed but unbowed.

24

The Prisoner

'Sir, we may have an important lead on the Fenian bomb,' said Sergeant Bill Thick having knocked on Inspector Reid's door and poked his head into his office.

'Really? That is good news Bill. The Special Irish Branch hasn't stopped bothering me. What's the lead?'

'I've just had a chat with P.C. Leadbeater, the young officer injured in the blast who's now well enough to talk after being at death's door for ages.'

'Good, what did he say?'

'He didn't remember too much about what happened but he did know that the men he saw with the bomb weren't Irish. They were locals – cockneys. He even recognised one of 'em and so we've nabbed him and got him in one of the cells downstairs.'

'Local villains, eh. That's a bit odd isn't it? The Fenian

Brotherhood, or whatever they call themselves these days, don't normally farm out their jobs to others, they always like their own to be fully in charge. Let's go and have a chat with him. What's his name?'

'Bill Blackwell, Sir.'

'That rings a bell, I've probably nicked him in the past.'

'Very likely, Sir.'

'Right let's see if we can loosen his tongue.'

The cells in the basement of Leman Street police station were cold, damp and dingy. Inspector Reid would never have said it out loud but he thought the state of the station's holding gaols were appalling and reflected badly on the overall policing system in London. The fact that prisoners could be kept locked up in them on remand sometimes for weeks on end before being taken to court was something that the prison reformers had not yet got around to. In the meantime those accused of crimes were held in conditions that were squalid in the extreme. As a result Reid hated going down to the cells; the stench coming from unemptied slop buckets was enough to put anyone off their dinner for the next week.

Reid, along with Sergeant Thick, stood outside the only cell to be occupied. The incarcerated man stood up as the two officers glared at him through the cell's bars.

'Blackwell? Yes, I remember you. You've been here before haven't you?' said Reid.

'I 'ave, Mr Reid an' these 'ere cells 'aven't changed much, an' that's the truth.'

'Sorry about that, if we had known you were coming we'd have had the decorators in especially for you. Who gave you the black eye?'

Blackwell smiled briefly before his expression changed to deathly serious: 'That was from yer sergeant when he nicked me, he's got a good left 'ook on him that un. Look, Mr Reid I'm a villain, I know it, you know it and your sergeant knows it but what 'e said about a bomb, that ain't my bag at all. Yes I'll rob people blind given 'alf a chance but I ain't no bomber. Ask anyone, I'd never do summat like that.'

'But you were seen by an officer standing next to a parcel that turned out to be a bomb. Presumably you'd carried it along and put it outside the back of this nick ready to explode and now you say you're no bomber.'

'I didn't know it was bomb, I swear on me muvver's life.'

'You ain't got a mother, she died last year,' said Sergeant Thick.

'Well, I'll swear on her grave then.'

'Who were the other two you were with?' said Reid.

'I don't know their names.' Reid looked skeptical. 'It's true, Mr Reid. They were just two blokes what was in the Princess Alice pub wiv me when this toff came up to us an' said 'e'd got a job for us if we wanted it, couple o' sovs each he said.'

'Who was this toff?'

''E never told us 'is name, Mr Reid, honest 'e didn't.'

'What did he look like then?'

'I dunno; very tall, clean shaven, grey hair, almost silver. Very well dressed like, bit out o' place in the Princess Alice to tell you the truth. Just walked up to me an' the other two an' said 'e 'ad a parcel that 'e wanted put at the back door of Leman Street nick, only 'e didn't say nick, 'e said police station cos 'e was a toff I s'pose.'

'When did he pay you the money?' said Reid.

'One sov before and one after we'd done the job.'

'So you met him again?'

'Yer, back in the Princess Alice the nex' day.'

'Have you still got either of the sovereigns?'

'Don't be silly, Mr Reid. Me an' the Missus spent it on beer an' gin in the pub. We 'ad a good week that week.'

'Was part of the job beating and kicking a young police constable senseless?' said an angry looking Sergeant Thick.'

'That was the work of the uvver two, 'onest, I never had anything to do wiv that. Mad they were, kicking 'im when 'e was down an' all. I don't like coppers but I ain't no basher like them blokes was.'

'Yes, I'm sure your conscience is as squeaky clean as a whistle! Have you seen the tall toff with grey hair again?'

'No, Mr Reid, not 'ide nor 'air of him.'

'Did you ask him at any point what was in the parcel?'

'No, Mr Reid, you know as well as I do that the likes o' me don't ask no questions. If some rich bloke wants to pay me good money to do a simple job then who am I to argue?'

'Didn't you wonder what was in the parcel?'

'No, Mr Reid, 'onest I didn't. I fort it might be one of them bloomin' missin' 'eads that you lot bin lookin' for an' it was left outside the nick for you to find. That bomb could 'ave gorn orf while I was bleedin' well carryin' it; I could 'ave been blown to bits.'

'Pity you weren't,' said Bill Thick, 'it would have saved a young lad a lengthy stay in hospital and he isn't right now.'

'I'm sorry about that, Mr Thick, but like I said that was nothing to do wiv me. It was the uvver two, 'onest, as God's me witness.'

"Hmm, I'm not sure that God would be very interested in

having someone like you as a witness to be perfectly honest. Is there anything else you can tell us about that night?'

'No, Mr Reid, I've told you all I know, that's the God's 'onest truth.'

Inspector Reid was about to walk away but remembered something: 'By the way, Blackwell, was the grey-haired toff Irish? You would recognise an Irish accent wouldn't you?'

'Nah 'e weren't no Mick. There are plenty of 'em around the East End, quite a few o' me mates are Micks but 'e wasn't one, I'm sure o' that.'

Edmund Reid stood in thought for a moment before turning and heading back upstairs to his office. On the way he stopped to tell the desk sergeant to get one of the cleaners to empty the slop bucket in Blackwell's cell.

'Do you believe him, Bill?'

'No, Sir, not at all, he's an inveterate thief who'll lie his head off if he has to. But, if he is telling the truth, that story about the sovereigns was very interesting. I wonder whether Blackwell met our counterfeiter?'

'My thoughts exactly, Bill. Get someone to go down to the Princess Alice and check out Blackwell's story about the other two villains and find out if the pub's landlord noticed whether the money that he spent with his wife was kosher or not.'

'I'll do that myself I think, Sir, if that's all right.'

'A good idea, Bill; let me know the result as soon as possible if you would.'

'Will do, Sir,' said Sergeant Thick before exiting Reid's office.

Reid sighed and then smiled. Maybe we're getting somewhere at last, he thought.

25

The Thread

'So what do we do now, Trevor?' After her unsuccessful foray into the house in Cleveland Street Atia looked gloomy as she and Ashto sat in their room at Mrs Smith's Select Guesthouse. Her telegraph boy uniform was discarded on the bed and she was dressed again in her Earth-female clothing.

'Well, Margot, we should return to our original plan and attempt to find out the origin of the piece of thread the police discovered on the body of the last murder victim, poor Constable Perkins.' Ashto attempted to sound as hopeful as possible to attempt to cheer up the miserable looking Apprentice Commander.

'That will take many weeks. And of course the thread might not even have the slightest relevance to the murders.'

'That is true, Margot, but it remains the only clue

we have as to the possible location and identity of the murderer.'

'Well, in that case, I suppose we should begin as soon as possible. We have a long list of locations to visit – where shall we start?'

'I have given that some thought. Our investigations will no doubt be seen by the police officer who follows us so we must make them look like part of our normal researches of course. I cannot think of any possible reason why our imaginary American readers would be particularly interested in taxidermy but they may possibly want to know how the planning and practice of funerals in this country operate in contrast to those in the United States. It is somewhat tenuous reasoning but I cannot think of a better strategy than visiting those undertakers we have on our list.'

'That is true, Trevor. We should perhaps begin by looking at those funeral directors closest to Cleveland Street, that would at least give us a starting point.'

'Agreed. Then we shall begin our task first thing tomorrow,' said Ashto, glad that Atia's usual enthusiastic demeanour had, to some degree, returned.

It was the early afternoon and Ashto and Atia both felt tired, hungry and somewhat deflated. During the morning they had visited six undertakers and funeral parlours in the Soho and Oxford Circus area and had been shown around the establishments asking questions about how the businesses operated while carefully looking around for possible clues that the murdered young men might have been there at some point in the past. Spurious notes had been made in their notebooks and feigned interest shown as the undertakers, with varying amounts of enthusiasm, showed the presumed American couple around workshops where coffins were made, plushly furnished rooms where grieving relatives could express their wishes for their loved ones' funerals and other areas where the recently bereaved were prepared for their laying out back at their family homes. Most of the individuals in charge were proud to explain their work and the various services they provided. Ashto and Atia had been particularly interested in inquiring about the chemical products that were used in the preparation of deceased bodies, which would ensure that not only would they be preserved for the period of time prior to their funeral but also how they were made to look as presentable as possible in the open coffins that most of the relatives seemed to favour for the laying out period. The Jaran pair certainly learned a great deal about the preservation of corpses and the widespread use of arsenic and formaldehyde in that process. They also realised that the purple thread that had been found on the body of constable Perkins could have come from any one of the funeral directors' premises as that particular coloured cloth was used extensively for curtains, table coverings and other decorative purposes in every one of the establishments they had visited.

'Shall we visit one more undertakers and then perhaps treat ourselves to a meal at Fortescues?' said a weary Commander Ashto.

'Yes, that is a splendid idea,' said Atia, trying to sound as upbeat as possible. 'The final undertaker on our list for this particular area is a Mr Percival Pell, located in Fitzroy Street.'

'Well, let us proceed there, I doubt whether we will find Mr Pell's establishment any different from the others we have visited today but at least we will be able to remove one more location from our list,' said the tired sounding First Commander.

'I have never met any Americans before and it is a pleasure to make the acquaintance of the two of you. I would, of course, be only too willing to assist you if I can help to further your researches,' said the undertaker.

First Commander Ashto had given Mr Pell his card and explained about the research he was conducting with the assistance of his wife. Pell had warmly greeted the Jaran pair in his office after the undertaker's assistant, Mrs Abberley, had showed them into his comfortable inner sanctum where the undertaker in sympathetic tones would quietly converse with the relatives of recently deceased family or friends.

'And you say that your eventual readers will be very much interested to read about the ways in which funeral directors like myself carry out our procedures in this country?'

'I believe so, Mr Pell. Any differences in the funereal traditions of Great Britain compared to those in the United States could be fascinating to potential readers, especially those planning to visit these shores in the future.'

Pell nodded. 'And this is your dear lady wife,' said the undertaker smiling. 'How useful it must be to have your loved one accompany you on your visit and indeed assist you in the writing of your book.' Mr Pell took Atia's hand and kissed it. There was something about the undertaker's overly unctuous manner that Atia did not like although she would not have been able to identify the reason behind her unease. She just felt that she would have liked to have immediately washed and scrubbed the hand he had just kissed.

Pell continued to wear his well-practised smile as he gestured for the Jaran pair to sit down on the pair of wing-backed chairs in his office. Behind his smile his mind was working hard to try to recollect where he had seen this very attractive young woman, who towered above him, before today. He never forgot a face; it was a skill he had had throughout his life. And then suddenly the penny dropped. The tall telegraph boy at the molly house in Cleveland Street yesterday looked exactly like this good looking young woman. Could it be the same person? The more he looked at the Apprentice Commander the more he was convinced it was. If it was the case that this woman had been disguised as a telegraph boy what would have been the reason? He knew very well that the police would sometimes send one of its officers undercover to investigate situations that were considered highly sensitive. Was this an example of the Metropolitan Police trying to outwit him? Did they suspect him? How could that be? A woman though, they must be getting very desperate.

'We are very keen to find out as much as we can about how a funeral director such as yourself operates. Would it be possible, if you are not too busy at the moment, for you to show us around your premises and answer a few of our questions?' said Ashto.

'Of course, Mr Ashton, it would be an absolute pleasure,' said the undertaker, whose mind behind his outwardly friendly and welcoming appearance was buzzing with many questions of his own. Could these individuals be police officers of some sort? Did the Metropolitan Police actually employ women to snoop around in such a way? What were they looking for? Why had they called at his establishment? Had he left some sort of clue that had been picked up by the police? He doubted that very much. His planning and execution of the murders had been meticulous; he had not left any sort of clue – had he? As he led Ashto and Atia, who both held notebooks and pencils, around his studio and workshop he was thinking hard about any possible reason why the police might be interested in him. He couldn't think of anything.

'I wonder if I can enquire as to whether you utilise the chemicals arsenic and formaldehyde in your work here, Mr Pell?' said Atia.

'Yes, I do. Both are very important in the preservative process, dear lady. When clients' loved ones are presented in open caskets it is required that they look as close as possible to how they appeared in life prior to their unfortunate demise. The chemicals you mention are among some of those that I, and all other undertakers I know of, use in our everyday work.' Mr Pell smiled in his usual fashion.

Atia nodded at the man although she could not find it in her to smile back at him. There was something about this individual that she did not like although she had no idea what the reason for her dislike was. Something about him registered at the back of her mind, but it was so far back she couldn't work out what it actually was. She was also somewhat disappointed with Pell's answer to her question, an answer that had been exactly the same as every other undertaker she had asked that day.

After being shown round the undertaker's premises the Jarans were about to leave when Atia noticed a door through which they had not been shown. 'Where does that door lead to Mr Pell, if you do not mind me asking?'

'Not at all my dear Mrs Ashton, it is simply the door

down to my cellar, which I use as a mere storage space. There is nothing down there that would interest you in the slightest I can assure you.' Pell carried on smiling although he had felt that his mask was slipping slightly. Had he sounded overly defensive in his answer? He was certainly relieved when he was able to show the Ashton couple out of the front door of his studio that led onto Fitzroy Street. He was able to breathe a small sigh of relief as he watched them walk, arm-in-arm, down the street.

Ashto and Atia were pleased to have been able to relax in the pleasant surroundings of Fortescues' restaurant. It was over their favourite meal of roast beef that the Apprentice Commander revealed her unease regarding Mr Pell.

'I cannot put my finger on the reason for it but I had a very strong feeling that there was something suspicious about that man.'

'I had no such sensation about him, Margot. He just seemed to be a friendly and rather helpful individual.'

'On the surface that would seem to be correct, Trevor, but there is something playing at the back of my mind that for some unknown reason makes me question his ... attitude ... his personality, I suppose. Something about his face and demeanour that ... oh, I do not know Trevor. I suppose it must simply be my imagination.'

'Well, Margot often in the past you have had a general feeling that something is not quite what it has seemed to be, a gut reaction so to speak. So when we are back in our guesthouse room I think we should look carefully at the video footage of our visit to Pell's establishment today and see if we can find the reason for your unease.'

'That would be a very good idea, Trevor. Thank you for taking my intuition seriously. Hmm, now what shall we have for dessert?'

Back at Mrs Smith's Select Guesthouse Atia and Ashto sat at their desk and carefully examined the video footage they had taken with their body cameras. Having looked at it all twice they could not find any cause for the deep unease that Atia had felt during the visit to Pell's premises.

Atia sighed. 'Right from the moment I first saw him I felt there was something about the man I did not like. Oh, I am sorry, Trevor I am not making any sense at all. I am being so annoyingly imprecise!'

'Do not worry, Margot. Intuition is often a vague, purely instinctive feeling. If you felt that there was something suspicious about the man Pell then there must be a logical reason for your feeling.'

'Hm, I do not know. Perhaps we could we take a look at the camera footage that was taken inside 19, Cleveland Street. Again I have a feeling – that is probably nothing at all – that there may be something there that is a link to this Mr Pell in some way.'

'Of course, Margot.'

The Jaran pair looked carefully at the video produced by Atia's body cam the day before at the house in Cleveland Street. At first sight they noticed nothing of interest and then suddenly Atia shouted: 'There! Pause it there, Trevor.'

'What have you seen, Margot?'

'That man on the sofa in the middle of the room – zoom in a little.'

Ashto zoomed in on the man who was sitting on the red

velvet sofa sipping champagne and talking to a large, blond haired man who was clad in colourful female clothing.

'It's him!' said Atia, triumph in her voice.

'Are you sure?' said Ashto. 'It's not a very clear picture.'

'It is definitely Pell, Trevor, I'd swear to it. I must have registered his face subliminally and then meeting him earlier today must have sparked something in my memory. We have a link between Pell and the house in Cleveland Street. He must be our murderer, surely.'

'Well let's not jump to that conclusion too quickly, Margot. For all we know he is just one of those men who seek an outlet for his perfectly natural feelings which in this society are unfortunately considered to be illegal. He might be completely innocent of any real crime as we would understand it.'

'Of course you are correct, Trevor, we will need to investigate further.'

'We will, Margot. Tomorrow we will send a fly drone to Pell's premises and attach a bug to his clothing. That will hopefully enable us to track his movements and we can see if he does indeed return to the house in Cleveland Street.'

Atia looked pleased. Finally they now had an important lead to follow up on that could bring the so-called Vampire Killer to justice. She was determined that she and the First Commander would do everything they could to catch this killer and avenge the death of Constable Perkins and the other victims.

26

Another death

Sergeant William Thick hammered on the door of the Princess Alice public house located on the corner of Wentworth Street and Commercial Street. In the cold light of an April morning the building looked almost attractive, a great contrast to its appearance in the evening when it was often full to bursting and smokily hellish with the noisy and the drunk. It was here, Sergeant Thick recalled, that last autumn he arrested John Pizer who was thought by some to be one of the main suspects in the Whitechapel murders. Pizer, a bootmaker and also known as "Leather Apron," had been accused of threatening prostitutes by holding a knife to their necks and as a result many of the locals reckoned he was definitely the Ripper. His arrest one night at the Princess Alice probably saved him from being lynched by an irate mob. Eventually he had been released without charge when it became clear that he had unimpeachable alibis for at least two of the murders.

In reply to the police sergeant's loud knocking the pub's front door opened slightly and a gruff voice from inside shouted: 'We're shut – bugger off!'

'Well you can damn well open up, Arthur Ferrar and let me in.'

'Oh, Mr Thick I didn't realise it were you. Come on in, you're most welcome as usual.

'I should think so,' said the detective sergeant entering the pub and removing his brown bowler hat. He looked for a clean table to lay it down on but eventually decided it would be better to keep hold of it.

'So what can I do you for? You ain't after Pizer again are yer?' laughed the burly, aproned landlord busily drying a pint beer glass.

'No, I haven't had the pleasure of dealing with that scoundrel recently,' said the Sergeant.

'I 'aven't clapped eyes on 'im since you arrested 'im last year, 'e must 'ave taken 'is custom elsewhere – thank gawd.'

'Hopefully he's left the East End completely, Arthur, good riddance to bad rubbish, eh?'

'Yer can say that again, Sergeant Thick. 'Ere, would you like a little tot of whisky to warm you up on this cold morning?'

'Very tempting, Arthur, but you know I never drink when I'm on duty. Save it for the next time I call in here one evening.'

'I certainly will, Mr Thick. 'Ere, they don't call you Upright Johnny for no reason do they?' said the landlord quickly tipping back a mouthful of whisky himself and having a little chuckle at his use of Bill Thick's nickname which was well known in the East End where the police detective was considered to be totally incorruptible as well as being the scourge of the area's criminal class. 'So what is it I can do for yer, Mr Thick?'

'I'm here to ask about a local thief and general toe-rag called Blackwell who drinks here.'

'Oh, 'im – 'e comes in here when 'e's managed to filch some ready money from somewheres.'

'A few weeks ago he came in here and proceeded to spend a lot on drinks for himself and his missus – do you remember that?'

'I do; 'e an' 'is wife 'ardly ever left the place. Drunk as lords every night for a week – spent a fortune on themselves and other like-minded sots. Mind you I wasn't complaining though, that's the truth.'

'Do you remember him handing over two sovereigns to pay for it all?'

'I do, gawd knows where he got 'em from, but in my line o' business yer can't ask such questions otherwise I'd soon go bankrupt.' The landlord gave a belly laugh and almost dropped the glass he was drying.

'Have you still got the two sovereigns here?'

'What? Nah, don't be daft, Sergeant. I don't get to see many thick uns an' certainly can't afford to keep 'em as souvenirs like.'

'Did you look to see that they were genuine?'

'Course I did, I wasn't born yesterday. I'd never trust a lyin' rogue like Blackwell on any day o' the week.'

'You didn't notice anything odd about them?'

'Nah, Sergeant Thick, they were completely kosher as far as I could tell. Why do you ask?

'There have been some counterfeit sovereigns turning up all around the East End for the last few months that's all. One more thing, did you notice Blackwell being spoken to by a well-dressed toff with grey hair a few weeks ago? He probably gave Blackwell the sovereigns.'

Ferrar scratched his head. 'Can't say as I did notice, Mr Thick. We don't 'ave many toffs coming in 'ere. Get 'em on occasions but they're usually young uns on the lookout for local jam tarts, if yer gets me meaning.'

'What about two other blokes Blackwell was drinking with in here one evening; they were also given money by the toff.'

'No, I'm sorry Sergeant. As yer know we're always crowded in 'ere at night an' I don't remember everyone who comes in. Besides Blackwell is the type to talk to anyone, usually tryin' to persuade others to buy 'im drinks like.'

'All right, Arthur, just keep your eyes open and if you remember anything give one of the local Bobbies a message to pass on to me.'

'I will certainly do that, Sergeant,' said the landlord escorting the policeman to the front door. 'An' don't forget that whisky on the 'ouse,' he shouted as the burly detective walked back down Commercial Street heading for Leman Street police station. The landlord watched him for a while and then went back inside the pub and carried on cleaning his beer glasses.

'That's disappointing, Bill. Is this Ferrar bloke reliable?' said Detective Inspector Reid when the sergeant had returned to Leman Street.

'Yes, I think so, Sir. As reliable as any Whitechapel pub landlord is ever likely to be,' replied Sergeant Thick.

'Hm, that's not saying much.'

'I think we can believe him though, Sir.'

'All right, Bill. Why don't you see if you can squeeze anything else out of Blackwell? Meanwhile I'll take another look at the list of undertakers in the area around Cleveland Street and we'll decide which ones we'll visit first. I thought we'd go to one or two ourselves and send uniformed men to the rest. It's a big shot in the dark really as we don't quite know what we're looking for. Nothing came from visiting those taxidermy places so I don't imagine that poking about in funeral parlours is going to be any different, but I suppose it needs doing.'

'Right, Sir.'

Reid scratched his head as he watched his sergeant leave his office. He picked up a file from his desk and took out a sheet of paper. On it were the names and addresses of undertakers around the capital. It would make sense, he supposed, to begin by singling out those around the Cleveland Street area. If there is a connection between the out of bounds molly house and the recent murders then starting with those relatively nearby would seems to be the best strategy. He was just about to circle the funeral establishment he should visit first when Sergeant Thick came running back into his office.

'Blackwell's dead, Inspector!'

'What?'

'I just went down to the cells, Sir, and found him lying on the floor – dead as a doornail.'

'What the hell...what has he died from?'

'Not sure, Sir... best if you come and see for yourself.'

Edmund Reid knelt down beside the body of Bill Blackwell. The dead man lay on his back, his wide-open eyes stared up at the ceiling of the cell. Sergeant Thick, along with three on-duty uniformed officers, looked on, surprise was written on all their faces.

'Looks like whatever he died from came on him suddenly,' said Reid feeling around the criminal's neck to ensure there was definitely no pulse evident. 'Hold on, what's this?' Reid carefully pulled an inch long narrow piece of shiny metal from the dead man's neck.'

'What an Earth is that?' said a shocked sounding Sergeant Thick.

'I've no idea… a needle of some sort?' said Reid holding the object out in front of him.

'Be careful with it, Sir, it could be poisoned.'

Reid took out an envelope from his coat pocket and dropped the object into it.

'Bill, have you ever seen anything like that before?'

'Never sir, how could it possibly have found its way into Blackwell's neck?'

'Has anyone else been down here in the last hour?' Reid looked up at the small group of watching policemen.

'I brought him a cup of tea half an hour ago, he was all right then; no one else has been down here,' answered one of the officers.

Reid noticed the empty tin cup on the floor beside the body. 'Somebody must have been down here. This needle or whatever it is didn't appear by magic did it?'

'Let me take it to get analysed in the lab,' said Sergeant Thick, holding out his hand and carefully taking the brown envelope from Reid.

'Thanks, Bill.' Reid looked at the uniformed officers: 'you three, get the body onto the bed. Let's see if you can manage that.' Reid sighed deeply. Was nothing going to go right with his investigations?

A little later, just after all the policeman had left the gaol cell, a flying insect of the size and shape of a dragonfly and which had secreted itself in a large hole in the wall in the corner of the room flew out of its hiding place and headed for the nearest open window. Its dull metallic body buzzed faintly as it was guided back by the individual who had sent it to the police station in order to eliminate the petty thief Blackwell with the poison dart it had ejected into his neck.

Report Number 0016 to the Glorious and Munificent Jaran Galactic Federation High Council (Planetary Exploration and Viable Exo-Planet Evaluation Committee – Sector 2007 Sub-Committee) by First Commander Treve Pacton Ashto.

My greetings and utmost felicitations to the esteemed members of the sub-committee.

I must apologise for the lack of reports I have filed recently. However, if I can be candid, I do find it strange that we have rarely, if ever, received any feedback about the reports I and the Apprentice Commander have sent in so far to the sub-committee in the almost nine Earth months we have been residing on this planet. I do realise, of course, that the sub-committee is very busy and has many duties and functions to carry out but surely an occasional comment arising from its deliberations about the possibilities for the Earth's eventual admittance into the Federation, even at this early stage in a five-year process, would be very encouraging for Apprentice Commander Atia and myself.

In any case we have continued to be extremely busy continuing to gather information and intelligence about the planet Earth. Apprentice Commander Atia and I have recently been continuing to monitor the local policing authorities in Britain's main city of London, particularly with regard of the new series of murders I mentioned in my last report. We have begun to help the police by providing them with the occasional piece of information (passed on anonymously of course) that will hopefully nudge them nearer to finding out the identity of the murderer who has been dubbed by the local written media "The Vampire Killer" apparently named after a mythical, half-dead, bloodsucking creature. Our own investigations into the murders, carried out as part of our overall research into the Earth humans and their various machinations, have continued with only limited success so far. However, we are always keen to develop new ways to study the local populace so even our lack of success so far in this area has not been unrewarding.

Recently Atia and I have been researching how the treatment and disposal of the recently dead in this region of the planet is undertaken, although we are aware that practices and traditions in other independent states on the Earth vary considerably. In Britain the burial of bodies in the ground or in specially constructed tombs is the norm, but as usual it is highly dependent on the wealth of the deceased person and their familial groupings. Periods of mourning before and after funerals have taken place is very common. (The aged Queen of this state went into a mourning phase after the death of her husband a number of years ago actually to the point where she disappeared from public view, attracting some criticism as a result.) Often the body of a deceased person will lie in an open coffin for a short time, prior to the funeral, usually in the family home. This allows friends and relatives to visit the corpse and say their final goodbyes (as humans often refer to this particular part of the process). Funerals are usually conducted with many religious trappings and are very unlike those ceremonies back home on Jara of course where dead bodies are integrated back into local eco systems without a great deal of fuss. All of this presumes that individuals and their families can actually afford to hold a funeral of this sort. Because there is such a lot of abject poverty in this country (despite, as I have previously mentioned, this being the wealthiest state on the planet) pauper funerals, often in unmarked and unrecorded burial places, are all too common.

That is all that we have to report at present. Hopefully the sub-committee will find the reports we have sent to be both interesting and informative. We hope to hear from you soon. I will report again in the near future.

With my utmost loyalty to the glorious Jaran Galactic Federation,

First Commander Treve Pacton Ashto.

Tracking The Vampire Killer

'Do you think Pell is on his way to Cleveland Street?' said Atia.

'That should become clear very soon, Margot,' replied Ashto.

The Jarans were hunched over the small computer screen that pictured a street map of London. Earlier in the day they had sent a fly-drone to Mr Pell's establishment in Fitzroy Street. The drone had planted a bug on the undertaker's overcoat, which had been hanging up in the hallway of his residence. Now it was the early evening and they were tracking the movements of the man they believed could well be the Vampire Killer who had just left his residence.

'He is walking, so it doesn't seem that he will be going very far,' said Atia.

'True, Margot; let us hope he is going to show his hand soon,' said Ashto using an Earth idiom he had recently discovered.

First Commander Ashto and Apprentice Commander Atia watched the undertaker's progress along Maple Street and as he turned into Cleveland Street it became obvious he was headed for number 19.

'I think I should put on my outerwear, Margot.'

'Yes you should, Trevor.' The Apprentice Commander was again dressed in her telegraph boy uniform. 'Trevor, are you going to say those words, you know those ones you like?'

Ashto smiled broadly. 'Yes, Margot, I think I should. As the famous detective, Sherlock Holmes says: "The game is afoot!"'

With a feeling of anticipation the two Jaran explorers left their room in Mrs Smith's Guesthouse. The First Commander exited the building first in order to attract the attention of the police officer assigned to follow them. Ashto had arranged to meet up with Atia again, once he had shaken off his police shadow. He took a circuitous route around the Whitechapel area and lost the man assigned to follow him easily enough in Brick Lane and Osborn Street. Ashto reunited with his Apprentice Commander outside Aldgate Street underground railway station thirty minutes later and the pair hailed a hansom cab.

The plan the Jarans had agreed on, somewhat reluctantly as far as Ashto was concerned, was for Atia to enter the Cleveland Street house, again in her disguise, and see if she could attract the attention of Pell, the undertaker. Ashto, waiting outside, would then be on hand to go to the Apprentice Commander's aid if or when necessary. How to ensure that Pell, if he was the Vampire Killer, could then be delivered to the police they had not, as yet, quite worked out.

'Good luck, Margot,' said Ashto who could not prevent a worried frown settling on his face.

'Thank you, Trevor.' Atia quickly looked around to ensure no one was watching and then gave Ashto a quick peck on the cheek. She then crossed the road and walked up to the front door of number 19, Cleveland Street quickly pulling on the bell-pull.

She smiled at the taciturn doorman as she gave the password in a deeper tone to her voice than normal and entered the house for the second time.

Atia looked about the large and smokily fragrant reception room. There was Pell sitting alone on the same red velvet couch, holding a glass of champagne and smirking. Taking a deep breath Atia walked over and sat beside him her face fixed in what she hoped what she hoped was her most beguiling smile.

Pell smiled back. He had recognised her as soon as she had stepped into the room, he had a photographic memory for faces, always had. It was probably one of the reasons why he had followed in his father's footsteps and become an undertaker. Being a connoisseur of faces and helping to make them look as attractive as possible as they lay in the coffin looking tranquil and at peace was one of the main challenges of his craft as far as he was concerned. Now this striking looking woman disguised as a young man had presented herself to him. Why was that? Should he add her fine looking head to his collection he wondered, even though she was, of course, far from his usual type?

'Good evening young man,' Pell said in his most mellifluous tones, 'have we met before, your face looks very familiar?'

'Nah, I don't fink so,' replied Atia, slightly alarmed by his question.

'No matter,' said Pell. 'I hope you are willing to indulge in some interesting activities at my personal residence this evening?' Pell clicked his fingers and indicated to a waiter to bring his new friend a glass of champagne. 'I'm sure you will enjoy some champagne, young man and there is plenty more back at my home as well. What shall I call you, by the way?'

'You can call me, Stevie.' Atia considered at this juncture that it would be in line with her imagined character and reason for being in this place to put her hand on Pell's knee. Having done so she took a large mouthful of the champagne she had just been given. She hoped it would help to relax her.

'And you can call me Jack,' said an amused looking Pell.

Atia did not like the way Pell smiled at her in what was a definitely predatory fashion. It was almost as if he could see through her disguise and she reminded herself that she needed to be on her guard. This man could be a killer; she had no doubt about that. Already he had demonstrated a number of traits that someone who could commit such heinous crimes would undoubtedly have. She knew she must not trust him one inch.

'Well, Stevie, drink your champagne up and we will retire to my house, which is quite nearby. There we can relax and indulge in a few of the activities at which you are, I am sure, extremely adept.'

Atia smiled back at Pell and was unutterably glad that her First Commander was waiting somewhere near ready to help her out. She drained her glass and stood up already feeling a little unsteady from the wine.

Outside in Cleveland Street First Commander Ashto had found a place to stand, away from the gas lamps and in shadows behind a large plane tree from where he could keep a careful watch on number 19. It was with some surprise and alarm that he felt a tap on his shoulder and turning around came face to face with a large, uniformed policeman.

'And what do you think you're doing here skulking about, if I might ask you, Sir?'

'Oh… officer… er, good evening… I was just…'

'It's quite all right, Bert, he's with me.'

Both men turned to see where the familiar voice had come from.

'Oh, it's you Mr Rogers. Still keeping tabs on the molly house then?'

'Yes, that's right, Bert. One day I hope to write up a story for the Standard that will shock the reading public rigid.'

'Well it won't shock me, Mr Rogers, I've seen all sorts of comings and goings from that building for the past year or so – couldn't believe my eyes at some of 'em – makes your hair curl it does – my missus can't believe the stories I tell her about some of them toffs what turns up here. I keep reportin' it to my sergeant but he tells me to ignore it. Glad to see you've got someone to help you, Mr Rogers; share the burden like.'

'It certainly helps a lot, Bert.'

'Well, I'll leave you to it then – must get on with the rest of my beat. Good evening to you, Sirs, and the best of luck with your newspaper work, Mr Rogers.'

'Thank you, Bert, I'm sure I'll see you again soon.'

The policeman touched the brim of his police helmet and carried on down Cleveland Street.

'Well, Mr Ashton it is good to see you again, but I must inquire as to what you are doing loitering about the most infamous male brothel in London,' William Rogers, the London Evening Standard journalist, said with a smile.

'To be very honest I am rather annoyed that it appears you have been following me again, Mr Rogers,' said Ashto as he tried to work out what to say to the reporter that would explain him being in the street and acting so suspiciously.

'Actually, Mr Ashton, I was already in the street when you arrived with the tall telegram boy who I presume is Mrs Ashton in a very good disguise.'

'How did you know that?'

'I didn't, Mr Ashton, although I do now,' said Rogers with a smile, 'besides, Mrs Ashton's obvious beauty is extremely difficult to disguise, if I can be bold enough to say so.'

The First Commander momentarily thought about delivering a punch to the grinning face of the newspaper reporter before thinking better of it. He had experienced jealous feelings before about the attention that Rogers had shown toward Atia in the past but now was perhaps not the best time to give in to those particular animal instincts. 'Mr Rogers, you know very well that my wife and I are collecting information for our book so surely you cannot be surprised that an exploration of the seamier side of London life would also form part of our researches.'

Rogers smiled at Ashto before pointing a finger at the doorway of number 19. 'Your good lady wife, in her disguise, appears to be emerging from the building and she seems to have a companion.'

Ashto looked across to where his Apprentice Commander, alongside Mr Pell, paused for a moment on the pavement before walking together towards Fitzroy Street.

'I would assume you are going to follow your wife and her… friend?' said Mr Rogers.

Ashto looked at the newspaperman before pushing him aside and crossing the street.

'Good luck,' said Rogers with a smile.

Atia had a quick look back down the street to see if the First Commander was following her. Mr Pell was very much shorter than she was and should be relatively easy to overcome him before there was any actual danger for her but she still hadn't worked out a plan for delivering him to the police in the likely event that she could prove he was the Vampire Killer. She certainly needed First Commander Ashto to be on hand ready to help.

There was a short walk in silence before Atia and Pell arrived at the house in Fitzroy Street. Inside Atia remembered the door that Pell had said led to his basement. Her intuition told her that it was down there she where she would probably discover any clues that could prove Pell's guilt. Somehow this evening she must find a way to explore the basement, find the proof that Pell was the Vampire Killer, before anonymously informing the police about what she had discovered. She felt happier now that she had decided what to do. So pleased did she feel that she did not see Mr Pell pick up the large metal poker from the fireplace in his drawing room where he had directed her and bring it down with a good deal of force on the side of her head.

Atia opened her eyes and immediately wished that she hadn't as a deep and sharp pain in her head made her want to quickly shut them again.

'Ah, you're awake my dear.'

Atia saw Pell grinning down at her. She worked out that she was lying on the floor in roughly the same place as she fell after being hit by something heavy and hard. She tried to move her arms and legs but found out that she couldn't; she didn't immediately know why.

'You cannot move, Mrs Ashton, as I have trussed you up in, I have to say so, a most professional and efficacious fashion. I am actually quite impressed with myself.' Pell looking down from above laughed out loud and then sat down in an armchair still grinning at Atia, as she lay prone on the floor of Pell's drawing room.

Atia frowned and then winced as that small muscle movement in her face caused her quite a considerable degree of pain. She assessed her situation quickly. She was unable to move and was obviously at the mercy of Pell who, most likely, was a crazed and sociopathic killer. She had an enormous ache in her head and it was likely that she was suffering from concussion. She could also feel a trickle of blood running down the left side of her face. Pell had just referred to her as Mrs Ashton so there was no way that she could continue with her disguise any longer.

'My husband... he was waiting for me... he'll be worried!' No, that was not good – why did she say that? She must be more definite in her threats. 'He will be here soon... he was following me... the police...'

'The police?' replied Mr Pell. 'Oh I've already sent for them – my neighbour has gone to get them – they'll be here soon. I know the local Bobby very well, Albert he's called, nice chap, always looks out for the local residents as we do tend to get a lot of burglaries in this area. Do you know in the future I think I might get one of those new telephone gadgets; they're the way of the future someone was telling me recently, liable to revolutionise the way people communicate with each other. It's all very exciting – the future. Don't you agree, Mrs Ashton?'

Atia, with difficulty, turned her head so that she could see Pell more clearly even though she was having trouble focusing her eyes properly. He was holding something up to show her, something small and silvery.

'And what exactly is this, Mrs Ashton, if that is indeed your name?'

Pell was showing her the disrupter weapon that since her encounter with the Ripper she always carried with her. 'Please do not toy with that... it's dangerous...' Again a stab of pain shot through her head and she was forced to close her eyes.

'It's very strange. How can it be dangerous my dear? Oh well, I'm sure I'll have plenty of time to work out what it's for after the police have taken you away. Now I'm going to put your hat back on your head – it may hurt you a little.' Pell, smiling broadly, bent down to where Atia was lying and scooping up her long dark hair fitted her telegraph boy cap back on her head. Atia winced with the pain.

'I'm sorry to cause you discomfort my dear Mrs Ashton but the narrative I am going to tell the police in a short time is dependent on me not knowing that you are actually a female. My story will be that you followed me to my residence and forced your way inside, presumably to burgle my home. Luckily, I shall tell them, I was able to render you unconscious by striking you with a poker before you could rob me. No one will be more surprised than me when the police inform me that you are indeed a woman called, apparently, Mrs Ashton. Oh, I will inform them, in a surprised fashion, that Mrs Ashton and her husband visited me recently presumably to prepare the ground for their audacious burglary attempt.'

Atia groaned. If she could think straight, if her head didn't hurt so much, she would be able to work out what she should do but her head was throbbing and the thing she most wanted to do was sleep. She shook her head to cause herself some pain and to stop herself dropping off. She had to stay awake and hope that First Commander Ashto would soon arrive at Pell's house.

Ashto watched from across the street as the policeman he had spoken to earlier, along with a second uniformed officer, stood at the door of Pell's house in Fitzroy Street. He had no idea what was going on and was unsure about what he should do. Presumably Atia was still inside the house so should he stay where he was and just observe what was happening or should he quickly rush up to the house and intervene in some way?

Ashto saw the front door open and Pell, the undertaker, invite the two policemen into his house. A short time afterwards he saw the door open again and there was Atia, her hands tied together, being led out by the two police officers and taken away to who knows where. Ashto followed, even more uncertain about what he should now do.

28

Atia Meets the Police Again

'Mrs Ashton, can you tell me and my colleague, in plain and simple terms, why you are dressed in male clothes and why this evening you attempted to rob a law-abiding member of the community?'

'Inspector, before I answer any questions I would like to speak to my husband.'

'You will of course be able to speak to Mr Ashton soon but first I must insist, Mrs Ashton, that you answer my question.' Detective Inspector Reid and Detective Sergeant Thick looked at Atia still dressed in her telegraph boy uniform, her long dark hair now freed from her cap cascading down about her shoulders. The two East End police officers had been summoned to Charing Cross Police Station by Chief

Inspector Abberline to interview the woman who seemingly had attempted to commit a serious crime.

Atia stared back at the two. She was trying to think clearly and ignore the pain that still thumped behind her eyes despite the bandage that that been placed around her head to stop the bleeding from the wound on her temple. What could she now say that would persuade the police that her actions this evening at Pell's house were reasonable, innocent and actually designed to help the authorities catch a criminal? 'I must speak to my husband. It is not fair to stop me from seeing him,' she said.

'I will tell you what is not fair,' said Inspector Reid, 'and that is the fact that you wore a telegraph boy's uniform this evening in order to illegally enter someone's home with the objective, presumably, to rob them.'

'No, Inspector Reid, that is not what happened. That whole notion is ridiculous!'

'Well, Mrs Ashton, then please tell me what *did* happen this evening.'

'I will answer whatever questions you wish to ask me after I have spoken to my husband.' Atia needed time to think. If only the throbbing ache in her head would stop so that she could work out what approach would be best for her to take in this enforced and crucial conversation with the police. If she said the wrong thing this evening she could endanger their entire mission on the planet Earth.

Edmund Reid looked at his sergeant and sighed and shrugged. 'Very well, Mrs Ashton, I will allow you to see your husband briefly but you must then answer my questions. Do you agree?'

'Yes, of course, Inspector.'

'Then Sergeant Thick will stay here with you while I fetch Mr Ashton.'

Reid left the room and found Ashto sitting in the entrance hall of the police station. He sat down beside him and the First Commander looked up expectantly. 'Mr Ashton, as you know we have taken your wife into custody on suspicion of planning to commit a crime. She is refusing to answer any questions about her movements this evening until she has spoken to you. Therefore I will take you to see her and will allow you five minutes alone with her before resuming our questioning. Is that acceptable?'

'Yes Inspector, of course, I am very confident that we can soon clear up this little misunderstanding and be on our way.'

Reid looked incredulous but stayed silent. He stood up and led the way to the room where Atia was being held.

'So you have had dealings with this American couple before, Edmund.'

'We have, Sir. To be honest I never quite know what to make of them.' Reid looked up at the tall and scowling figure of Chief Inspector Frederick Abberline, who had asked him the question.

'Well, they certainly look like a rum pair at the moment,' said Abberline looking through the window into the interview room where Ashto and Atia had embraced, kissed and were now engaged in conversation. 'Has she come up with an explanation as to why she's dressed like that?'

'Not yet, sir but I'm hoping she soon will.'

'Well, they're obviously working out what to say. I'd get

in there if I was you and get some real answers.' Abberline was annoyed; Reid didn't blame him.

'Yes Sir, will do. I'll let you know what they have to say. Sergeant, let's go and ask them some questions.'

Abberline, still looking annoyed turned and left Reid and Thick, 'I'll be in my office, Edmund.'

'Well, Mrs Ashton, I believe it is now time for you to answer a few questions.'

'Of course, Inspector, what would you like to know?' Atia smiled beatifically at the police detective.

'First of all will you please tell me why this evening you are dressed in the uniform of a telegraph boy?'

'Of course, Inspector, although I would have thought it was completely obvious.' Atia looked from Inspector Reid to Sergeant Thick and back again, a seemingly confused look on her face.

'Please, I will need you to enlighten me, Mrs Ashton,' said Reid.

'Inspector you already know that my husband and I are researching all facets of everyday life in this country with a view to writing a book that will, in the future, assist travellers from the United States to appreciate the many aspects of Britain.'

'Yes, Mrs Ashton, I know that, please go on.'

'Well, Inspector, that explains everything about this evening surely? What else do you need to know?'

Reid looked baffled and rubbed his eyes as if he was waking up after a particularly confusing dream. 'Mrs Ashton, please tell me why you are dressed as you are and why you ended up in the home of a Mr Pell, a resident of

Fitzroy Street? If you do not answer my questions I will have no alternative but to arrest you for obstructing the police in the pursuance of their duties.'

'Inspector, I adopted the uniform of a telegraph boy to enable me to legitimately enter a house in Cleveland Street where I could observe certain aspects of life in modern day London. I was then planning to report back to my husband so that he could make notes about what I had discovered which could eventually be included in the book he is planning to write.' Atia looked relaxed as though her explanation would satisfy the most curious of questioners. Inside she felt tense and wondered if she could possibly extricate herself from this mess. Her head still throbbed which made clear thinking difficult.

'Inspector, it is obvious that my wife is suffering from a concussive injury and needs medical treatment. Will you now let us be on our way?'

'Mrs Ashton, your wife has agreed to answer my questions and I would very much appreciate it if you would allow her to do so,' replied Reid. 'Now, Mrs Ashton, please explain to me what you were doing in the house of Mr Pell?'

'Certainly I will, Inspector Reid. In the course of our researches recently my husband and I have come to the conclusion that Pell is the Vampire Killer. I was in his house this evening, having earlier been invited in by him when I met him at the building in Cleveland Street. At his house I intended to look for evidence to prove that he was guilty of the terrible crimes that have been committed recently, evidence that we hoped could then be presented to you so Pell could then be apprehended by your officers.'

The Inspector looked confused. 'That is, I must say, a

very serious allegation you have made against Mr Pell. Do you have any of the evidence you say you were seeking this evening?'

'No, I am afraid I was rendered unconscious by the blow to my head that Pell inflicted on me before I could uncover any, but if you search his house, in particular his basement, then I am sure that you will find the evidence that you need to charge him with committing the so-called Vampire Murders.'

'Mrs Ashton, we can't just waltz into someone's home and search it just on your say so. I will need definite facts from you as to why you suspect this Mr Pell of having committed murder.'

'He was at the house in Cleveland Street. That was where he met at least two of the unfortunate young men I believe he killed. That is why, of course, this evening I disguised myself as a telegraph boy to see if he would invite me into his residence and attempt to deal with me in the same way.'

'Wasn't that rather dangerous if, as you suggest, he had already murdered four individuals?'

'Yes, Inspector, but my husband was on hand to come to my aid. Unfortunately Pell rendered me unconscious before we could act.'

Edmund Reid rubbed his eyes again. He bore an expression of weariness on his face. He glanced at his sergeant who looked equally confused. 'I'm sorry Mrs Ashton; your story makes little sense to me. Why would a pair of travellers from America who are, according to you, in this country to undertake research for a travel guide decide to involve themselves in such matters? We have a police force here and it is our job to find criminals – not yours.'

'With all due respect, Inspector, I would have thought that you would welcome any help with your investigations. After all your police force were not very successful at catching last year's serial killer.' Atia was immediately annoyed with herself. She had let her anger and her sadness at the events surrounding the Jack the Ripper murders, a victim of whom she had known and had been closely involved with, get the better of her. She had said things that were not part of the strategy she and the First Commander had quickly agreed on in their brief conversation before Reid and his sergeant had returned to the room.

Inspector Reid looked thoughtful. He had not heard the term *serial killer* before and considered how well it fit the description of Jack the Ripper and the murders he had committed in the autumn and early winter months of the previous year. He wondered where she had come up with such a phrase. There was something about this woman and her husband he had always been unsure about, something he could never put his finger on. The best thing he could do, he quickly decided, was to let them both go but put them under increased surveillance. He wanted them watched carefully and their movements intricately monitored. He also had decided that Mr Pell would be put on his list of closely watched individuals too. If there was more to the Ashtons than met the eye the same, his intuition told him, was also true about Pell, the undertaker from Fitzroy Street.

'Well, Mrs Ashton, thank you for answering my questions; you have given the sergeant and me much to consider. You and your husband may now be on your way but I must insist most strongly that you stay in London.'

'Thank you Inspector, we will of course remain on hand

to answer any more questions you have for us in the future,' said the First Commander. Holding Atia's hand he led her from the interview room and out of the police station.

Reid and Thick watched them as they left.

'I have to say, Sir, I'm quite surprised you let them go so quickly.'

'Well, Sergeant, although there's a lot about their story that doesn't make much sense I am quite intrigued to learn that there's another link between the murders and the Cleveland Street house.'

'Do you mean the fact that the undertaker was a visitor to the molly house?'

'I do, Bill, I do. And that he is in the habit of picking up telegraph boys and taking them back to his own house.'

'But he told us that he did that because he had recognised that it was Mrs Ashton in disguise.'

'True enough, Sergeant, but I wonder... if he's done that once perhaps he's done it before. We're going to watch Pell and his movements carefully and we'll put an extra man on to watch the Ashtons – get someone reliable to do that. I think that just maybe we may have made a breakthrough in this case. We can't go into 19, Cleveland Street but we can watch those that come and go from the place! Right let's go and report back to Fred Abberline and see if he agrees.' For the first time in a long time Edmund Reid actually felt optimistic.

29

Percival Pell

Pell looked through his upstairs window onto the street below. So the police are watching me, he thought, having noticed the man on the pavement opposite who had been stationed there all morning and was now lighting a cigarette. 'Well,' he said aloud, 'I'll have to give them something to watch.' Pell smiled. Throughout his life he had always been very good at assessing what others would do, he considered it one of the very many skills he possessed, along with being extremely confident in everything he did. From an early age he knew that he was definitely superior to most people and that he considered himself to be expert at presenting a certain image to the rest of the world that did not in any way display his real self. In the guise of a mild-mannered, caring and sensitive funeral director he could get away with a great deal that was considered outrageous and nefarious in this muzzled and restrained society in which he was forced to live.

He smiled as he thought about the ineptitude of that American woman's disguise from the day before. She certainly wasn't very clever if she thought she would get away with such an amateurish effort. The way her long dark hair had spilled out when he had caused her cap to fly off. It had been very satisfying to deliver a hard blow to the silly woman's head and see the dribble of blood appear as she lay on the floor of his drawing room. He had been tempted to lick up the life-giving substance but restrained himself from doing so. Actually it was a great pity he hadn't caused a little more damage to her skull; he would have liked to witness more of her blood leak out and perhaps he could have then saved some of it. He licked his lips at the thought. Later today he would see if he could dismantle the small metal device she had carried in her pocket and about which she had been so concerned. What on Earth was it? He'd soon discover its purpose however; he was skilled at finding things out – that was another one of his talents. He smiled; perhaps he should have been a police detective; he would have been good at that he mused. He was certain that he would have caught Jack the Ripper if he had been in charge of the investigation. He would have certainly been better than the current group of useless and inept police officers who were in charge of things.

He would often ask himself why he had decided to become an undertaker and the answer was always clear to him: it was because it gave him ultimate power over other individuals. When corpses lay in his mortuary they were his to do with whatever he wanted. As long as they looked at peace when relatives viewed them and when they were lying on display in open coffins everyone was happy. What happened to the lifeless bodies in the privacy of his funeral parlour was his business and no one else's. After all, he needed a release for his pent up emotions just like everyone else; that was surely only fair. He had always been totally disdainful of marriage. Why would he want to spend every day of his life with a woman who would probably chatter incessantly about totally unimportant matters? The dead didn't talk and couldn't complain; one of the many things he liked about them.

He thought back to the day he had discovered how to instill the appearance of life into those deceased individuals that found their way into his establishment. Most of his *customers* were old, wrinkled and worn out looking but the transfusion of 'new' blood into their dead bodies, along with a concoction of chemicals of his own devising, revitalised them, at least in terms of their outward appearance. How the deceased's relations would exclaim with surprise and delight at the lifelike appearance of their dead loved ones. How they would fawn over him and extol his skills and virtues. His very high fees were certainly worth every penny they would invariably say when they recommended his work to others.

And so it was only fair that in return for the highly thoughtful and skillful services he provided he should be allowed to seek his own pleasure with the bodies of the dead, at least with the deceased females that came under his purview. He certainly did not want to 'interfere' with the men and boys he dealt with of course, the very idea of that was completely disgusting and totally perverted. However, once he had discovered that the blood of young males was required to help him with the presentation of the deceased he had no choice but to seek them out, bring them to his residence and his basement laboratory and utilise their bodies to provide for his scientific needs. And if the young men's blood helped to give a lifelike appearance to the dead then perhaps it would also give extended life and vigour to the living – himself in particular. It was certainly worth a try he had decided. At this stage in his experiments with imbibing fresh blood himself it was early days but he had promised himself that his research would carry on just as long as he could find young men to 'help him out.' He had at first simply drunk the blood of his 'helpers' as he liked to think of them it but just lately he had begun injecting himself with the life-giving substance that he had drained from the young men. He had to be careful of course that he did not take too much, he did not want to be affected by the drug with which he had rendered the young men and boys insensible. So far he had not noticed any difference in his own appearance; his thinning hair had not yet begun to grow back and he was still somewhat diminutive in height, but it was very early days in his experimentations. However, he did feel that his inner self was changing. He felt even more determined and sure of himself than ever before and his intellect, at a high level to start with he believed, was developing and improving at speed. He would certainly persevere with his experiments; it was definitely the right thing to do, even though it meant having to visit that disgusting den of vice and perversity in Cleveland Street.

And there was very little chance of him being caught; that was a conclusion he had reached right at the beginning of his interactions with the young men and boys, the police being worse than useless of course. Transporting the headless bodies of those he had utilised around had been very easy. No one ever questioned why he would be driving around in his hearse with a coffin in the back; people just looked solemn as he passed by as they doffed their hats. No, he felt invincible and untouchable. People like himself should be what the future ought to be about. In ten years or so it would be the start of a brand new century. Inevitably the future would bring about a time when great thinkers and men of action like himself would undoubtedly thrive. To spill the blood of those who were weak and degenerate was completely necessary if the world of the future was to progress and accommodate such forward-thinkers as himself. Without doubt the twentieth century would belong to people like him. The newspapers had christened him "the Vampire Killer," that was stretching the truth somewhat, but on the whole he liked the nickname and revelled in it. One day he would announce himself to the world; then he would be universally acknowledged as a great innovator, a modern day pioneer and hero in fact, someone who, through a baptism of blood, would help save a country that had become weak and mediocre and inhabited by little people of no importance. Everyone would thank him for their collective deliverance.

Pell looked in the mirror that hung on the wall of his bedroom. In it he beheld not a man of small stature, a very ordinary looking, insignificant and balding individual but instead he saw reflected back at him a great man who personified triumph and genius, a Napoleon for the modern age. What he failed to recognise, of course, was the growing look of abject madness in his wide, unblinking and psychotic eyes.

30

Another Plan From Ashto and Atia

'It will be very dangerous, Margot.'

'That is true, Trevor, but it is vital that we retrieve the disrupter weapon before Pell tries to dismantle it, or worse fires it accidently and kills someone.'

'That is an accurate assessment of the situation, Margot, but I have one slight change to your plan to break into Pell's residence and take back the disrupter device.'

'What is that, Trevor?'

'That I should be the one to secretly enter Pell's house, and not you.'

'No, Trevor, it should definitely be me to carry out this task as it was due to my ineptitude that this situation was caused in the first place.'

'No, Margot, I have to insist and, if necessary, as this mission's First Commander, issue an order to the effect that it is my responsibility to find and bring back the lost weapon. Besides you still need to recover fully from your head wound that was inflicted by the dreadful Pell only a few days' ago.' Ashto did not make a habit of developing a hatred of another living creature but as far as the undertaker was concerned he was prepared to make an exception. The blow he had inflicted on Atia could have been far more serious than it was, fatal even. He would not let the human known as Percival Pell get away with that and looked forward to ensuring he would soon to be apprehended by the police and hopefully charged with the terrible murders of the young men. He intended to ensure that as well as retrieving the disrupter he would also uncover the evidence that the police would need to prove that Pell the undertaker was also the Vampire Killer.

Atia looked downcast. 'Trevor I am now fully recovered from the blow to the head I suffered. The tests you carried out with our medical kit showed that I am fine to go ahead with this plan.'

'No, I'm sorry, Margot and that is absolutely a final order.'

'Very well, First Commander, I can do nothing else but obey your direct order, but I would like you to know that I do not agree at all with your decision.'

'Margot, please... I could not bear it if something were to happen to you at the hands of that terrible man. Remember your confrontation with the Ripper last year when you almost died. I would never recover from... losing you.'

Atia smiled. 'You are right, of course, Trevor. But you must let me be on hand to help out and intervene when necessary. We must use all means available to us in order to defeat this man and retrieve our equipment. We must employ body cams, audio, fly drones, tracker devices and anything else we can think of to keep you safe and to bring this man to justice.'

'Of course, Margot.' Ashto leant across and kissed Atia. He knew that as every day passed he was more and more in love with her.

The Jaran pair watched their small computer screen carefully as Atia controlled the fly drone as it moved from room to room in Pell's home and his funeral director's establishment.

'He is definitely in his office speaking to clients of his at this moment. His female assistant is in her adjoining room at her desk undertaking paper work and, as we know from our observations, it is Pell's housekeeper's day off. There is no one in his residential rooms at present,' said Atia.

'In that case now is the time to act,' replied Ashto checking that his earpiece and tiny cameras attached to buttons on his jacket were firmly in place.

The First Commander and his Apprentice Commander were seated on a bench beneath an oak tree in Fitzroy Square and were being very careful to conceal their computer behind a newspaper, which to any passers-by they appeared to be studying avidly.

'I will continue to monitor your progress, Trevor, and will soon be with you if you need my assistance.'

'I have every confidence in you,' said Ashto, leaning over to give Atia a peck on the cheek. 'I will complete the mission and be back with you very soon.' He quickly left and made the short walk to Pell's house in Fitzroy Street.

Atia looked at his disappearing figure and against all her professional instincts felt extremely concerned as she again gave her attention to the scene of the inside of Pell's house via the camera on the fly drone. She maneuvered the mechanical fly so that she could monitor the door at the back of the house, which was, they had decided, the easiest and safest place for the First Commander to break into the building unseen.

Ashto inserted the tool that the Jaran pair had designed to enable him to unlock any door he was liable to come up against. Closing the door quietly he quickly waved at the fly drone, which he could see was perched on the wall opposite in the scullery where he had entered the house.

'Margot, as you can see I am now inside and ready to begin my search for the disrupter,' whispered the First Commander. 'As we have so far been unable to find its location using the drone I am going to go down to the basement of the house, the most likely place for Pell to have secreted it.'

'Very well, Trevor, I will observe you as you do so.'

Once he had found the door to Pell's basement he used the tool to open it. 'Margot, I have unlocked the door and will now go down to the cellar area to see if I can retrieve the weapon. As we planned you will keep a look out and warn me of anyone coming through from Pell's offices.'

'Yes, Trevor, I understand.' Atia still felt quite nervous but was sure that the First Commander would soon complete his task and be out of the house in Fitzroy Street returning to her having found the disrupter weapon. Her sigh of relief was cut short by a familiar voice.

'Ah, Mrs Ashton, what a pleasure it is to meet you yet again.'

Atia looked up and saw the smiling face of William Rogers, the reporter for the Evening Standard. She quickly hid the computer beneath the copy of The Times. 'Mr Rogers, this cannot be a coincidence?'

'Only partially so, Mrs Ashton, I was heading for Charing Cross Police Station to interview one of the officers there when I noticed you sitting here and wondered what you were doing? You seem to be thoroughly engrossed in your newspaper.'

'Well, Mr Rogers, it is a fine morning and I thought it would be pleasant to sit quietly and look at today's newspaper. I was extremely interested, as a matter of fact, in reading a review of a concert last evening at St James Hall where the great Russian composer Tchaikovsky was conducting a selection of his own works. Of course, Mr Rogers, it could be argued that what I am doing is actually none of your business,' said Atia attempting a carefree sort of smile while wondering what Ashto was doing at that moment.

'That is quite true, Mrs Ashton; I am very sorry for being so presumptuous. Is Mr Ashton carrying out his research around here.'

'Presumptuous of you again Mr Rogers?' said Atia forcing herself to smile.

'I apologise once more, Mrs Ashton. Please put it down to my overwhelmingly inquisitive nature as a newspaper reporter.'

'I will, Mr Rogers. And now I would like to be left alone to read my copy of the Times.'

'Of course, but first can I ask you about your adventure the other evening in Cleveland Street when, I am sure you will remember, you were dressed as a telegraph boy for some reason known only to yourself.'

'Again, Mr Rogers, I must insist that the "adventure" as you term it is something that is my business and is most definitely not yours.' Atia desperately wanted to get back to her computer and monitor the progress that Ashto was making in the premises in nearby Fitzroy Street and was frustrated that she was unable to reply to his questions she was receiving in her hidden earpiece.

'Ah, but it *is* my business, Mrs Ashton, inasmuch that the readers of my newspaper may be interested in why a beautiful, female, foreign visitor disguised as a telegraph boy would enter an infamous male brothel, go to the house of a well-respected local businessman, unfortunately sustain a head injury and then get arrested by the police on a charge of attempted burglary.'

'I see your contacts with the local police authorities are still thriving, Mr Rogers. In that case can I make a suggestion?'

'Of course, Mrs Ashton, I am full of anticipation.'

'If you leave me alone now I will agree, at some time in the near future, to accompany you to Fortescues' restaurant where I will tell you anything about the said evening that you care to ask me. Is that agreeable to you?'

'It is very agreeable to me, Mrs Ashton. I will therefore leave you to your newspaper just as soon as we arrange a suitable date for that assignation.'

'Would tomorrow evening be a suitable time, Mr Rogers?'

'It would indeed, Mrs Ashton. I will be on veritable tenterhooks until then. I shall call for you at your guesthouse at 7 o'clock tomorrow evening.' Rogers smiled, looked triumphant, doffed his hat, turned on his heels and walked off in the direction of Cleveland Street.

Atia breathed a quick sigh of relief and quickly looked back at her computer that lay beneath her newspaper.

First Commander Ashto descended the steps down to Pell's basement after first turning the knob on the wall, which activated the electric light. Pell might be a murderer, Ashto thought, but he was keeping up with the latest technological developments on this primitive planet. In this year of 1889, even in such a wealthy country as Britain, it was very unusual for electric lighting to be installed in people's homes. It was certainly not a luxury the two Jarans had in their guesthouse room where everyday they had to deal with some frustratingly temperamental gas lamps.

At the bottom of the stone staircase Ashto stopped and looked around the large cellar space that Pell had said he used as a simple storage area. In the rather dim electric lighting from the one bulb, which as well as buzzing quite loudly, created shadowy nooks and crannies around the room, Ashto found it quite difficult to make out any details and it wasn't until he stood close that he could see there were several large glass jars lined up along a shelf on one of the cellar walls. At first he not able to work out what the jars contained and then suddenly his eyes widened and he gave out an audible gasp. 'Can you see these, Margot? Margot? Margot can you hear me?'

Ashto was alarmed at not getting an immediate reply from his Apprentice Commander. He tapped his small hearing device that he wore in his right ear; there was still no reply. No time to waste then, he thought, it's possible that Atia is in some sort of trouble or that the audio equipment he wore had stopped working for some reason. His attention was drawn back to the horror of what was contained in the big cylindrical glass containers. Four heads, one in each jar and floating around in some sort of preservative liquid, peered out at him with lifeless eyes. He hoped that his body cams were working properly as he slowly moved down the line of horror stopping at the last one and shaking his head as he recognised the face of poor P.C. Perkins, the young policeman who had followed them to Whitby and whose headless body was later found by the police.

Ashto moved away from the horrors on the shelves and went across to what was obviously some sort of workbench that was covered by a threadbare purple cloth and on which were various tools of indeterminate nature as well as glass vials, beakers and test tubes, some of which were connected by rubber piping. A greenish liquid seemed to be dripping into one stoppered glass vessel causing Ashto to recall the play at the Lyceum theatre the previous year where the character called Dr Jekyll turned into his frightening alter ego of Mr Hyde by drinking a similar looking green concoction.

'Margot are you receiving me?' said Ashto trying his sound equipment again but as before getting no response.

The First Commander could not see the disrupter weapon lying around on the bench but there were two drawers, which he carefully opened. There Ashto saw the weapon and he breathed a sigh of relief. He picked it up and carefully examined it to see if Pell had tampered with the dangerous device. Seeing that there was no obvious damage to the outside of the weapon he then checked its settings and discovered that it was still fully charged before slipping it into one of his pockets.

Moving to the other side of the cellar he was intrigued to see a tall A-shaped structure that went up to the basement's ceiling. Dangling down from the substantial wooden framework was a series of chains and, at the top, some sort of pulley device. Ashto was in the process of working out what the function of such a structure could be when an alarmed Atia shouted in his ear: 'Trevor, Pell has left his funeral director's offices. He is returning to his residence!'

Atia, after her extremely annoying conversation with Rogers, had quickly looked back at her computer screen and immediately saw that Pell was no longer sitting down talking to clients, presumably carrying out his undertaker duties, but had moved perhaps to go back to his residence. Feeling panicky she quickly activated the fly-drone, which had been perched on the ceiling of the undertaker's office, and flew it into the other rooms of his funeral studio. He was not in his room that displayed a number of different types of coffins, nor in the adjoining mortuary where a corpse lay covered up. Atia breathed a sigh of relief when she discovered the undertaker standing by his female assistant in her office and having a conversation pertaining to his recent meeting, which apparently was about an order for the delivery of some new coffins.

And then Atia watched with alarm as Pell did not return

to his own office but instead began to make his way back to his residence.

'Margot, I've been trying to contact you. Where exactly is Pell?'

'I'm following him with the drone and… oh no!'

Margot, what is it?'

'He has just seen that the door to his cellar is open. He has stopped by it and… now he has gone to his drawing room… he's returning to the cellar door… Trevor, he's carrying a weapon, a pistol of some sort!'

'Margot, I must have left the door open.'

'Trevor, be careful. I'm on my way to help you.'

Slow deliberate footsteps on the stone staircase sounded as Ashto vainly looked for somewhere he could conceal himself. He decided that all he could do was stand there and watch as Pell, pointing a gun, came down the steps towards him. At the bottom the undertaker smiled as he recognised the Jaran First Commander.

'Ah, it's Mr Ashton if my eyes do not deceive me,' said Pell. 'To whom were you talking just now?' Pell looked around the cellar in the half-light of his electric bulb to check that there was no one else in the room.'

'Just conversing with myself, Mr Pell, it is an old habit of mine.'

'Well, Mr Ashton, it is often said that talking to oneself is a sign of incipient madness,' replied Pell smiling.

'I think that madness is a subject you would know something about, Mr Pell.'

'Ah, touché, Mr Ashton; is your very pretty wife not with you today? Oh, and by the way, if you are wondering,

I do know how to use this revolver. One cannot be too careful these days with incidents of crime, especially violent burglaries, on the increase apparently. I have to admit that I sometimes wonder what the world is becoming! Now, please, if you do not mind, would you move over to my workbench and raise your arms above your shoulders.'

Ashto did what Pell had asked. He had momentarily thought of reaching into his pocket and pulling out the disrupter but was certain from how Pell was poised with his gun held in a steady hand that he would not be able to use it before the undertaker had put one or two bullets into his head.

'Now, Mr Ashton, you see the beaker containing the green liquid? I want you to take out its stopper and drink the contents.'

'I am sorry Mr Pell, but I do not intend to do that. The substance would obviously poison my system and lead to my demise.'

'Not so, Mr Ashton; the liquid is simply a drug that will temporarily induce paralysis. It will render you harmless while I contact the police. The alternative is to shoot you and do the same to your wife who is, I assume, now on her way here to provide you with some assistance. Now, Mr Ashton, please drink it.'

Seeing no alternative the First Commander did what he was told.

# 31

A Chase

Apprentice Commander Atia ran as quickly as she could to the house in Fitzroy Street where it seemed the dangerous Mr Pell would soon discover First Commander Ashto in the cellar. However, hampered by the many layers of the ludicrous outfit she was wearing she found it impossible to move with any great speed. She momentarily thought about tearing off her skirt to allow her legs to move more freely but quickly assessed that such an action would create more problems than solutions and would probably lead to her arrest on a charge of indecent behaviour.

Arriving at Pell's residence she was about to access the back of the house and the unlocked door Ashto had used to enter the property when an authoritative voice, strong and deep in tone, called out to her.

'Excuse me, Miss, what exactly do you want here?'

Looking around Atia saw that the gruff voice belonged to the same local beat officer who had escorted her to the police station following her encounter a few days ago with Pell the undertaker and a heavy poker.

'Ah… good morning Constable, I was just looking for my husband.'

'It's Mrs Ashton is it not? It took me a while to recognise you, what with you wearin' proper women's clothes an' all. So what is your husband doing here at Mr Pell's house then?'

'Well, Officer… er, he is attempting to clear up the recent misunderstanding we had at this location recently and… I was… er, here to support him… in what he had to say.'

'Mrs Ashton, I hope I don't have to arrest you for a second time but your behaviour again seems to be very suspicious. I must ask you to move along sharpish like or I will indeed be forced to take you into custody again.'

Atia was in a state of indecision about what she should do. The sound from the First Commander's audio equipment had ceased and she knew that he must be in grave danger at the hands of a known murderer. As far as she could see she would have no alternative but to deal with this policeman and temporarily put him out of action while she entered the house to help Ashto overcome Pell. She was just about to reach out to locate the pressure points in the police constable's neck when the large gates of the stable attached to the undertaker's house suddenly swung open with a loud clang. Both Atia and the policeman looked towards the gates and saw two large black horses emerge pulling a smart, shiny black hearse in the back of which, behind glass, had been laid a coffin. The policeman instinctively removed his helmet in deference to the hearse as it passed the pair. Atia at once noticed that Percival Pell, the undertaker, whip in hand, was driving the hearse.

'Trevor, can you hear me. Where are you? Speak to me!' said Atia speaking into the microphone attached to her jacket.'

'Miss, who are you talking to?' said a confused police constable.

Seconds after he had drunk the green liquid Ashto felt that he was no longer able to control his limbs. His knees turned to jelly and he slowly crumpled to the floor. He wanted to let Atia know what was happening but all that emerged from his mouth and into his hidden microphone was a guttural, retching sound.

As he lay on the floor he was conscious of everything but totally unable to move any part of his body. A small part of his mind acknowledged he was experiencing an interesting sensation but the other parts told him he was in grave danger of losing his life. He hoped that Atia, who would doubtless be entering the cellar very soon, would take extreme care with an adversary they had both underestimated. Ashto watched with unmoving eyeballs as a smiling Pell walked over to him, bent down and felt for his pulse.

'Well, Mr Ashton, you appear to still be alive. I'm very surprised. That amount of the drug should have killed you instantly; they must make individuals very resilient in the United States of America. Do not worry, however, the drug *will* lead to your death as it eventually causes your heart to stop working. It will I believe be a completely painless process, at least I think that will the case; you will know soon enough I suppose. Now I have to deal with your soon to be lifeless body, just in case your wife is accompanied here by a policeman or two; she does seem to attract them doesn't she?'

Pell, while carrying on talking, had grabbed Ashto's ankles and pulled his large frame towards a coffin that lay in the corner of the cellar. It was with great difficulty and much huffing and puffing that the undertaker removed the occupant of the coffin and replaced it with Ashto. Had he been able to do so the Jaran explorer would have registered a look of absolute horror on his face as the coffin lid was put back in place and nailed shut by a profusely sweating Mr Pell. For the First Commander everything went very dark.

Pell dusted himself down and walked out towards the stables at the side of the house where his horses and his hearse they pulled were kept. Here, by luck, the two black horses that Pell privately called Plague and Pestilence, had been hooked up to the carriage earlier in the morning in preparation for a funeral in the afternoon. The stable hands as usual had done a wonderful job of preparing the horses. Pell was always impressed with their work, particularly the way the horses looked so magnificent with their shining coats and the large black plumes they wore on their heads.

Calling for the stable boys he explained to them that he needed the coffin to be placed in the hearse and for the wooden gates at the top of the slope and which led out onto the road to be opened. 'A last minute change of plan,' he said to the surprised stable hands who quickly manhandled the coffin into the hearse.

Pell climbed up to the driver's position at the front of the hearse, donned his shiny top hat which was adorned with a black crepe ribbon and, cracking his whip, urged the large and powerful horses forward up the sharp slope and out onto the road outside. As he passed them Pell smiled at Atia and the policeman, doffing his top hat at them in seemingly friendly fashion.

Atia feverishly tried to work out what exactly what had happened and decided that it was unlikely that Pell would have left the First Commander in the house and so therefore he must have taken Ashto with him in the hearse. 'Oh no,' she said, 'the coffin!'

'What is it, Miss?' said the policeman, confused by the sudden burst of activity and Atia's words.

'I'm sorry, Constable, but I must go after that carriage,' said Atia, taking out her computer from her handbag and checking that the tracker on Ashto's person was indeed on the move and heading towards Oxford Street. The body cameras he wore were all registering total blackness.

'I can't let you do that Miss, I…' the policeman's words were cut off as Atia quickly pinched carefully selected nerves in his neck and gently laid him down behind the railings and shrubs at the front of Pell's house.

'I apologise, Constable, but I have no time to put forward a reasoned argument,' said Atia who, without any qualms at all on this occasion, lifted up her skirts and ran off in the same direction the hearse had taken.

Atia realised that she must cut a very unusual figure as she ran at top speed down Maple Street and turned right into Tottenham Court Road and then left into Bayley Street and Bedford Street towards Russell Square. As she passed the elegant frontage of the British Museum at Montague Place a number of bystanders observed her with mouths agog as she sped past them. 'What on Earth is the world coming to?' said one portly gentleman who had never before seen a well-dressed woman actually running in such a way, her skirts hoisted above her knees, displaying her legs to public view. As Atia ran, occasionally apologising to the people she inadvertently bumped into, she formulated a desperate plan that she hoped would result in her rescuing the First Commander who was currently being taken by Percival Pell to some unknown destination.

By the time she arrived quite breathless into Russell Square she sighed with relief when what she had hoped to find was actually there. Beside the small, wooden, black and white structure, which was one of sixty-one hansom cabmen's shelters around the city, places where cab drivers could have a break, a meal and a cup of tea, there stood two hansom cabs with their horses serenely munching on bags of oats.

'I'm very sorry to interrupt your well-deserved rest,' said Atia to one of the horses as she detached its nosebag, gently patted its neck and untied its reins from the railings they were hitched to, 'but we have a very important task to undertake.'

Without hesitation Atia lifted her skirts again to allow her to raise her leg onto the high step that enabled her to hoist herself onto the driver's seat at the rear of the horse drawn carriage. She took hold of the reins and hoped that she would instinctively be able to control the large equine creature and get it to propel this vehicle in the correct direction. She had been in hansom cabs many times since arriving in London the previous year and had witnessed the techniques the drivers used for controlling their horses but now as she was actually going to attempt to drive one herself she felt far from confident. She shrugged realising that there was no alternative to what she had planned and gently urged the horse forward feeling pleased when the creature did what she wanted. As she continued down the road she heard shouts from behind her and wondered what the penalty was for stealing a hansom cab. She shrugged. 'One problem at a time,' she said aloud as she took out her computer and looked to see where the tracker attached to the First Commander's clothing was currently located. She saw that Pell and his hearse were on the street known simply as Holborn heading towards Whitechapel and the East End. At least he will soon be in an area I know quite well, thought Atia.

As the Apprentice Commander had expected the midday traffic made her progress along the byways of London exceedingly slow and she gained plenty of practice stopping the well-trained horse and getting it to go forward again; control is really all in the reins, she thought. If her mission had not been quite so desperate she would no doubt be enjoying her adventure immensely. On occasions people on the crowded pavements would hail her cab and were surprised and annoyed when she sailed past them, suddenly realising with shock that there was actually a woman driving it.

Constantly keeping one eye on the computer screen and the tracker display she saw that Pell's hearse had turned off Whitechapel High Street and was now on Dock Street heading for the river. Urging her horse on as quickly as possible on the busy streets she fervently hoped that she would be in time to rescue Ashto from the clutches of

Pell. She tried not to think too deeply about what the mad undertaker planned to do with the coffin and its contents.

Following the route that was being taken by Pell, Atia took her hansom cab around the streets that encircled the London Docks with its many workers loading and unloading goods from various boats and ships. The area was a dark and forbidding place, a veritable rabbit warren of narrow roads and alleyways. Atia had to concentrate hard to keep control of the horse in the noisy and busy atmosphere of a place where it seemed the sun seldom shone and where most Londoners from the West End never visited. Around the Wapping Basin Docks was an area of the city that was renowned for its lawless nature and its many criminals, its rowdy public houses and its hard drinking inhabitants. It was also the location of many opium dens that catered for rich young thrill seekers as well as inveterate drug addicts who were beginning to create a real problem in staid Victorian London. Atia and Ashto had promised themselves that when they knew a little more about the Earth and its humans they would immerse themselves in this dark nether world and find out much more about the aspects of London life evident there. However, Atia thought that unless she was able to rescue her First Commander very soon it would be unlikely they would ever get the chance to do that.

Looking at the computer Atia saw that Pell had stopped his hearse at a place called Gun Wharf. She knew that along this part of the river there were many dark, anonymous warehouses where the undertaker could conceal the hearse and easily dispose of the coffin in which Ashto currently lay. She reluctantly picked up the horsewhip that lay in its holder and cracked it above the horse as she had seen drivers do many times when they were asked to speed up by impatient passengers. She felt sorry she had to do that to a horse that had negotiated the streets of London so well as she urged the compliant creature to go faster, its iron horseshoes sparking on the cobbled streets.

After a few minutes careening at speed around the streets that surrounded Wapping Docks, Atia and her cab approached Gun Wharf with caution. She knew that Pell had a weapon, which he would be very happy and willing to use on her. On the other hand she also knew that Pell would not be expecting her and so she felt confident that she would have surprise on her side. She stopped the cab and looked at her computer screen. Pell, and presumably his hearse, were inside the warehouse directly ahead of her, its large wooden doors closed.

Atia got down from the cab and tied the horse's reins to a large mooring post at the river's edge. She patted the sweating horse on its neck and felt sorry that she had no food or water to give it after its long and exhausting journey. 'Apologies my fine equine friend,' she said quietly, 'I will ensure you will be fed and watered as soon as possible.' She smiled at the horse and patted it again before moving off towards the building where it seemed Pell had taken Ashto.

Keeping to the edge of the warehouse she searched for a window so she could discover exactly where Pell was. Her search was in vain, however, and so she headed for a wooden staircase at the side of the warehouse that would take her to the top storey of the building. As she climbed the steps as silently as she was able she sincerely hoped she would not be too late to save the First Commander, a man she called Trevor and with whom she was in love.

32

The Police Spring Into Action and Atia Faces Danger Yet Again

'So, Constable, what exactly happened to you?' Detective Inspector Edmund Reid and his sergeant, Bill Thick, were standing in the street outside Pell the undertaker's house. They looked at the uniformed police officer who was rubbing his eyes and who seemed extremely groggy.

'I'm sorry, Inspector Reid, I don't rightly know. One minute I was standing talking to that Mrs Ashton woman who told me she wanted to go inside to meet her husband and then all of a sudden I found myself waking up on the ground. I was lying in front of Mr Pell's house feelin' decidedly odd and Mrs Ashton was nowhere to be seen.'

'So what did you do then?'

'I blew my whistle to get help, sir.'

'Sergeant, what about the plain-clothes officer who was assigned to watch Pell's house?' said Inspector Reid.

'He was called away on other duties and so far hasn't been replaced,' answered Sergeant Thick.

'Wonderful! Do we know where Pell went?' said Reid.

'According to the Constable here and the stable hands who work for Pell he left unexpectedly in his hearse with a coffin in the back. It's not known where he was going.'

'Have we any idea where Mrs Ashton has got to?'

Sergeant Thick consulted his notebook: 'According to various bystanders she was seen with her dress hitched right up displaying her ankles and legs, running all the way to Russell Square where she proceeded to steal a hansom cab from outside the cabmen's shelter.'

'Running eh? That's very odd behaviour, Sergeant. Was she able to drive the cab she stole?'

'Apparently she could – she was seen by a number of witnesses.'

'A woman running down the street showing everything she's got and then driving a hansom cab. It seems that America produces some very unusual women!' said Edmund Reid who couldn't help smiling. Turning to the still dazed looking constable Reid put his hand on the officer's shoulder and told him to go back to the station and have a cup of tea to settle his nerves. 'All right, Bill, let's see what we can find out in the Undertaker's house.'

Mrs Abberley, Pell's grey-haired secretary and assistant, opened the front door to the two Police Officers and invited them into her office.

'Do you know where Mr Pell has gone?' said Inspector Reid to the rather confused elderly woman.

'I'm afraid not, Inspector. It's very unlike him to dash off in such an unpremeditated fashion,' replied Mrs Abberley.

'Do you mind if we look around Mr Pell's rooms?' said Sergeant Thick.

'I suppose that would be all right,' said Mrs Abberley sounding very unsure. She had not had anything happen like this before and she found it all very unsettling. If only Mr Pell were here to advise her what she should do.

'In that case we would be very grateful if you would be kind enough to guide us around the house, Mrs Abberley,' said Reid.

'Well, yes, I suppose so, Inspector, although I do have work to do in my office.'

'I'm sure you do, Mrs Abberley,' said the Inspector, smiling benignly, 'but it won't take us very long and I'm sure Mr Pell would want you to help us as much as possible.'

'Very well, Inspector, please come this way.'

Mrs Abberley conducted the two Metropolitan Police detectives through to Pell's residence. When they got to the still open cellar door Inspector Reid stopped: 'Where does that door lead to, Mrs Abberley?'

'It goes to the cellar, Inspector, although I have never been down there. It is extremely odd because Mr Pell normally keeps that door locked and I have never seen it open before. He uses the cellar for storage apparently although I have to say he has never asked me to fetch anything from down there.'

'Do you mind if we go and take a look?' said Sergeant Thick.

'I suppose that would be all right; oh, if only Mr Pell was here, I'm certain he would be far more use than I at answering your questions.'

'That's all right, Mrs Abberley. Don't worry, we'll only be a jiffy I'm sure and then you can get back to your work,' said Inspector Reid.

Reid and Thick ventured through the door and down the stairs. 'One of those electric light gadgets,' said the Detective Sergeant pointing up at the buzzing bulb that hung from the ceiling and which had been left switched on.

'Can't see them catching on. A bit too noisy I would have thought,' replied the inspector.

As the eyes of the two police officers became accustomed to the dim light source they slowly moved across the cellar towards some shelving on the far wall. As they approached they began to stare in utter disbelief at the glass jars on the shelves and both gave out involuntary gasps as the full realisation of what they were seeing registered on their minds.

'Bill,' said Inspector Reid continuing to stare at the horror that lay on the shelf in front of him, 'let's get some uniformed officers down here to guard this awful place and then we'll go and find Pell and make him pay for what he's done here!'

At the top of the stairs Atia went through the door that led into the warehouse, wincing at the sound of its rusty, squeaking hinge. Inside it was completely dark so she took out the small but powerful torch she had in the pocket of her long outerwear jacket and shined it in front of her. She moved slowly and carefully through the top floor of the warehouse aware of every creak and crack of the bare wooden floorboards beneath her booted feet.

And then she heard a voice from below and carefully moved towards where the sound seemed to come from. Kneeling down, hampered again by her many skirts, she peered through a small gap in the floorboards. There she could make out the disturbing scene below. First Commander Ashto lay with eyes open but unmoving in the opened coffin with Pell sitting next to him cross-legged, talking and gesturing. A guttering candle caused shadows to dance around the large room occasionally illuminating the stationary hearse and horses nearby.

'… and having weighted down the coffin with those large rocks I'll soon be pushing you into the river where you'll sink without trace. However, before I do that and wish you a final farewell, Mr Ashton, what I'm going to do is take some of your blood – quite a lot actually – as you certainly won't be needing it in the near future.' Pell chuckled. 'You know I am really quite amazed you are still alive, Mr Ashton. I'm extremely impressed with your bodily constitution and I am seriously thinking your life-giving blood must have some special properties that I will be able to utilise in my experiments in the future. I will draw some of your blood using this… ' (Atia could see that he held up a large syringe that was connected via a tube to a glass jar) '… but first I will avail myself of some of it in a rather more direct way; I hope you do not mind,' said Pell continuing to chuckle.

Atia watched as the obviously deranged undertaker took from a box a small, shiny, metal object with two sharp pointed prongs that looked almost like … and then Atia's eyes widened as she watched Pell place the object in his mouth with an audible click. Now, when the undertaker smiled at Ashto, two bright metal fangs protruded from his mouth like the teeth of some alien robotic animal. Atia watched with abject horror as Pell reached forward into the coffin and bit into the First Commander's neck. A horrible slurping and sucking noise emerged from Pell as the terror-stricken Atia, now unbothered about the noise she was creating, quickly stood up and ran to a flight of wooden steps that led down to the floor below.

Pell raised his head disturbed by the sudden noise as Atia dashed down the stairs as swiftly as her skirts would allow her. Pell, wide eyed, stopped his grisly work and stood up. Seeing the Apprentice Commander he smiled at her, his metallic fangs dripping blood onto the white collar of his shirt and also onto the pistol he pointed at her.

Detective Inspector Reid and Detective Sergeant Thick had hailed a cab and were in the process of travelling full pelt towards the East End where witnesses said both Pell's hearse and Atia's hansom had been heading.

'Sir, do we have any idea where Pell and the Ashton woman were going?' said the sergeant, scratching his head.

'Where would be the best place to quietly get rid of a coffin with a body inside it?' replied the inspector.

'The river, of course! Down by the docks where there's not too many that's going to ask any questions.'

'Precisely, Sergeant, the only problem is whereabouts. There are so many places along the river where a coffin could be quietly slipped into the water never to be seen again.'

'Do you reckon Mr Ashton was in the coffin?'

'Yes, Bill, I'd put money on it. He wasn't in the house and why else would Mrs Ashton risk life and limb to follow Pell and his hearse?'

'Very true, Inspector, now we know that Pell is our murderer we need to get to him before he does Ashton in as well.'

Reid looked worried. He opened up the hatch in the roof of the hansom cab: 'Driver, go to St Katherine's Dock Basin as quick as you can,' he shouted. 'We'll try there first,' said Reid to his sergeant, 'we just might get lucky.' The inspector didn't look or sound very optimistic.

'Do not move, Mrs Ashton. This revolver is fully loaded and, believe it or not, I am an expert shot with it; my father taught me very well. He was in the army you know and this is his trusty service revolver he bequeathed to me when he passed away.'

Atia looked over to Ashto lying in the coffin. His shirtfront was bright with fresh blood that leaked from two small holes in his neck. 'You've killed him,' she said. Tears began to roll down her face as she realised that she had lost him forever.

'No, Mrs Ashton, not yet, your husband appears to have a remarkable constitution, he even seems to have a double heartbeat, which is of course impossible. In any case I was planning to first extract some blood from your husband, which would have been utilised in my vitally important experiments into ways to make people appear young again. My work will signal a great advance in science and see the end of the aging process as we know it and I'm sure you would agree that scientific endeavour should always outweigh the fate of any one particular individual. But unfortunately, now that you have appeared with, I assume, the police close behind, I can no longer carry out that little procedure. A pity but there you are.' As he spoke Pell felt a little groggy, he realised that he'd probably taken just a little too much of the drug-laden blood from the man he knew as Mr Ashton.

Atia noticed that the revolver in the deranged undertaker's hand had begun to shake slightly and droplets of sweat had broken out on his brow. It was obvious that the First Commander had been drugged and that Pell had imbibed some of that drug when he had bitten into Ashto's neck and sucked his blood. Rather unsteadily, while still holding the gun trained on the Apprentice Commander, Pell opened up a large trap door in the wooden floor. When the hatchway creaked open Atia could see the dark waters of the River Thames flowing beneath. As the Undertaker started to drag the coffin containing Ashto, with some difficulty, towards the trap door he smiled between his huffing and puffing. 'Please stay where you are, Mrs Ashton, as I wish you to witness your husband's demise. As you can see I have weighted your husband's coffin down with chains, dumbbells and some large rocks so that it will sink very quickly to the bottom of the river. Ha! I doubt whether even Mr Ashton's wonderful constitution will be able to cope with that!' laughed Pell.

As Pell prepared to slide the coffin through the trap door and into the water Atia realised she must act immediately if she wanted to save the First Commander's life. As Pell transferred the gun he held from his right to his left hand to enable him to get a firmer grip on the edge of the coffin she turned on her torch, shined its bright light directly into the mad Undertaker's eyes and then leapt at him. Had she been wearing her tight fitting and flexible Jaran explorer service uniform her athletic leap would have been successful in reaching Pell, hitting him in the chest and easily knocking him backwards, but the fussy, female Earth clothes she wore badly hindered her and she was only able to strike Pell a glancing blow. The undertaker's left arm was knocked upwards, his revolver went off causing a shower of sparks and splinters to fall from the floorboards above his head and Atia found herself sprawled half over the coffin and half over Pell's legs.

It took a crucial few seconds for the undertaker to gather himself and bring his gun to bear once again on Atia who, seeing the danger she was in, managed to grab Pell's wrist and violently force it backwards. Pell screamed in pain as his left wrist dislocated and the gun he had been holding flew out of his hand and skittered across the floor. Pell looked angry and opened his mouth displaying his shiny metallic teeth he still wore and which were still stained with the First Commander's blood. 'Well, Mrs Ashton, I will have the pleasure of tasting your blood as well as that of your husband, which will be an interesting experience to say the least.' With his left arm hanging limply Pell grabbed Atia's hair with his right hand and yanked it downwards. Momentarily surprised by his unexpected strength Atia was forced to the floor allowing the mad and maddened Undertaker to clamber on top of her, forcing her arms down with his knees. He grinned maniacally at the Apprentice Commander, his metal fangs making him look like some demented and hellish creature: 'You seem to have put an end to my little game, Mrs Ashton, and for that I will kill you by draining every last drop of blood from your body. You are very tall so you must have lots of the life giving liquid flowing around your veins. I will fill myself up with it, I will gorge upon it and, I can assure you, I will enjoy it more than you can ever know!'

Using her strength and equally great determination Atia managed to free her right arm from Pell's knee and with the open heel of her hand hit Pell directly in the nose as his head was on the way down to her neck. There was a soft crunching noise and Pell screamed and fell backwards, blood beginning to stream down his mouth and chin.

The undertaker scrambled around on the wooden floorboards dripping copious amounts of blood from his broken nose. He had, despite his pain, noticed where his revolver had come to rest and, on his hands and knees, scrambled over to pick it up and pointed it again at Atia. This time he looked malevolent in the extreme as blood continued to flow from his nose and his left wrist dangled uselessly by his side. His deranged looking eyes were full of hate for this woman who had caused him so much pain and he would very much enjoy putting a bullet into her head. He carefully aimed his gun at the Apprentice Commander.

Atia, sitting up from her prone position on the floor, was too far away from Pell for another attempt to leap at him. She realised that there was nothing else left for her to do but close her eyes and wait for the bullet from Pell's pistol to cruelly smash its way into her skull and her brain and instantly kill her.

Then she heard a sharp whooshing sound. She had experienced the sound once before when she had been in another life and death situation with Jack the Ripper a few months before. Opening her eyes she saw the shocked and bloodied face of Percival Pell, the undoubtedly crazed undertaker and the man the newspapers had christened the Vampire Killer, mouthing a soundless scream as the atoms in his body dispersed and flew apart as he was slowly vaporised by the beam from a disrupter weapon. She looked around at where the powerful stream of molecular destroying neutrons had come from. There sitting up in the coffin in which he had been placed was the First Commander squinting and still pointing the disrupter at the now empty space where Pell had existed just moments before.

Atia got up and rushed over to Ashto and threw her arms around him. 'Trevor, my dearest darling, I thought I'd lost you,' she said.

'I'm all right I think, Margot. Rather weak from loss of blood and still somewhat affected by Pell's drug, but still alive.'

'Oh, Trevor, I have never been so scared. I thought we were both going to die. You had the disrupter with you, where did it come from?'

'I found it in Pell's cellar and put it in my jacket pocket. Luckily he didn't discover it and I just about managed to retrieve it before he was able to use his firearm on you.' Ashto dropped the disrupter and looked distraught. 'Margot, I'm so glad that Pell didn't harm you but I have just realised that for the first time I have taken a life… I have killed a sapient individual!'

'You had no choice, Trevor, it was him or us and…' Atia stopped as she heard a loud noise. Someone was battering down the gates of the warehouse and shouting.

33

An Explanation

It had been a frantic dash to the docks for Detective Inspector Reid and Sergeant Thick. They had looked in vain for signs of Pell and Mrs Ashton around the St Katherine's Dock area before moving on to the Wapping Basin. It was there they found two uniformed officers who were investigating the sightings of a mad woman who had been seen driving a hansom cab in a reckless fashion through the streets around the Basin. Reid and the other policemen had then discovered the stolen cab, its horse tied to a mooring post alongside a deserted looking warehouse at Gun Wharf. When they heard gunfire come from inside the building a large metal bar had been found which enabled them to force open the bolted gates of the warehouse and, led by Inspector Reid, the small group of police officers entered the building.

Shining bull's-eye lamps into the inside of the dark

warehouse what they saw was mystifying. As well as Pell's hearse and the two black horses standing placidly by, sitting up in a coffin, was Mr Ashton, seemingly bleeding badly and covered in a great deal of blood, his arms chained to two heavy looking dumbbells. The coffin itself seemed to contain not only a chained up Mr Ashton but also some large rocks. Next to Ashton, kneeling beside him and with her arms lovingly around him, looking somewhat dishevelled and very much the worse for wear, was Mrs Ashton.

'Where's Pell?' said Reid, concerned that a crazed killer was still on the loose somewhere.

'Er…' Atia was not sure what she should tell the police and for once was unsure about what to say.

Ashto nodded his head towards the open trap door: 'down there, Inspector. My wife managed to push him and his gun into the river and I believe he has gone for good.'

'We'll see about that,' said Reid, 'bodies that go into the river usually end up being washed up on the foreshore further down stream.'

'Or washed out to sea,' said Sergeant Thick. Reid nodded.

'The gunshot we heard, what was that?' said Reid.

'That was Pell's gun. Margot managed to grab his arm before he was able to target her.'

'Mr Ashton, how are you, you seem to be bleeding very badly?' Reid indicated to the uniformed officers to help free the undercover Jaran from the chains.

'It probably looks worse than it actually is,' said the First Commander, feeling his neck and then examining his bloody hand.

'We'll need to get you to hospital and get that wound seen to. It looks nasty; what did Pell do?'

'He bit into my husband's neck and drank – sucked up in fact – rather a lot of his blood,' said Atia, her voice quavering. She had rarely felt quite so emotional as she did at that moment.

'A hospital visit is unnecessary, the wound looks much worse than it actually is, Inspector.' Ashto pulled out his handkerchief from his top pocket and held it firmly against his injury.

'Well, if you are absolutely sure, Mr Ashton,' said the inspector somewhat skeptically. Reid then looked at Atia. 'Mrs Ashton, you will need to answer a few questions about your actions today.'

'What actions would they be?' said Atia.

'For a start, Mrs Ashton, how about hindering and perhaps attacking a police officer in the course of his duty, taking a hansom cab without the owner's permission and driving it illegally and recklessly through the streets of the city endangering the lives of others.'

'I am very willing to answer any questions you might have, Inspector but first you must let me look after my husband.'

'Of course, Mrs Ashton, that goes without saying. We will return the hansom you, shall we say for now, borrowed and provide you and your husband with transport back to Whitechapel. We will interview you both at Leman Street police station tomorrow morning, if that is acceptable to you?'

'That is completely acceptable and thank you Inspector for being so understanding,' said Atia smiling, pleased that she would have some time to enable her and Ashto to come up with a plausible explanation for the various events of the day.

'How does your neck feel now, Trevor?'

'It is fine, Margot, and does not hurt. I am extremely glad I did not have to attend one of the London hospitals. The likelihood is I would never have come out alive.'

'Yes, medical practise on this planet has a very long way to go yet before they can be considered to be anything other than primitive. And also they might have been overly interested in your Jaran anatomy, particularly your two hearts.'

'That is certainly true, Margot. Well, are you ready to enter the lion's den again?'

Atia smiled at the First Commander's usage of another Earth idiom. Just lately he was becoming very adept at employing them in an appropriate way. She was glad to see that every day he, like she, was becoming more and more immersed in the culture and language prevalent in this part of the planet Earth.

The two undercover Jaran explorers stood on the pavement outside Leman Street police station before giving each other a fond, supportive smile, climbing the steps and entering the building.

'Good morning, Mr and Mrs Ashton, I hope you have both recovered from the extraordinary events of yesterday.' Inspector Reid stood as the Jaran couple was shown into his office by the desk sergeant.

'Thank you, Inspector, we have both fully recovered I am very pleased to say.'

'That is very good news indeed.' Reid's smile suddenly changed to a quizzical look. 'Mr Ashton, the wound on your neck appears to be almost healed up!'

Ashto's hand went up to where Pell's artificial fangs had torn painfully into his neck. The basic med kit they had brought with them from their explorer-class spacecraft had proved to be very effective in repairing the damage that Pell had caused to the First Commander's neck quickly healing up the puncture holes the crazed undertaker had inflicted with his artificial fangs. The pink scar tissue that had been left was already beginning to fade. 'Er, well, Inspector, as I intimated yesterday the injury did appear to be far worse than it actually was; the amount of blood was, I believe, somewhat misleading.'

For a moment Reid looked highly skeptical and was about to question Ashto further about the wound and how it had healed up so soon before thinking better of it and shrugging. More important issues at hand, he thought. 'Now, Mr and Mrs Ashton, as you know I have a number of questions about what went on yesterday. At this point I am not going to charge either of you for any crime, but depending on your answers to my questions that may very well change. Do you understand?'

'Perfectly,' said the First Commander. Atia nodded in agreement.

'Very well, now please excuse me. I am just going to fetch my Sergeant who will make some notes on our conversation. I will not be long.' Reid got up and left the room.

'Do you think the inspector will believe our story, Trevor?'

'I think so, Margot. After all it is more or less the truth.' Ashto winked at his Apprentice Commander, another Earth affectation that he had picked up recently.

In minutes Reid returned with Sergeant Thick in tow. Both policemen sat down and looked at the Jaran couple.

Reid began: 'Mr Ashton can you tell me what you were doing in the house of Mr Pell?'

'I would have thought that was obvious, Inspector. Pell was a murderer and my wife and I wanted him caught and brought to justice.'

'Why did you not just inform the authorities about your suspicions and leave it to the police to arrest him?'

'Well, Inspector, we needed to provide some proof for that to happen effectively.'

Reid looked bemused. 'Mrs Ashton, can I ask you what you did to Constable Evans that caused him to collapse outside Pell's house?'

'I did nothing, Inspector. He just fainted away soon after we saw the undertaker's hearse leave the premises. Unfortunately I did not have the time to revive him, as I needed to follow Pell, so I left him lying comfortably on the ground. He will probably need to consult a medical practitioner if his fainting fits become more regular.'

Reid shook his head out of puzzlement. 'Mrs Ashton, you were seen speedily running down the street towards Russell Square where you drove off in a hansom cab that you took without the permission of the driver. You do not, I presume, have a cabbie's license, which would enable you to drive such a vehicle, so these are two crimes you definitely committed yesterday both of which could result in you being charged. Do you understand?'

'I do, Inspector, and let me apologise for both of my actions but they were the only possible measures I could take under the circumstances because, as you know, my husband's life was seriously in danger.'

Inspector Reid sighed. 'Mrs Ashton, in this country we

do not take the law into our own hands. That may be the way they do things in the United States of America but your actions yesterday were completely unacceptable here if not to say outrageous. As a result you, as a foreign national, may find yourself being deported out of this country and never allowed to return.'

'That would be completely unfair, Inspector,' said the First Commander. 'My wife performed those extraordinary deeds in order to save my life; surely she should not be punished for that?'

'Mr Ashton, can I ask you what you witnessed in the warehouse which, as we have discovered, was rented by Pell and where you were taken by him?'

'Inspector, I am afraid I witnessed very little of what took place. I had been drugged at gunpoint by Pell at his residence and was therefore unable to move. I was placed in a coffin and taken to the warehouse in, I assume, Pell's hearse. At the warehouse I was eventually able for the first time to sit up where I saw my wife bravely deal with Pell and the gun he was holding by pushing him through the trapdoor and into the river. By the way, has his body been washed up yet?'

'Not as yet, Mr Ashton, sometimes it takes many days for bodies in the Thames to reappear again. Mrs Ashton, can I ask you how you, a member of the weaker sex, if you don't mind me saying so, managed to overpower Mr Pell, who was armed with a revolver I believe?'

'Indeed he was armed, But as you can see, Inspector, despite my belonging to the weaker sex as you put it, I am tall and I have always tried to ensure that my strength and fitness levels are as high as possible. Pell on the other hand was rather short in stature and also suffering at the time from the effects of imbibing some of his own drug when he bit into my husband's neck and drank some of his blood. I therefore had no problem at all in dealing with the odious man by pushing him though the open trapdoor and into the river.'

Reid nodded. He looked at Mrs Margot Ashton. She was definitely the most remarkable looking female he had ever seen; of that there was no doubt. In fact he had never come across a woman who was almost six feet tall and who looked quite so strongly robust as she did, while also being so very attractive looking. As he sat there staring at her he thought he would not fancy his chances engaging in an arm-wrestling contest with her. 'Mr Ashton and Mrs Ashton, I still do not understand why and how you became involved with the undertaker, Pell, in the first instance. How did you discover that he was responsible for the series of murders that have taken place recently, including the murder of one of our own officers, PC Perkins?'

'Well, Inspector Reid it was the cruel death of Constable Perkins that persuaded us to see if we could discover who the murderer was. We had become quite attached to the young officer when he had followed us around for so long including when we left London for an extended journey to the north of the country.'

'How did you know he was following you?' said a surprised Inspector Reid.

'Oh, come now, Inspector, your officers may be very skilled in the various roles they are ordered to undertake by you but undercover surveillance is an area where, I believe, more training needs to be provided by yourself and the police authorities in the future,' said Atia.

Reid glanced at his sergeant and shook his head in a resigned way. He looked back at the Apprentice Commander. 'Mrs Ashton, I am sure we will consider your suggested improvements, but I would still like to know why you suspected Pell in the first place?'

'Inspector, you will recall that I was detained by the police whilst wearing the disguise of a telegraph boy and after I had been struck on the head by Pell in his house.'

'I do recall that incident, Mrs Ashton, how could I possibly forget it? Please go on.'

'Well, Inspector, I had adopted that disguise to enable me to gain entrance to a house in Cleveland Street that we believed, my husband and I that is, to have been the location where the so-called Vampire Killer had met some of his victims prior to murdering them. It was there I saw Pell, who we had briefly met previously, and begun a conversation with him. He invited me back to his residence, but unfortunately it seems that he had seen through my subterfuge and struck me on the head with a rather heavy poker before calling the police and claiming I was a burglar.'

'I see, Mrs Ashton. Can you tell me how you came to find out about the building in Cleveland Street, which is a location the police have been interested in for some time due to possible illegal activities that had been taking place there?'

'Inspector, I am loathe to criticise this society's views towards homosexuality and freedom of expression generally but making such practises illegal has done nothing else but drive certain individuals to seek out such harmless pleasures underground and in secret. It is little wonder that such deranged individuals such as Pell would be drawn towards such an unnecessary and secretive world and take advantage of the situation. And besides it has to be said the police seemed to be done very little with regard to investigating the goings-on in the Cleveland Street house despite knowing that some of the murder victims had visited the building.'

Edmund Reid felt a sudden sense of frustration on hearing the words of Mrs Ashton. She had just said exactly what he had been saying about the Cleveland Street house for some time and he was still annoyed that had been stopped by those higher up the chain of command from investigating the activities there. 'Mrs Ashton, there are reasons why the property in Cleveland Street is not subject to our immediate investigations that I cannot divulge,' said Reid sharply. 'I would very much like to know from where you obtained your information. You seem to be privy to a great amount of detail that has not, as far as I know, been made public.'

Atia felt that she had probably said too much about the situation. She had thought that her explanation so far would have satisfied her police interrogator but now realised that she would have to come up with a believable reason for why she and the First Commander knew quite so much about the man the newspapers had named the Vampire Killer. 'Mr Rogers, the journalist who works for the Evening Standard, was conducting his own investigation into the activities in Cleveland Street. He passed on to us most of the information we know.' First Commander Ashto looked at his Apprentice Commander and raised a questioning eyebrow.

'I see, Mrs Ashton. I do believe we will need to talk to Mr Rogers and discover who his informant in the police service is.'

'Inspector,' said Ashto, 'Mr Rogers is a highly intelligent young man. I believe he came to his conclusions about the importance of the house in Cleveland Street without very much help from the police and by simply observing the comings and goings at the building.'

Reid thought that Ashton was probably right in his reading of the matter but was annoyed that his superior, Chief Inspector Abberline had not let him conduct a raid on the Cleveland Street property when he had originally wanted to. Deaths, particularly that of PC Perkins, might well have been avoided if he had had his own way. 'That's as may be, Mr Ashton, but there are still the charges pending against Mrs Ashton. The idea that foreign visitors can go around London purloining hansom cabs for their own use is not something we can take lightly.'

'But you now know, Inspector, that my wife did that to save my life. The undertaker, Mr Pell was clearly insane and would have killed me if Margot had not driven the cab to the docks to search for me. If she had not acted in the way she did I would now be dead and you would still be looking for a ruthless killer.'

'That is completely true of course, Mr Ashton, but the law is the law and a number of laws have obviously been broken by your wife.' Reid looked at Atia who smiled benignly at him. He was just about to officially charge the woman he knew as Mrs Margot Ashton with taking a cab without the owner's permission and with driving a hansom illegally and without a cabman's licence, when the door to his office was flung open and in walked the impressive figure of Detective Chief Inspector Frederick Abberline: 'A word please, Edmund,' he said in a booming voice.

34

Chief Inspector Abberline Pulls Rank

'Sit down, Edmund,' said the tall, bewhiskered Detective Chief Inspector.

Reid had followed Abberline into a nearby interview room closing the door behind him.

'What's this about, Sir?' said Reid.

'Edmund, how long have we known each other?'

'A long time, Sir; ever since we were both young detectives at Leman Street nick.'

'That's right Edmund – call me by my first name by the way – we've both seen a lot of villains and crooks come and go over the years in Whitechapel and beyond, far too many to name I should think.'

'That's certainly true, Fred.'

'Locked up a lot of 'em and sent a few to the gallows too.'

'Certainly, Fred, can I ask what this has got to do with…?'

'Don't interrupt, Edmund. There are some important things happening in the background that you have no idea about. You know, just lately, I've been thinking ahead to my retirement – it's only a few years off now – thought I might do a bit of travelling with the missus. They say Monte Carlo is very nice; warm and sunny there I believe, or so people tell me anyway. Afterwards I thought I might settle down in Bournemouth – I was born near there y'know – the air down south will be good after all the dirt, smoke and pea-souper fogs in London… I'm looking forward to it… so many pressures in this job… can't do it for too long… it'll drive you mad eventually.'

'Fred, what's all this about?'

'Yes, Edmund, let me come to the point. You know that in our job there are many people we must consider when we take our actions regarding the law. Sometimes there are people, important people, we have to listen to carefully before we make our decisions.'

'Fred, is this about Cleveland Street?'

'It is, Edmund, it is. Orders have come from up on high regarding that blasted and benighted place. For the time being, as I've said to you before, we are to leave it alone and untouched. There are certain individuals, one in particular, who have shown up at that building who really shouldn't have and it is not in the public interest that they should be identified. We do not want to stir up a hornets' nest that could even lead to the fall of the Government and a state of general anarchy.'

'Meaning?'

'Meaning we are to ignore it for the present and leave it out of any such investigation regarding this Vampire Killer person, as the press have ridiculously christened him.'

'You say "for the present" – what do you mean by that?'

'There *will* come a time, Edmund, at some point in the future, when that molly house in Cleveland Street will be raided and its owners and participants arrested and some of them, undoubtedly, will be locked up behind bars. But for the time being we must wait until the individual I referred to earlier, and his friends for that matter, are not present in London but out of the country enjoying the sunshine in some far off foreign haunt. Then we will, I promise you, bring the full force of the law down on those who frequent that den of iniquity.'

'This individual you speak of?'

'Do not enquire any further, Edmund. The less you know the better it is for you.'

'Very well, Fred, but how does this affect my current case involving the two Americans?'

'Edmund, you will let them go without any charge. The less fuss about the events surrounding this case the better; we do not want to give the gentlemen of the press any reason to speculate further on such matters. We will forget about that barmy undertaker, Pell. Sadly, he seems to have been just another individual, one of many, who has decided to take his own life in the Thames, his body never to be recovered. Just another sad statistic I'm afraid. Those *items* in his house will be taken away and disposed of without any fuss or publicity. No one will ever know the ins and outs of this case, Edmund. There will be no more talk of the Vampire Killer ever again!'

Edmund Reid shook his head. 'Fred, this is not how things should be. No one should be above the law, whoever they are. If this important person you speak of is guilty of a crime then he should be punished just like anyone else.'

'You are correct of course, Edmund, in theory. But in reality the world is not like that. There is a certain elderly lady, who sometimes resides in this city of ours, who would not be at all amused if details of this individual's peccadillos were revealed to the public's gaze. So you, like I, will do as we are told and drop this case like a very hot potato and move on to something else. There are plenty of those to choose from I believe. Concentrate on those bomb outrages and threats by the Fenians; that always gets the public's attention away from more, shall we say, delicate matters. A bit of terrorist activity invariably gives the police, and the government for that matter, plenty of public sympathy. And what about those counterfeit coins eh? Are they still turning up?'

'They seem to have stopped. The counterfeiters must have eventually realised their stupid mistake I suppose. Is that all, Fred? I'll get back to my two American guests if that is all right by you.'

'Yes, Edmund that is all, but remember what you have been told.' Abberline sighed loudly.

Reid nodded at the Chief Inspector and left the room. Abberline watched him go, looked down at his pocket watch, tutted and, looking thoroughly annoyed and downcast, left Leman Street police station.

'Well, Trevor, that outcome was very surprising,' said Apprentice Commander Atia.

'It was, Margot. I was convinced that Inspector Reid at one point was about to charge you with committing two crimes which would have led to our mission on Earth to be cancelled,' replied First Commander Ashto.

The two Jarans had left Leman Street and were on their way back to the guesthouse room in Bell Lane.

'Why do you think the inspector let us go, Trevor?'

'I'm not sure, Margot. It would be interesting to find out. Perhaps we should search out Mr Rogers and ask him, as he seems to know everything that takes place at Leman Street police station. I have also noticed that he seems to be paying you plenty of attention again.'

'Trevor, do I detect a hint of jealousy in your voice?'

Ashto smiled. 'Just a little, Margot, mainly due to the fact that you and he are due to meet again for dinner at Fortescues.'

'Yes, Trevor, but as I have already mentioned to you that was unavoidable in the circumstances.'

'I know, Margot,' said the First Commander, smiling broadly at the woman who the world viewed as his wife.

'Oh, and Trevor.'

'Yes, Margot?'

'This time at Fortescues' there is to be no surreptitious use of the fly drone.'

'I understand, Margot. I will ensure that no errant fly will disturb your dinner companion on this occasion.' The First Commander could not suppress a chuckle as he thought back to the previous occasion where Mr Rogers had taken Atia for a meal and he had distracted and annoyed the newspaperman with a fly drone, causing him to shout out and disturb the quiet atmosphere of the exclusive dining establishment. This time he would have to leave the young and handsome journalist, annoyingly taking Atia for dinner, unbothered by Jaran made mechanical flying insects.

Atia smiled at the First Commander as the Jaran couple waited to cross the busy Whitechapel High Street. As they walked across the road, arm in arm and carefully avoiding the large piles of horse dung that as usual littered the street, both felt pleased that their mission on Earth would now be able to continue. They had much to see and do and over the next four years and they would endeavour to ensure they had no more dealings with the police or crazed psychotic killers. Walking up Goulston Street towards Mrs Smith's Select Guesthouse both of the Jarans silently hoped that their days of investigating crimes perpetrated by Earth humans were definitely over.

35

Fortescues' Restaurant Again

Apprentice Commander Atia looked around at the ornate dining room of Fortescues' restaurant. She was relieved to see there were no signs of flies, real or drone-like, flitting around the crowded but quiet room where only restrained conversation, the clinking of wineglasses and the occasional metallic chink of cutlery could be heard. Atia smiled at William Rogers, the Evening Standard reporter, who had called for her in Bell Lane at a prearranged time and who now sat opposite her at the table, which was covered with its gleaming white linen. Mr Rogers and Atia had enjoyed their main course of roast beef and were now nibbling on grapes and a selection of cheeses and contentedly sipping red wine.

'So, Mrs Ashton, after all your exploits you escaped the

clutches of the Metropolitan Police with only a warning?' said Rogers.

'That is correct, Mr Rogers. Inspector Reid had realised I believe that I had had no alternative but to commit two minor crimes in order to save the life of my husband and so he let me walk free without any charge to blacken my reputation.' Atia smiled broadly at the young newspaperman as she popped a small piece of Stilton cheese in her mouth.

'I would so love to publish the account of your exciting and madcap dash through the city in a stolen hansom cab. It would make a wonderful story for the readers of my newspaper.'

'Now, Mr Rogers, you have promised that you will not write about what happened to my husband and me in your paper. I would, of course, vehemently deny anything that appeared in print and I am also sure the police authorities would be extremely annoyed with you if that should happen. You would doubtless lose all the exclusive privileges you have gained with the local policing authorities as a result.'

'I know, Mrs Ashton. In fact the police have already given me a very explicit warning about what would happen if any reference is made to your amazing story of derring-do in print. But still it is indeed a great pity that your exploits of the other day will never be revealed to the reading public.'

'I am sure you will soon have plenty of other stories to write about in the future, Mr Rogers.'

'I do hope so, Mrs Ashton.' Rogers took a sip from his wineglass and smiled at Atia. 'I believe that in the not too distant future I will be given exclusive rights to a story regarding that infamous house in Cleveland Street.'

'Was that part of Inspector Reid's bribe to stop you writing about any more about the Vampire Killer?'

'That is quite correct, Mrs Ashton, although I would prefer the term incentive rather than bribe. By the way isn't it about time we were on first name terms… Margot?'

'I do not think so, Mr Rogers. There are certain proprieties that ought to be observed and maintained in a civilised society, do you not agree?' said Atia smiling again at the young reporter.

'I suppose that is the case, Mrs Ashton,' said Mr Rogers sounding disappointed.

'So, Mr Rogers, what will happen to the Cleveland Street establishment, do you think?'

'Well, Mrs Ashton, at some point in the future it will be raided by the police. That will result in its owners being arrested and many of its cliental named and inevitably subsequently shamed and vilified in some sections of the press.'

'And when will this raid take place?'

'My guess would be in the summertime when a certain individual, who is known to frequent the house, along with his friends, will be away on his annual holidays in the South of France and a scandal of epic proportions will therefore be avoided.'

'And this all-important individual would be?'

'I'm surprised that you do not already know of whom it is I speak. His name has been bandied about for all sorts of reasons in the past two years or so and is widely known in Fleet Street, although no reputable newspaper would ever print his name and risk being closed down for good.'

'Are you referring to a member of the Royal Family?'

Rogers took a glance around the room and leaned across the table to be nearer Atia. Whispering he said: 'indeed I am, Mrs Ashton, to be precise none other than Prince Albert Victor Christian Edward, grandson of the Queen and Heir Presumptive to the throne. It has been well known that the young man has certain proclivities that would not be deemed acceptable to the general public and a scandal involving him and his friends would inevitably bring down the government and perhaps even threaten the stability of the throne itself.'

Atia sat back looking thoughtful. 'Tell me, Mr Rogers do you not think that the persecution of individuals because of their sexual orientation is the result of an unfair law that ought to be abolished.'

William Rogers considered himself to be very broadminded but to hear such words and views put forward by a well brought up woman still shocked him and made him blush.

'Er, Mrs Ashton, I have never heard the phrase "sexual orientation" before' (he blushed even further) 'but I assume you are referring to male homosexuality, the practise of which is considered to be a crime punishable by imprisonment and hard labour.' Rogers had leant forward again and whispered to Atia. He had never ever thought that he would be saying such words aloud and discussing such matters with a woman as refined as Mrs Ashton. He sat back again in his chair as he was interrupted by a waiter who brought coffee to their table. Rogers was surprised to see Atia smiling at him.

'Mr Rogers, there are many aspects of your... our society that should be improved in my opinion. In the future I am sure that such matters regarding an individual's sexuality will become far more acceptable and that love and affection between members of the same sex will eventually be decriminalized.'

'Decriminalised is another interesting word I have never before encountered, Mrs Ashton. Your American idioms are something I must utilise far more often in my writing in the future. And can I say how very unusual, open-minded and progressive your views are, particularly for someone of your social status. There are many of us who would like to see such changes take place in what we consider an extremely over-conservative, old fashioned and repressed society.'

'Well, Mr Rogers, you should not stop working to improve society. Progress can only be made by well-meaning individuals continually striving to bring about such improvements. As visitors to your country, Mr Ashton and I have found many aspects of your current society in want of fundamental change. We have very often commented, for example, on the huge and quite immoral differences there are in Britain between the rich and poor and we… what is it, Mr Rogers?' Atia had noticed that the young newspaperman was staring at her and smiling broadly.

'Mrs Ashton, you are without doubt the most unique woman I have ever met. Not only very beautiful but also highly intelligent. You really are a credit to your sex and I'm so very glad that I know you. If only you were not already spoken for I would be…'

'Mr Rogers, that is quite enough. I am a happily married woman and although I may hold views that would be considered by many to be highly progressive in regard to many aspects of life in the world at large, I still know how to maintain certain modes of decorum and behaviour.'

Atia looked sternly at the young reporter to emphasise her words before smiling at him again. 'However, Mr Rogers, I still regard you as a friend and I am sure that our friendly relations will continue into the future. Now I do believe that my husband is waiting outside with a cab in order to accompany me back to our residence and I would not like to keep him waiting for any length of time.'

Rogers looked puzzled: 'Mrs Ashton, how do you know he's outside?'

Atia tapped her nose. 'That particular insight is for me to know, Mr Rogers. Goodbye and thank you for tonight's meal and also a most pleasant and enlightening evening.' Atia stood ensuring that the small earpiece, which was disguised as an earring and through which Ashto had just contacted her, was still firmly in place.'

As she left the dining room Rogers stood staring after her. Not only was Mrs Ashton beautiful and highly intelligent, he thought, but she was also the most mysterious and intriguing woman he had ever met.

'I heard what Rogers said to you, Margot. I can't say that I'm very pleased with his behaviour towards you to say the least. He is, in my opinion, far too forward in his attitude.'

Atia smiled at Ashto's seeming adoption of the norms of this restrained Victorian environment in which they now lived. 'He is a very young and impetuous individual, Trevor and you will also have heard what I said in reply to him. I think that he remains a very good contact for us to have regarding our mission here on planet Earth.' Atia, still smiling fondly at Ashto, held his hand and sat back and relaxed in her seat in the hansom cab as it travelled through the busy London streets towards their guesthouse in Whitechapel.

'Besides, now that my debt of honour to Mr Rogers has been paid by agreeing to dine with him this evening, I'm now back here with you and it is you who will have my constant attention for the rest of the evening, particularly once we have retired for the night and we are in bed together. That is something I am looking forward to immensely,' said Atia with a very large twinkle in her eye.

Ashto smiled back. He felt very happy now that Atia's meeting with the newspaperman was over and he had Atia all to himself again and he also looked forward to the rest of the evening. Jarans, on the whole were not passionate individuals in their normal environment, but life here on the Earth over the past few months had made both Ashto and Atia feel far more emotional and loving towards each other than ever they could have imagined before. Both sat back feeling happy and expectant as the horse pulling their cab clip-clopped its way towards their adopted Whitechapel home.

Report Number 0017 to the Glorious and Munificent Jaran Galactic Federation High Council (Planetary Exploration and Viable Exo-Planet Evaluation Committee – Sector 2007 Sub-Committee) by First Commander Treve Pacton Ashto.

My greetings and utmost felicitations to the esteemed members of the sub-committee.

Again I must apologise for my lack of reports recently but Apprentice Commander Atia and I have been inordinately busy of late. As well as our continuing task of the gathering of information and data regarding this planet known as the Earth we have, as I alluded to in my last report, also been involved in the tracking down of another local and mentally unbalanced serial killer. This psychotic individual seemed to have had an uncontrollable urge to imbibe the blood of his victims prior to murdering them and then draining their bodies of their remaining blood to purportedly use in completely insane experiments aimed at restoring youthfulness in humans. Thanks to the Apprentice Commander I was very fortunate to escape from his clutches after he had drugged and threatened to kill me.

On Jara of course such an unstable individual would be treated for his obsession and eventually cured and rehabilitated, but on this planet very little is known about the treatment of any sort of mental illness. Those who suffer from psychological disorders, both mild and profound, are not offered any efficacious treatment at all but are often merely locked away in, what are called here, lunatic asylums. Many are never released and spend their entire life in such places, where conditions are notoriously abysmal. This is obviously an area of study that the Apprentice Commander and I will need to conduct more research into in the future.

Hopefully there will be no more serial murderers emerging in London and particularly here in the Whitechapel district, in the near future. This part of the city has very much become our adopted home and we have grown to appreciate its general atmosphere as well as the people here, most of whom battle against a background of extreme poverty the like of which would be difficult for those back on Jara to even comprehend. Despite this most of the residents of the area are optimistic and determined to survive and prosper against all the odds. Crime is high of course but the majority of criminals are no more than petty thieves who are not generally prone to violence. Indeed there is much to admire in the physical and mental make-up of Earth humans and I am beginning to believe that the inclusion of this planet into the Galactic Federation would be a very positive development for all those concerned. Over the next few months the Apprentice Commander and I will hope to provide the sub-committee with plenty of evidence to support this view.

That is all for now, I will report again soon. Just one final point – Atia and I have still not yet received any kind of feedback from the sub-committee regarding our findings so far. Is everything back home all right? Is there anything we need to be briefed about? Please let us know at the earliest opportunity.

With my utmost loyalty to the glorious Jaran Galactic Federation,

First Commander Treve Pacton Ashto.

36

A Second Visit to the Beefsteak Room.

'Welcome, Mr and Mrs Ashton, Trevor and Margot, I am so pleased to see you again.' Bram Stoker had greeted the Jaran pair with genuine warmth at the front of the Lyceum theatre.

'And we feel very much the same, Bram. How are you?' said Ashto, shaking Mr Stoker's hand. Atia smiled and nodded her agreement.

'Very well, very well indeed, Trevor. As you know the theatre is currently closed for the summer with Henry Irving away on holiday somewhere in Europe – Bavaria I believe on this occasion. Do you know he is so determined to discover what the architecture in that region is like that he has taken the Lyceum's main scene painter, a chap called Harker with him in order to make sketches with a view of reproducing them as accurate backdrops for a future production at the theatre? Henry really is quite incorrigible and very adept at spending the theatre's money.'

'I imagine that adds certain complications to your business manager's role at the Lyceum?' said Atia.

'Indeed it does, but to be fair Henry usually knows what he is doing in that regard. Anyway, how are you my dear lady?' said Stoker, taking Atia's hand and kissing it while looking longingly into the eyes of the Apprentice Commander. Atia was reminded how she seemed to have become a focus for Bram Stoker's amorous attentions.

'I am very well too,' said Atia smiling inwardly again at the rather silly Earth custom of the kissing of female hands. 'Can I inquire how your writing and your researches into the superstitions of Eastern European countries are progressing?'

'Very well, Margot, very well I must say. As you know our visit to Whitby gave me a great many ideas that I have been thinking about since then and with the theatre closed I have had plenty of time to sit in my office and write in an undisturbed fashion.'

'Are you still planning to write a story about mysterious counts, wolves that are half-human and things that go bump in the night, Mr Stoker?' said Atia.

'I certainly am, dear lady, but please call be Bram. I shall endeavour to tell you more about my poor scribblings this evening but shall we make our way to the Beefsteak Room? We have another guest who I think you will be very keen to meet.'

Bram Stoker led Ashto and Atia down the plushly carpeted corridor to the rear of the Lyceum theatre and into the ornate oak panelled dining room that was the inner sanctum of Henry Irving and his closest staff at the theatre. It was a place where excellent food would be served, fine wine and brandy would be drunk, cigars smoked, and plays and literature would be discussed at length and where some of the great and good of Victorian literary society would occasionally be invited to dine with Irving and Stoker. As the Jarans and Stoker entered the Beefsteak Room, with its paintings and beamed ceiling, a tall, rather portly man, with unusually long hair and dressed in a deep blue, velvet suit put down his cigar and rose to greet them.

'May I introduce the writer, Mr Oscar Wilde. I believe, Mrs Ashton, that you have expressed a desire to meet him.'

In spite of herself Atia felt a little overwhelmed to come face to face with a man about whom she had recently read so much and who she had admired from afar. Notoriously flamboyant in his dress and actions Wilde bowed extravagantly to the new arrivals, his hair flopping over his face, and gently took Atia's hand and kissed it before shaking Ashto's hand and smiling broadly.

'I am so very pleased to see you, Mr and Mrs Ashton. Bram has told me so much about you and I am looking forward to hearing your very vivid descriptions of your home in the United States, a wonderful country in which I spent many months touring a few years' ago,' said Wilde.

'I believe the Americans did not quite know what to make of you, Oscar,' said Bram Stoker.

'That is so very true, but I have to say that one of the outstanding memories of my lecture tour was drinking some rather rough whisky with the miners of Leadville, Colorado. Have you ever visited there, Mr and Mrs Ashton?'

'I'm afraid we haven't had that particular pleasure,' said Atia.

'Well you really ought, it is a most fascinating place. Although the miners there are uneducated working men they showed a great deal of genuine interest in not only my ideas about the English Renaissance in Art, which was the subject of my lecture, but also in my capacity to consume a great amount of their so-called rotgut whisky to the extent that I was indeed the last man standing at the end of the evening. They were also most impressed the following morning when I suggested we should resume our whisky drinking as part of our breakfast. But probably the main thing about your country I discovered on my tour was that America has never quite forgiven Europe for having been discovered somewhat earlier in history than itself,' said Wilde smiling in a disarming way that seemed to suggest that nothing he was going to say during this evening should be taken too seriously, although it would undoubtedly be highly entertaining.

Atia was able to discern that, like Bram Stoker, Oscar Wilde had preserved just a small part of his Dublin Irish accent. Overcoming her nerves at meeting the great man Atia was keen to ask him about his recent writings. 'I so enjoyed the fairy tales you published last year, Mr Wilde, they gave me a great deal of pleasure.'

'*The Happy Prince and Other Stories* gave me an equal amount of pleasure whilst writing them, I can assure you, Mrs Ashton. But I hear from Bram that you are both researching a travel volume about our country, a task that sounds quite fascinating.'

Oscar Wilde sounded so sincere in his comment that

Atia immediately felt saddened that the book they had told so many they were planning to write would never actually be written. There was something about Oscar Wilde's openness that she almost wanted to own up to the fact that they were merely interplanetary travellers, explorers from another world who were researching the Earth's future potential as a member of the Jaran Galactic Federation. She had a feeling that this large, friendly and genial man would actually believe her and take it fully in his stride.

'That is true, Mr Wilde, although this evening we would much rather hear about your and Bram's writing than our own poor attempts at producing something of literary value,' said Ashto.

'Well, Bram I know is thoroughly hell-bent on writing a terrifyingly gothic tale about dark castles and huge bats that turn into voracious vampires. Every so often he tells me about some of the ideas he has come up with and although I love superstitions I have had to ask him to stop talking before he causes me to have nightmares. But, as I have said before, nothing succeeds like excess.'

Stoker laughed loudly at Wilde's comment and Ashto and Atia quickly joined in despite not fully appreciating Wilde's bon mot.

'I wonder if you could tell me, Mr Wilde, about what you are working on at the moment?' said the somewhat starstruck Apprentice Commander.

Wilde lit a cigarette after carefully inserting it into his cigarette holder with his long fingers. He smiled at Atia who had noticed that Oscar Wilde, despite his wit and seemingly confident repartee, constantly smoked probably in order to offset his nerves at meeting new people she reasoned. 'Well,

Mrs Ashton, although I always make it a rule that I never discuss anything about my works in progress, however, for one so sublimely beautiful as yourself I will make a unique exception. I am currently writing a number of articles for magazines of one sort or another, notably *The Pall Mall Gazette*, which always pays better than the others and then there's my diary, which I always have near me, particularly when I'm travelling and require something sensational to read.'

Atia and the others laughed.

'And then, of course, I am planning to write more fiction,' Wilde continued. 'For example I want to write plays that will doubtless eventually be performed at this very theatre under the auspices of our generous hosts.' Wilde looked at Stoker and smiled broadly. 'And, very much against my better judgement, I am planning to write an extended work of fiction that will, I assume, be serialised in one or other of the magazines that tediously pester me for such work. It will tell the story of a sublime looking man who makes a Faustian bargain to never grow old and to always remain utterly beautiful. However, since I have maintained many times before that modern novels, despite having many good points, are quite unreadable I very much doubt that anyone will want to read the one I produce.'

'You underestimate yourself, Oscar,' said Stoker.

'That in itself would be a virtual impossibility, my dear Bram' said Wilde leaning back in his chair, blowing a long line of cigarette smoke from his mouth and looking very pleased with himself.

'Well, I shall certainly read it as it sounds so intriguing,' said Atia.

'Does your wife ever accompany you in your visits to evenings in this dining room, Mr Wilde?' said First Commander Ashto.

'Please call me Oscar and I will call you Trevor, if I may. Only very rarely in fact will Constance join me in a visit to this wonderful dining establishment. We do have two small sons and although we employ a nanny Connie does like to see the rascally pair as often as possible and actively enjoys putting them to bed herself. She will even occasionally direct me to read stories to Cyril and Vyvyan a task, which I have to say, I always relish and enjoy more than anything else imaginable. However, I will always bear in mind that children will begin by loving their parents but eventually end up judging them. Rarely, if ever, do children actually forgive their parents.' Wilde leant back in his seat and sucking deeply on his cigarette, looked satisfied while the others chuckled.

'Oscar, I do believe you are a friend of Mr Conan Doyle,' said Ashto.

'Perhaps more of a valued acquaintance, I would say,' said Wilde. 'Why do you ask?'

'Well, I very much enjoyed his novel called *A Study in Scarlet*, in which he wrote about the brilliant consulting detective Sherlock Holmes. I was wondering if he had mentioned to you whether he intends to write more about the great detective in the future.'

'Trevor, I do believe that Stoker is far more likely to know the answer to your question. Indeed I think I'm accurate in saying that he is distantly related to Arthur Conan Doyle. Is that not correct, Bram?' said Wilde.

'It is Trevor. In fact Arthur occasionally dines with us

here when he visits London and I do believe he plans to write more stories about Sherlock Holmes. Although he has a medical practice in Portsmouth at present to tell you all the truth I think he actually dislikes being a doctor and intends to become a full time writer in the future. In my opinion he will doubtless end up living in London, sooner rather than later.'

'That is very exciting news. I look forward to reading more about Mr Doyle's clever detective. I think the police would appreciate having such a man helping to solve crimes in London in reality,' said the First Commander.

'Talking about crimes,' said Oscar Wilde, is it true that you, Margot, found yourself recently commandeering a hansom cab in order to drive it around the East End?'

Atia was surprised: 'how did you come to hear about that, Mr Wilde?' she said blushing.

'Ah, that would be telling, Margot, and I'm afraid I cannot disclose my sources although I have an unerring ear for gossip especially the sort spread by the gentlemen of the press. But I would have to say if you are concerned about people discussing you and your exploits, Margot, I firmly believe there is only one thing worse than being talked about, and that is not being talked about,' said Wilde lighting another cigarette.

'Well, Mr Wilde... Oscar I mean, we were hoping that my little legal infraction would go unnoticed. It was, I have to say, a moment of madness that caused me to take the hansom cab and attempt to steer it through the streets of London. Luckily the police were able to see the amusing side of the matter and decided not to prosecute me for my foolish behaviour.' Atia looked at the First Commander who gave a nod that reassured Atia that she had handled the unexpected conversation in an acceptable fashion.

'What an amazing outcome, Margot,' said Wilde. 'It is highly unusual for the Metropolitan Police to ignore such shows of personal freedom! I would so love to have seen you, whip in hand, scattering pedestrians left, right and centre as you careened through the byways of the capital. Can you do it again please, so I can observe what must have been one of the true wonders of the age?'

'I do not think so, Oscar. My cab driving days are hopefully behind me forever.'

'What a pity, Margot, young women these days seem to make it the sole object of their lives to be always playing with fire, and you should not be left out,' said Wilde.

'No, Oscar, it was purely a one-off event I can assure you,' replied Atia.

'Margot, this is the first I have heard of your escapade,' said a surprised sounding Bram Stoker.

'It is not something of which I am proud and I have been trying to forget about the incident ever since it took place.'

'I understand, Margot. I have but one question however and then I shall never mention anything about it again. How on Earth did you learn to drive such a vehicle as a hansom cab?' said Stoker.

Atia paused for a few seconds while she quickly consulted her neural implant for some information. 'Well, er… back home in the United States of America there are plenty of opportunities for anyone to learn to drive such a horse drawn vehicle.'

'But a woman being able to control such a vehicle is very unusual to say the least,' replied Stoker.

'I think that in the future, Bram,' said Atia, 'there will be many areas of life that women will become adept at and will be able to display their skills in all sorts of ways. Hopefully the days when women are only seen as decorative items who leave all difficult tasks to males are soon to be numbered.'

'Hear, hear!' shouted Wilde. 'That's put you in your place, my dear Bram.'

Smiling, but looking rather abashed by the Apprentice Commander's words Stoker looked for a way to quickly change the subject: ringing the small bell on the table which was there to tell the waiters to spring into action he said: 'er… I do believe it is time for us to eat.'

37

A Very Unexpected Dining Companion

First Commander Ashto and Apprentice Commander Atia were relishing another pleasant evening in Fortescues' restaurant. Winter in this part of planet Earth had now passed and a few early signs of summer had begun to arrive. In a few months' time the Jaran pair would be celebratingced the first completed year of their mission and both felt satisfied about what they had so far accomplished and the data they had managed to gather in such a relatively short time. Yes, their forays into the tracking down of two serial murderers had been something of a distraction from their main mission but even the events surrounding the killers they had dealt with had told them a great deal about Earth humans and their psychological make-up. They had also learned much about how the policing authorities operated in London – both their successes and shortcomings.

The Jaran pair had just finished their roast beef dinner and were enjoying a very nice French red wine while smiling fondly at each other when they were interrupted by a tall, raven-haired and very distinguished looking woman in an expensive dark blue dress who, without any sort of introduction, seated herself at their table. The Jarans were now so very well adapted to how things were done on Earth that both felt suitably affronted by this sudden example of such rude behaviour.

'Excuse me, Madam, can I ask you why you have interrupted my wife and me in such an impolite manner?' said Ashto.

'Ah, we'd suspected you might have gone somewhat native, as the Earth humans might say, First Commander Treve Pacton Ashto, and you've certainly seem to have mastered all the correct phrases in this rather complicated language they call English. But although you may fool the primitive inhabitants of this planet with your disguise and your conversation you do not in any way fool me. So get off your high equine quadruped, First Commander Ashto, and allow me to introduce myself: I'm First Supervisor Draga Mo Cragio and I believe that you and Apprentice Commander Atia Mo Margo have a little explaining to do.'

Ashto and Atia had never quite fully appreciated the English language idiom of jaws hitting the floor up until this point as they both took in the fact that the impressive looking female now sitting opposite them, who had such a disarming smile on her face, had just spoken to them in the Jaran language.

'Please do not stand up and salute, you'll draw unwanted attention from everyone else in this eating establishment. You have been consuming a naturally produced meat product I presume?'

'It is called beef in the local language... er, esteemed Madam,' said Ashto speaking in his native Jaran language for the first time in several months. It felt strange to do so.

'Have you looked into the process of how such food is produced on this planet? I was observing the production methods yesterday in the area of this city known as Limehouse and it was not a very pleasant experience to say the least. But I must say the large joint of meat that is being wheeled around on the serving trolley does look extremely appetising,' said First Supervisor Draga.

Atia who had felt that she had been struck dumb by this sudden and very surprising curtailment of their evening's celebration was just able to murmur a question: 'Supervisor Draga... esteemed Madam... er, can I ask you what brings you to this planet and how long you have been here?'

'I have been residing on this small and rather undistinguished minor planet for the last Earth week,' said the Jaran supervising officer in her native language apart from her use of the English word "week". I have been staying at an adequate hotel in an area of this city called Bloomsbury and have discovered a rather nice restaurant and tea room in Baker Street by the name of Speedwells'. Do you know it?'

'Erm, no we do not, esteemed Madam,' said Ashto.

'Pity, I think you would like it, although of course it's not a patch on this place. I must remember to dine here before returning to headquarters. I have to say I have taken a liking to the Earth drink known as tea, I find it very refreshing. I must take some of the leaves home with me so that I can replicate them.'

'Yes, First Supervisor, you must,' said Ashto, looking questioningly at Atia.

'You ask what brings me to this planet,' said Draga.

'Yes, esteemed Madam,' said Atia.

'Well, the short answer is, in fact, you two. The sub-committee has examined some of the information you have been sending back to Jara and to tell you the truth a number of its members are not at all happy with some of your actions and interventions since you arrived on this little planet. And what with the cutbacks in funding that have been announced recently… '

'Cutbacks, First Supervisor?' said Atia.

'Yes, didn't you know? There is rather a large financial crisis going on at the moment, as well as various political shenanigans, and the war of course. This has inevitably led to the explorer outreach programme budget being drastically reduced. For the foreseeable future we're going to be pulling back from exploring unimportant backwater planets like this one and concentrate on those that will be far more beneficial to the Federation's financial situation in terms of trading opportunities. As well as that there may be important strategic military considerations which will need to be in the forefront of our thinking from now on.'

'War?' said Ashto and Atia in unison.

'Yes, you didn't know about that either? I'm sure you should have been informed about it.'

'No, esteemed Madam, we know nothing about any war. We have not received any briefings from the sub-committee for some time now,' said the First Commander.

'Well, there has obviously been a major bureaucratic oversight on someone's part.'

'So what exactly has taken place?' said a wide-eyed Apprentice Commander.

'About six months ago, as time is measured on this planet, a militant breakaway organisation on the planet Ballardia in the Verran system declared war on the Galactic Federation and attacked the Jaran diplomatic city of Discovery, killing many thousands of its peaceful inhabitants. If you know your history Ballardia was the first exo-planet visited by Jaran explorers half a millennia ago and this terrorist outrage came as a huge shock to the High Council. Since then the war has spread as the rebel group's operatives have travelled to many other planets in the Federation sewing seeds of rebellion and causing terror related incidents that are aimed at disrupting Federation activities. As a result our military forces have been dispatched to as many trouble spots as possible in order to bring those responsible for the outrages to justice. As you can understand such actions are very expensive in terms of personnel and resources and so many of our more outlying explorer missions will have to be curtailed. It is sad but there you are.'

'And what does that mean for our mission on Earth, First Supervisor?' asked Atia, fearing the reply.

'Well, I'm afraid your mission is to be prematurely concluded and you will be expected to return to Jara as soon as possible.'

'But we have over four Earth years of our mission to run,' said Ashto.

'A fact that is unfortunate but one which cannot be helped I'm afraid,' said First Supervisor Draga, 'but as I have said we are currently on a war-footing across the whole of the Galactic Federation.'

'Esteemed Madam, you said something about some members of the sub-committee not being happy with our actions. Could you enlighten us as to what exactly you mean by that observation?' said Atia.

'Ah yes. It is to do with your interference in the local business of the natives on this planet.'

'Our interference?' said Atia.

'Yes, Apprentice Commander Atia, it has been made very clear in your reports to the sub-committee that you have been interfering in various local policing matters in this city and have influenced the outcomes of certain events in the locale where you have been based. The information you supplied about – what were they called again? Oh yes, the Jack the Ripper murders, was most graphic and in some ways very entertaining and enlightening but unfortunately your actions contravened at least three of the guidelines regarding the non-interference protocols of the Federation's Explorer Executive when interacting with native peoples in primitive environments. My goodness I believe that you, Apprentice Commander, even deliberately caused the death of one of the individuals of this planet. Can you imagine the furore that would have been caused if the disrupter you used to dispatch the Earth person had fallen into the hands of the local authorities? It could have precipitated a major interplanetary incident – another one!'

'To be absolutely exact, First Supervisor, the Apprentice Commander did act in self-defence and sustained a serious injury in the process,' said Ashto, glad that he hadn't owned up to dispatching the Vampire Killer more recently.

'That is all very well but could you tell me what would have happened if the Apprentice Commander had been taken to one of this planet's so-called medical facilities. The whole aspect of the undercover nature of your mission here would have been compromised had local medical staff, such as they are here, been able to examine her and discover that her anatomy was not indigenous to this planet.' First Supervisor Draga looked at Ashto and Atia in turn, a serious, determined and questioning expression on her face. When no answer emerged from either of the Jaran explorers she nodded. 'I think your silence conveys a great deal,' said the First Supervisor. 'There is, however, another impediment to your continued presence on this planet,' said Draga.

'What is that?' said Ashto.

'Our intelligence sources have indicated that this planet, like others where we have explorer personnel present, has also been targeted by Ballardian terrorists and that one of their operatives is actually now at large in this city.'

'But why would they be interested in the Earth?' said an incredulous Atia.

'I'm afraid we do not know the answer to that question. Whatever the motive of the terrorist faction is in sending someone to this planet, having you two here as a target for their machinations is not something we are prepared to risk. The knowledge both of you have, not to mention the technology you have access to, is potentially too important to be ignored And so, for that reason as well, you are ordered to leave Earth as soon as possible,' said Draga. 'Anyway, now that matter has been decided,' she continued, 'I've suddenly come to the conclusion it would be appropriate for you two to buy me dinner at this very pleasant restaurant this evening and then later we can discuss your timetable for withdrawal from this planet. Now, this deep red coloured liquid you are drinking, I believe it is called wine is it not?'

First Commander Ashto nodded before calling for a waiter to bring another wineglass and, still with a stunned look on his face, poured the Jaran First Supervisor some of the wine. She sipped from her glass and sat back in her chair. 'That is very pleasant,' she said, 'can you order me some of this roast beef you were telling me about?'

Later that evening Atia and Ashto lay in bed, both still shocked by their surprise meeting with First Supervisor Draga.

'Er, Margot.'

'Yes, Trevor.'

'As you know I have been a loyal member of the Explorer Executive for most of my adult life.'

'Yes, Trevor, I know.'

'And I've always done my utmost to exactly follow their orders in the past.'

'Yes, Trevor.'

'But I have to say the news delivered by First Supervisor Draga this evening has shaken my faith somewhat in the wisdom of the decisions made by my... by our superiors.'

'I feel the same way too, Trevor, most definitely.'

'It's good that you feel the same, Margot, because I have a proposition to put to you.'

'What proposition is that, Trevor?'

'Well, Margot, this is very difficult for me to say, and is something that goes against the grain of everything I have believed in for a very long time...'

'Yes, Trevor?'

'Margot, I think that we should ignore the orders of the sub-committee and stay on the Earth in order to complete our mission. If in the course of our continued work here we should unmask the Ballardian terrorist and the reason for his or her incursion into the affairs of this planet so be it,' said First Commander Ashto.

'I agree, Trevor.'

'You do?'

'Oh yes, I completely agree.'

'Oh, Margot, I am so glad.'

'Good, Trevor, now please kiss me.'

Ashto smiled broadly and kissed Atia.

The End (for now)

Historical Notes

Most of the main events in this story are fictional and, as far as I know, two alien explorers did not visit London in the 1880s. There certainly was no such person as Percival Pell, aka the Vampire Killer, although there were a number of headless murder victims found around London by the Metropolitan Police shortly after the Jack the Ripper murders which was another series of crimes that would remain unsolved. At the same time the authorities were very worried about the resurgence of an Irish separatist bombing campaign by the so-called Fenian Brotherhood.

Some of the individuals mentioned in this novel were actual historical figures.

Edmund Reid and William Thick were police detectives based at Leman Street police station in Whitechapel and had been among those involved in the hunt for Jack the Ripper in the autumn of 1888. Frederick Abberline was another who had tried and failed to track down the infamous serial killer. All three were excellent policemen by the standards of the time, however, and were no doubt a credit to the Metropolitan Police.

Isabel Wells was also a real life person and was actually

engaged to her cousin, the writer H. G. Wells at the time she and First Commander Ashto inadvertently met in the story. Handily, when she and H. G. Wells were married a year or so later, she did not have bother changing her surname. You may expect another meeting between Miss Wells and First Commander Ashto to take place at some point in the future.

Bram Stoker, the author of the influential novel *Dracula*, was the business manager at the Lyceum theatre and a close friend and devotee of Henry Irving, the greatest actor of the age. It is very possible that Stoker based his description of Count Dracula on the tall, charismatic and rather gaunt figure of Irving, who he imagined, wrongly in fact, would eventually want to play the part on his own Lyceum stage. The Stokers visited Whitby on many occasions and it was in the small Yorkshire fishing town that some of the action of Bram Stoker's famous horror novel is set. Today the delightful and busy town of Whitby makes much of its association with the fictional Transylvanian vampire as well as its ruined abbey and church, which overlook the town, its famous 199 steps and its picturesque harbour. A tongue-in-cheek notice recently on the door of St Mary's Church in Whitby tells visitors not to bother searching the churchyard for the grave of Dracula, as he was a fictional character. Such is the power of literature.

The writer and wit Oscar Wilde was a frequent visitor to the Beefsteak Room, Henry Irving's private dining room at the Lyceum. In 1889 Wilde was at the beginning of his career and was busy working on his novel, *The Picture of Dorian Gray*, which caused a sensation when it was published in 1890. Wilde eventually was another who was found guilty of transgressing the draconian laws on the prohibition of male homosexuality and, at the height of his glittering career, in 1895, he was sentenced to two years imprisonment with hard labour. His poem *Ballad of Reading Gaol* is one of his most heartfelt pieces of writing. He died in exile in Paris just five years later at the age of 46, a penniless and broken man.

Novelists Arthur Conan Doyle and Hall Caine as well as the painter James McNeill Whistler were briefly mentioned in the story and were of course also real people, although sadly Sherlock Holmes wasn't!

Frederick Treves, an eminent doctor at the London Hospital in Whitechapel was an actual person, as was his patient and friend, Joseph Merrick, also known as The Elephant Man. Sadly Treves was correct in his assessment that his friend would not survive very long as Joseph Merrick died in April 1890 at the age of 27.

Most of the other characters in this novel are completely fictional and bear no relation to any person living or dead.

Number 19, Cleveland Street *was* a male brothel – a *molly house* in the slang of the time. Legislation passed by Parliament in 1885 had strengthened the law that made sexual acts between males illegal and had only succeeded in driving such activities underground. The Metropolitan Police were criticised by some in the press for failing to act sooner to close down the Cleveland Street establishment. This was in order, it was thought at the time, to protect certain very important people from scandal. It was indeed widely rumoured that the "house of assignation" as it was called in the newspapers *was* visited on a number of occasions by Prince Albert Victor, son of the Prince of Wales, an individual who was eventually to die of influenza at the age of 28. His convenient death in 1892 saved Queen

Victoria and the rest of the Royal Family of the time a good deal of embarrassment. The Police eventually raided the house in Cleveland Street on the 6th July 1889 and arrested a number of people, although the brothel's owner, Charles Hammond and one of its patrons, Lord Arthur Somerset, an equerry to the Prince of Wales, had fled abroad before they could be prosecuted. A number of young male prostitutes, who also worked as telegraph messenger boys for the General Post Office, were arrested and punished.

Atia and Ashto, the two aliens living undercover in the London of the late 1880s, will return and continue to have some further adventures, when they will discover more about the Great Britain of the time, meet more eminent Victorian figures and perhaps even solve a few more intractable problems.

Finally, if you have enjoyed this novel please think about writing a review of it on Amazon, Goodreads or the publisher's website. Thank you.

Neil Coley
Lichfield 2024

This book is printed on paper from sustainable sources managed under the Forest Stewardship Council (FSC) scheme.

It has been printed in the UK to reduce transportation miles and their impact upon the environment.

For every new title that Troubador publishes, we plant a tree to offset CO_2, partnering with the More Trees scheme.

For more about how Troubador offsets its environmental impact, see www.troubador.co.uk/sustainability-and-community